REMEDY

REMEDY

EIREANN CORRIGAN

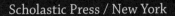

Scholastic Press / New York

For Rob Franzmann—
our warrior in so many ways

CHAPTER ONE

Some days, when I first wake and the hazy light filters through the blinds, striping my white blanket like there were bars on my window, I try to remember what it felt like to be well. I was so little then. Maybe seven or eight? It wouldn't have occurred to me to feel lucky. I wouldn't have noticed that nothing hurt.

I was still discovering all of my body's potential—the lengthening bones, the coiled muscles. Every so often I could stretch and touch a shelf that I hadn't been able to reach before. My teeth fell out and grew in. Once in a while, I'd have a skinned knee.

We used to play with scooters and parachutes and hula-hoops in gym. Back when I was still allowed to take gym. And one Field Day, they brought out the second grade and we hula-hooped in front of the whole school. One by one, each hoop faltered and clattered down to the blacktop. Except mine. I kept it spinning until the principal stood next to me and caught the hoop with her hand. The second-grade hula-hoop champion. I could have twirled for hours.

They gave me a certificate. I remember tracing the gold seal embossed on the heavy paper. I would have saved something like that certificate. But I probably didn't pack it for the move. Definitely not for the second move.

I'd have left the award behind because it would have made my mother sad to see me treasuring it. If she noticed me folding it between the pages of a book or tucking it into a shoebox, she'd think I was feeling sorry for myself. My mother has sacrificed so much on my account. I couldn't hurt her. Besides, we are Wakely women, after all. We do not feel sorry for ourselves.

That is what I remind myself while lowering my two feet onto the slats of the wood floor. Brace myself and heave the rest of my body to a standing position. I try to ignore the fog in my brain, the thick coating of sickness in my mouth. I yank the cord to the blinds and the bars of light break and scatter into dapples of sun.

It's morning. The glare makes my eyes ache. I try to feel grateful the way I've been taught to be.

CHAPTER TWO

Every day opens with the same question.

"Cara Jean, how did you sleep?"

"Four."

We have a rating system for sleep and appetite, fatigue and pain. For sleep a four is good—great even. Deep and undisturbed. We rate out of five for sleep and appetite. But pain and fatigue go to ten. This means that all fours count as a good score. That's where I hover at this morning: relatively well rested, ready to eat. Stiff and sore but not in the kind of pain that sometimes has me burrowed under blankets, gasping to breathe through the bile rising in my throat. Four.

I hold up my fingers as I say it, because Mom's busy juicing. She's lined up the beets and carrots, the kale and spinach. The machine chomps and growls. Its screech vibrates my teeth.

"Good, good!" she shouts, and pours us each a cup of green froth.

When I reach for my glass, she lightly smacks my hand. "You know the drill, sunshine. Vitals first." So I perch on the stool and hand over my arm.

My mom operates efficiently, expertly. Before I was born, she worked as a nurse in an emergency room, but then I came along. She says that life turns out the way it's meant to. She says she would have studied even harder in nursing school if she'd known her only patient would eventually be me.

The blood pressure cuff constricts and loosens and she leans over me to write the numbers on the chart hung on the kitchen wall. Next she tucks the thermometer under my tongue and then presses her fingertips to my wrist to take my pulse.

Everything gets written down. We've got the kitchen chart but also spreadsheets and a thick folder full of all my records—the hospital intake forms and prescriptions and waivers. My mom saves all of those so carefully. Sometimes I catch her with all of it spread around her on the table like a map directing her to the distant island of my good health.

There are other spreadsheets—money in, money out. She keeps a folder full of bills and applications for medical debt relief. Mom doesn't want me to focus on those numbers. Today is a four. That's the number that's supposed to matter to me.

Mom hands me my glass and tips hers toward me. I raise mine and say, "Cheers!"

"Salud!" she corrects. We both smile at the stupid joke, sitting at the counter and drinking to our happy and healthy lives. "Think you can make it to school today, baby?" She looks at me expectantly, so I say yes before I think it all through: the reading I haven't completed yet for Japanese class, the lack of anything remotely decent to wear. But the mom machine is up and running. "Good, good! That's great news." As if she can light my way forward with the brightness in her voice.

The green juice settles in the glass. Then I can feel it on my upper lip like a monstrous mustache. I'm already preparing for the slow climb back upstairs to get ready, steadying myself in the shower. Mom flips through the tiny plastic compartments of my pill case, moving meds. "Let's hold off on Big Blue until you come home, then." She holds up the familiar capsule. "It sometimes makes you so drowsy. If your pain's only at a four, I bet you can power through." The case rattles when she passes it over to me.

Today is Thursday. It's the first time I've tried to go to school this week. I open up the compartment labeled *TH* and gulp the three remaining pills down with my juice.

Sometimes I genuinely don't know what creeps at a more glacial pace—my own body readying itself in the morning or my mother's Toyota. We used to live outside Hubbard, Ohio, and I swear the Amish horse-and-buggies would occasionally pass us. We've been pulled over for taking the highway too slow. That time, Mom pointed out my travel oxygen to the policeman. "Precious cargo, Officer. Precious and fragile."

"My apologies, ma'am." That time, the officer rapped his knuckles gently against the car door. "God bless."

Today I don't have the travel oxygen tank at my feet or tubes up my nose. My backpack feels light because Mom won't allow me to strain my back carrying books. In my locker, I keep a second set I can bring to my classes.

"How're you feeling?" she asks again. "Any nausea?"

I shrug. Out the window, the town passes by like a flipbook of strip malls. Sometimes I want to tell my mother that it's the car's unhurried crawl that turns my stomach. I feel every bump and jolt.

When she needs to, she can drive fast. The last time we moved, Hubbard receded in the rearview in a blur. I remember gripping the armrest beside her and marveling at her focus on the road, how she'd suddenly learned to gun the engine and change lanes like a stuntman in a spy movie. Sometimes my mom surprises me.

But not today. We take each turn slow. Mom pulls up in the handicapped spot, right at the front entrance, so I try to propel myself out of the car quickly, before anyone sees.

"Do you need me to sign you in?" she asks, her fingers already closed around the door handle.

I don't. She knows this. Parents have to sign their kids out to leave early, not to drop them off late.

"No worries," I call out, slinging the bag over my shoulder.

"Text me if you need me."

I nod. Who else would I text?

Immediately, I regret braving the front office alone. The secretaries stop chatting the second I open the door.

Mrs. Arsenault, the gray-haired lady who sits farthest back, leaps to her feet and disappears into the vice principal's office.

That leaves me with Mrs. Oakes, whose hair is colored a deep shade of cranberry. She studies me carefully.

"May I have a pass to third period, please?" I ask.

Her brow furrows. "Third period is over."

Okay. Deep breath. Already I am so very tired. "May I have a pass to fourth period, please?"

Mrs. Oakes taps the clipboard. "Sign in. Make sure to write the reason for your tardiness."

I carefully write my name in the space provided. Under *reason*, I print *illness* the way my mother has instructed.

Mrs. Oakes reads as I write. "Illness? Are you sick?" We have had this conversation so often, I almost answer before she asks.

"I have a chronic illness. It's not contagious." My voice sounds automatic, like a robot version of me. The school edition.

"Ummm-hmmm." Mrs. Oakes starts carefully lettering the hall pass as Mrs. Arsenault swoops back to her seat.

"Mr. Brinks would like to speak with you . . ."

"Cara." I supply her with my name.

"Cara." Mrs. Arsenault sounds triumphant.

"Now?"

"What?" Mrs. Oakes asks. She stares at me blankly. I don't know if it's my brain that's cloaked in fog or hers.

I try again. "Would Mr. Brinks like to speak with me now?"

Mrs. Oakes glances at Mrs. Arsenault, who calls behind her, "Mr. Brinks, are you ready to speak to Cara . . ."

"Wakely." I supply that one too. I'm on a roll.

"Wakely?" Mrs. Arsenault calls into the office behind her. I feel as if I'm waiting to audition for a part in a play about a kid who has the audacity to cut class.

When Mr. Brinks pokes his head out of his office, he smiles directly at me. His eyes crease kindly. "Cara?" I'm prepared to list symptoms, discuss diagnoses. Mrs. Oakes and Mrs. Arsenault settle in their chairs. I am used to starring in this show.

Mr. Brinks doesn't order me into his office, though. Instead he says, "I think you should attend fourth period. How about coming back later?"

"You mean like after school?" I ask. "Do you want my mom here?"

"How about lunchtime? Did you bring a bag lunch today?" I nod. "Great! We can chow down together. I'll see you at twelve thirty." Mr. Brinks disappears back into his office. Show's over. The secretaries seem disappointed.

"You should get a move on," Mrs. Oakes prods. "That pass is time-stamped."

I'm not very accustomed to walking fast. Just getting to fourth period is an obstacle course. I stop at my locker and need to look up the text I sent myself with the combo. It's English class and I'm not entirely sure which novel we're reading. But Mr. Durand is one of those inspiring teachers, a self-designated lighthouse in the storm of our adolescence. He always wears colorful shoelaces and makes us write journals. So I grab three books and stuff them into my bag, knowing Durand won't examine the time stamp on my pass too closely. He won't roll his eyes and sarcastically say "Nice of you to join us today, Cara" the way other teachers might.

Everyone's still milling around in the classroom as Durand fusses with his laptop and the projector. He doesn't even ask for the pass in my hand. "Hey there, Cara," he says. He is the only one who acknowledges my arrival. The eyes of my classmates barely flicker in my direction.

But that's okay. That's understandable. I grab a seat in the second row and wait to see which book Libby Gilfeather retrieves from her bag.

This is how I manage most school days: I find a kind person who attends on the regular and take my cues from them. If there's a test or a quiz, I fill in every answer and hope occasionally one lands right. School is full of tests that don't matter—quadratic equations, battles of the American Revolution. Mom says that my classmates have the luxury of learning a little at a time, that once we figure out my health I'll catch up. For now I try to absorb as much as possible in the few hours I can hold my body upright in a desk.

Libby sees me eyeing her book. She points her finger to the chapter number and nods and smiles. There are people on this planet who are instinctively generous. That's one silver lining of sickness—it gives those people a reason to flex their compassion muscles. I turn to the correct page, meet Libby's eyes, and smile. For a second, I let myself imagine having a best friend. Libby Gilfeather and I would study at the kitchen table together. We'd ride our bikes to the Dairy Queen on Hanover Avenue and text each other photos of questionable outfits before school.

But I know how that goes. My ketogenic diet doesn't allow for Dairy Queen. I'm not sure I could actually propel a bicycle forward. And I am everyone's nightmare partner for group projects. Libby would understand the first few times I canceled. She'd probably even swing by my house and pretend to be fascinated by my potassium levels. But really the first rule of friendship is that you have to show up. I can rarely show up.

Mr. Brinks and I sit across from each other at a round table in his office at lunchtime. He's come out from behind his oversized desk, probably to avoid intimidating me. Or maybe he didn't want the mayo from my turkey-and-spinach wrap smeared on his important papers.

Mr. Brinks is eating yogurt—three of them, which seems like an awful lot of dairy but what do I know?

"What do you know about the attendance policy at Middlefield High School?" he asks, pitching the first emptied carton into the trash can.

"I'm not sure." I nibble on my wrap, stalling for time. But Mr. Brinks is pulling that adult trick of letting the silence sit, waiting for me to fill it. So I trot out my own overplayed card. "To be honest, I'm just really focused on my health right now."

"Tell me about that." Yogurt: The Sequel pops open.

"I have a chronic illness." My robot voice crackles.

"Right." Brinks lets the quiet stretch.

Fine. "It's called unidentified autoimmune syndrome. I first began experiencing symptoms in the third grade: joint pain, fatigue, muscle depletion."

"Third grade. That's a long time to be sick."

Out of the corner of my eye, I can almost see that younger version of myself, twirling her hula-hoop over and over. "Well, I've had periods of remission. My mom says that if we consistently work on it, my health might become more consistent."

Brinks nods into his yogurt. "Make sense." He looks up. "What does your doctor say?"

"Which one?" My laugh is half robot. "We see a lot of doctors."

"But you have a pediatrician? Someone who oversees all your care."

"I guess so. My mom is a nurse—she used to work at a hospital. So she's able to coordinate my appointments and make recommendations. We're lucky for that. Some parents don't know enough to even question doctors."

"Should we do that? Question doctors?" Mr. Brinks sounds genuinely curious.

It takes me a moment to chew on my bite of turkey wrap. I think of how often the medicine I've been prescribed has done nothing but introduce new side effects. How doctors would examine me, but not really listen to me. How often my mom would scorch the phone lines, insisting, "She's not getting any better. Do something." Sometimes we'd need to move on to the next office and hope someone new might help us.

"Lots of times we assume that doctors have this authority, but they don't always know everything," I say. Mr. Brinks listens intently. "My mom has tracked my symptoms for years; she's basically an expert. But people underestimate nurses."

"That's how she feels?"

"That's how I feel."

Mr. Brinks nods. His fingers steeple together in front of him. "I'm not an expert in autoimmune disorders." His last yogurt sits on the table unopened. "But I have a lot of experience getting kids through high school. I'm worried that you're not off to a great start." He reaches to the giant desk behind him for his laptop and taps the keys. "It's November fourteenth?" he asks me.

11

I want to tell him that I have no idea. For me, the day's number is four: four out of ten for pain and fatigue; four out of five for sleep and appetite. But it's starting to seep into my dull brain that I've already spoken too freely to Mr. Brinks. My mom would remind me that health is a private matter. There are laws in place to protect us from nosy and judgmental people. So I don't even nod. I don't need to help him along.

"Right," he says, as if I've contributed. "We've just completed the first marking period. We've been in school forty-five days so far. Do you know how many you've attended?"

"I've been really struggling this fall."

"You've attended eighteen days of school."

I want to ask, *That many?* Instead I just set my lunch down and say, "Yes."

"Less than half."

"I've worked really hard to keep up with my assignments."

"I know you have. All your teachers report that." Well, that's something. "I see from your middle school transcript that you've moved a lot. My concern, Cara, is that you are so used to playing catch-up that you don't realize how your frequent absences are eroding your educational experience."

My head nods thoughtfully. I am so, so tired.

Mr. Brinks goes on, "High school counts in a different way. Colleges will wonder about that kind of pattern. And there's the matter of state mandates. I'm legally bound to report truancy. Now, I know you're not a truant. You complete your work diligently. Your mother is an involved parent who communicates with our office frequently. But the end result is the same—I can't give you credit for classes you haven't actually attended."

"This is the best I can do." My voice cracks and I almost throw his last yogurt against the door in frustration.

Mr. Brinks sits back in his chair, studying me. I press my lips together, willing myself not to cry.

"Okay," he says. "It's good to know that. After all, we're here to support you. But part of supporting you is making sure you understand our limitations. If a student misses twenty percent or more of her classes, the state recommends a repeat of that grade level, regardless of ability or performance."

"What are you saying? Should I not even bother coming anymore? If you're going to hold me back anyway." My voice sounds too surly—the robot version of me pulses a silent alarm. *Get a grip.* "I'm sorry—this is just a lot to take in. I'm not feeling very well."

"The state recommends. It does not require. But my concerns remain—about your attendance, about you. Is there anything else you'd like to tell me, Cara?"

Yes, I want to say. I want to tell Mr. Brinks that in second grade I was in the Cardinal reading group and they ran out of chapter books in the library for me. I was the first girl to climb to the top of the rope in gym class and once insisted that my mom drive me through a snowstorm because it was the Math Festival and I couldn't believe they would cancel school.

But then the headaches started. And sometimes the pain would jolt me badly enough that I'd throw up. Sometimes I threw up so violently my body shook uncontrollably. There were mornings I'd wake up feeling like my limbs had been set on fire from the inside, like my veins contained gasoline and not blood cells. There were days when my mom would turn on a light and it would sear my skull even through my sealed eyelids.

13

I could tell Mr. Brinks how it felt to slowly find myself sitting out. From gym, from recess. From class trips and end-of-the-year picnics.

But I'm tired even of talking about that.

"There's nothing else," I tell him. Then I even manage to smile. "But I appreciate knowing that you're here to help."

"Great. Then we've accomplished a lot with this talk." Mr. Brinks sounds pleased.

I stand and feel the rush of blood to my brain, grip the edge of the table so that I don't fall down.

Mr. Brinks looks worried. "You okay? Would you like me to call the nurse?"

Mom wouldn't want me to go to the nurse. School nurses meddle and their offices are teeming with germs. Nothing good has ever come from me landing in the nurse's office.

"I'm just fine," I say. I let go of the table in order to prove it and barely wobble. "Really." Mr. Brinks studies me. I straighten my posture and try to look more alert, continuing, "I have Japanese class next period. It's important to attend language classes as regularly as possible, right?"

"That's what the research tells us, yes." Mr. Brinks raises both hands as if surrendering. "I'm going to have to rely on your judgment here, Cara. After all, you've been handling these health challenges for—my goodness—half your life, correct?"

"Yeah. I guess so."

On the periphery of my vision, I can see that younger version of myself spinning the hoop around her waist. When Brinks words it that way, the hula-hoop rattles to the floor. She hangs her head in dismay.

14   Half my life.

CHAPTER THREE

I don't know if they have special car showrooms specifically for moms, but every middle-aged lady circling the school parking lot seems to pilot an SUV in the same shade of maroon.

Ours is more banged up than most, with a Jesus fish sticker peeling off the bumper—a remnant of whoever donated it to the Catholic charity that passed it along to us. I open its door and heave myself inside, taking care to avoid slamming anything. I don't feel ready yet to describe the day's frustrations. I plaster a smile on my face and clip on the seat belt as if my shoulders don't ache from turning slightly in the seat.

Mom fusses over me anyway, saying, "You look tired." As if on cue, my eyelids feel leaden. I allow them to close briefly and then force them back open. She taps the pill case on the console and I take my three o'clock meds, washing them down with the bottled water she keeps in the console.

"I'm fine." My voice sounds weary though, and I study the view of the roadside stores like a kidnapping victim memorizing every turn. Maybe she will just let me rest. My head falls against the seat's back, hoping.

"You push yourself too much—we have discussed this, Cara." Her voice drills. My head hurts.

"I said I'm fine."

"I know what you said." The lines around her mouth seem to crease more deeply. I take three calming breaths and remind myself: *She cares about you.* "It breaks my heart to see you looking so defeated. You've got to learn how to advocate for yourself."

"I did." It slips out before I consider the energy it will take me to tell the whole story.

"What do you mean? Did someone give you a hard time? Was it that European history teacher again?"

"Mama, can we just talk about it later? I keep spacing out."

"Sure." We drive in silence for a while, but she can't help herself. "I will tell you that this is not the life I expected for myself." My shoulders wilt. I know what's coming. "When I was a teenager, I was self-absorbed too—that's a natural development. I put everything into my skating." I picture the medals hung from the bedpost in my mother's room. She keeps talking. "That was my mistake—thinking all that applause would just follow me." I know this story well: the championships, the injuries. I picture my mom at my age, circling the ice rink and gathering up dozens of thrown roses.

"Not everyone gets to be extraordinary." Mama seems to shake off her memories. "And you know, you might not be an elite athlete, but you are stronger and more determined than most people I know. Grown women and men haven't survived the kind of pain and suffering you have. Those stuffed suits at school have no idea. So don't even give them a listening ear."

"I got called into the vice principal's office," I explain. "I wasn't in trouble—he said he was concerned." Mama goes positively pale then. Sometimes just watching her react to the world is tiring. "Mr. Brinks was helpful. I explained about my absences. I told him a little bit about my medical issues."

"I have already explained your absences. I have discussed your medical condition with Mr. Brinks. At length. He has no right to call you into his office like you're some kind of delinquent. He must not have enough work to do if he has the time to harass a child with serious medical challenges."

"It wasn't like that. He really seemed worried." *And aren't we used to worry?* I want to add. For as long as I can remember my mother and I have existed in a cocoon knit from the concern of others. They are generous; we are grateful.

But my mom is having none of it. "He can express that concern in a phone call—to your parent." She flounces out of the car. "We have gone over this. You don't have conferences without me present, Cara. You need an advocate. I'll go in with you tomorrow—if you are feeling up to going in tomorrow."

"That's just it." I try to make my voice as light and carefree

17

as possible. "I have to go in tomorrow. Mr. Brinks is monitoring my attendance so closely—I might not get credit for the first semester of ninth grade if I miss any more classes."

"We will see about that." Inside, Mama plants herself at my homework station, tapping away on the computer. The tentacles of my mother's online influence extend across Ohio and beyond. It's a sight to behold. She perches on the computer chair with her feet tucked beneath her and a clipboard of notes in her lap. I hear the keys clicking and think of circuits blinking throughout the country—a network of moms mobilized on my behalf.

It makes me worry a little for the vice principal. Mr. Brinks won't know what hit him.

I also know not to interrupt my mom when she's like this—not even for homework. I shuffle by her at the little desk and she calls out "Drink your juice" almost absentmindedly. But my health is never off my mother's mind. "You have one hour before it's time for the green pill," she reminds me as her fingers frantically click. She looks up, sees me pause. "What?"

"The green pill makes me feel foggy."

"Don't be ridiculous. That loony doctor from the urgent care put that in your head. Most side effects manifest through the power of suggestion. You've got to take your meds, Cara."

I tread carefully. "It's just that I have homework."

Mama shakes her head, concerned. "I don't like the congestion in your voice. We'll need to set up the breathing machine tonight."

"I'm breathing fine—"

But she holds one hand up to quiet me. "That's what you always tell me—right before we rush you to the ER with pneumonia."

She's right. I know she's right. But I hate the breathing machine even more than I hate Mama's podcasts. Both feel like they suck all of the air from the room. There is no way I'll sleep well with the rubber mask tight around my face and the tubes tangled around my neck. And then tomorrow I'll drag myself through another day of school with the outline of the stupid mask imprinted under my eyes. Awesome.

Mama turns back to the computer and after hitting a few keys starts using her video voice: "Hi there, friends and fellow wellness warriors. We wish you a good day and good health. Just behind me, you might catch a glimpse of my girl wonder. She made it through a whole day of school today, despite facing discrimination and harassment by senior school officials. You all know how that goes with invisible illness. They don't know and, worse yet, they don't care. And there's my girl, not even home for half an hour and already pushing through the pain to complete her homework. Cara, honey, give a wave to all our subscribers. Let them know how you're feeling today!"

I make sure my smile is wide and toothy. Sometimes she makes me say "Good morning and good health!" but it's almost 4:00 p.m. and Mama lets me get away with an enthusiastic thumbs-up.

"Isn't she amazing?" Mama asks the screen. "What impresses you most about your children, wellness warriors? Shout out their bravery in the comments as we talk about insurance issues. Let's review what treatment an ER must provide to your child, regardless of coverage."

I suppose that Mama's channel helps people. We surpassed fifty thousand subscribers a while ago and we always get tons of comments. Sometimes she watches our old videos and that's hard to handle. I don't always know what I actually remember or what

I've seen on a screen. Me in a hospital gown printed with tiny teddy bears. Me using a tiny walker, trudging along the driveway of our old apartment. For a while, after she and my father first got divorced, Mama wouldn't put anything about us online. "You never know who's watching, Cara Jean," she'd tell me. I guess he's not though, since she broadcasts us all over the internet now.

When my mom is finally done and it's my turn for the computer, I log on to the school's online learning portal. It's the first time all day I actually feel like a real student, toggling between my class pages and ticking off the task boxes of homework. Some kids learn best like this, Mama tells me. I remember Mr. Brinks and his skeptical eyebrows. It wouldn't be the worst thing—earning my diploma remotely. But it would feel like giving up. I see the notification banner on top of the website while I'm filling out my reading response for history, then click on it and read what the school has posted to my account.

"Mama?" I call out.

Mama rushes into the kitchen. "Cara, darling, are you okay?"

"I'm sorry, Mama. I'm fine." I wave off her worry and point to the screen. "But look, the office sent an alert—they don't have my physical form?"

"Of course they do."

"It says they don't, that it was due on September sixth."

"Well, this constitutes harassment. First Mr. Brinks summoning you to the office today and now this. This constitutes bureaucratic abuse. He probably set the nurse up to it the second you walked out that door."

"I don't understand."

"We're strong women, and some people don't like that, Cara."

"But I have a completed physical form, right?" I think of all the doctors' offices I've visited in the past year. "Maybe you forgot to send it in?"

Mama looks at me incredulously. "Who are you talking to?"

"I'm just reading what the school says here."

"Correct. And that school also says you're too sick to attend. Or maybe just lazy. That school says you won't pass ninth grade. Are we believing everything that school says now?"

She's right. I know it. I've seen her deliver what feels like hundreds of forms to different schools over the years. All of them with different required signatures. Mama keeps track of everything. And schools—well, schools tend to lose paperwork.

She goes on. "It's not your fault we have to put up with this, Cara. Not your fault at all. I don't understand why schools can't understand how to treat ill children. This does not deserve our energy. Thank God, I have my support group tonight. Surely one of the other moms has gone through this. It will help even just to vent a little bit." Every Thursday, Mama sits with her parent support group at Tri-Point Medical Center, talking about the challenges of my thick medical file and her relentless worry.

She shuts down the computer. "We've had enough of Middlefield High School's intrusion in our lives today," she says. "You need to rest."

Reflected on the black screen, my face looks grim and worn. I know she's right. I would keep going, making myself sicker, if I didn't have my mom around to remind me to take a break.

Now that I've stopped, now that I let myself feel the exhaustion, I'm grateful.

21

Mama leaves the room and comes back with the green pill in her palm as a peace offering.

"Why don't you go and lie down?" she says.

I know better than to argue anything now.

The lavender wrap feels like the weight of defeat on my shoulders—all the arguments I don't have the energy to pursue. But it's warm and it helps.

Before Mama leaves she says, "There's some leftover vegetable stir-fry in the fridge. Please try to eat. I'll ask the group tonight about alternative schooling options. Unless you don't want me to go?"

"No," I say. "Go."

"Text me if you need anything." She's put on makeup; silver earrings gleam in her ears.

"Thank you, Mama." The thing is, I do mean it. There are worse things a parent can do than take care of their kid, after all.

I lie there with my eyes squeezed tight and listen for the door to shut and the van to start up with its rumbling cough. I think I'll fall asleep, but my body surprises me by resisting that. *At least do your homework*, it says, even though I'm pretty sure she took the laptop with her. We only have one and Mama takes copious notes, especially when the support group welcomes guest speakers. I bet when she was my age, my mother always completed her homework. She believes in excellence. I think about the secretaries at school and their meaningful looks, Mr. Brinks and his theatrical concern. I think about the kids at school, who scan me as if I have all the potential of a piece of furniture.

Prove otherwise, my body insists. It's like I have a weird, sudden burst of energy. So I do something completely crazy.

I go outside.

CHAPTER FOUR

I'm sure Libby Gilfeather has a house key of her own, but I need to leave the side door of our place unlocked.

It takes me a moment to let go of the doorknob, to step off the small cement stair. It's dusky already, even at four thirty, and the wind knits itself through the stitches of my sweater. If I go back inside for a jacket, I probably won't come back out, so I tell myself the cold will clear the fog from my brain and plow forward. Two middle schoolers breeze by on their bikes—one farther ahead and the other hunched forward, determined to catch up.

The library is three blocks to the right and four streets over.

23

I think it has to be open because Mama and I have gone there for alternative medicine evenings and once for a Lyme disease screening. I know there are computer terminals there.

Propelled by the cold wind and the possibility of Mama's meeting ending early, my feet move more quickly than I'm used to. And honestly, it's a little thrilling—to be out in a fall night, to find my own way there.

When the doors slide open at the library, I feel so hopeful. It's warm and busy and the hush seems industrious rather than sickly. But when I go to sit down in the horseshoe formation of computers, the screen at my terminal immediately requests my ID number. I raise my hand, like I'm in class or something. No one comes to help.

To my left, there's a kid, maybe a little younger than me, working behind an enormous stack of science magazines. He scribbles on a clipboard and studiously ignores me. Across the horseshoe, a couple spills all over their terminal. She's balanced on his lap. His arm coils around her waist and her fingers twirl strands of his hair. They look like a rope puzzle, impossible to unknot. I can't imagine my body that tangled with another.

"There's no teacher here." It takes me a moment to realize it's the young scientist speaking to me. He pronounces the words carefully, as if he's considered whether or not I will understand them.

When I answer, it probably doesn't help clarify the possibility of language issues. I just say, "Librarian?" As if you can order one, like a latte.

He shakes his head. "At night, they don't leave the front desk."

"I can't log on."

"Switch computers."

"I don't know my ID number."

"It's on your library card."

I pat my pants, like there's a pocket there. "I lost my card."

The science kid sighs like he'll personally have to replace it. "Go to the front desk. The librarian will look it up for you."

"Thanks for the help." It comes out sharp, but it's not Science Kid's fault I don't have a library card. He doesn't know me or understand that, at fourteen, I've not yet achieved the level of independence of a second grader.

I make a show of stopping by the desk, but no one pays attention to me. The couple is still absorbed in each other and Science Kid is still absorbed in his clipboard. Outside, the air feels even colder. I check my phone, in disbelief that I have actually risked another argument with Mama to sit in the public library for four minutes. I hear my mom's voice in my head: *Cara, November is the peak of cold and flu season. And there you are at the public library, touching computer keys that God knows how many other people have handled. You are immunocompromised. Your body simply doesn't have the ability to fight germs the way other bodies do.*

I know this. I just wish sometimes I could unknow it. But that kind of unknowing isn't good for me. That's probably why I need my mother's voice in my head to remind me.

Doing what I want to do and doing the healthy thing to do are not the same thing.

I hate it, but there it is.

I leave the library. Crossing the street, my chest tightens and my legs ache. My skin feels itchy with all the antibodies in my blood busy practicing defense. Sweat suddenly breaks out on the small of my back as if the temperature of our little main street just surged. What was I thinking? I look for someplace to rest a moment. I could just sink down on the pavement.

Across the way is a place called Mud Matters, which has a bench I spot through the window. When I step inside, a deep ringing sounds and I look up to see a string of clay bells draped over the door. They clang again when I shut the door, but otherwise it's more silent than the library. The floor feels gritty, and when I step forward, I kick up a small cloud of dust.

"Hey there." I hear the lady before I see her. When she moves toward me, even larger clouds gather at her feet. "What can I do for you?"

I'm still taking everything in. Shelves line three walls of the store, with rows and rows of glazed dishes, cups, even tiny houses. The woman matches the store—all browns and pinks. She has two black braids and even then her hair might be the longest I've ever seen. Over her khaki pants and pink thermal, she wears a brown canvas apron and hiking boots splattered with white. She has a kind face, a patient face.

"Have you been here before?" she asks.

I force my head to shake as I sit down on the bench. "Well, that's wonderful. I'm so glad you found us. Mud Matters is a pottery studio. We sell the work of local artists, but you can also create your own pottery here." She gestures to the long tables covered in brown craft paper. "We offer classes and camps. We even do birthday parties."

She is so friendly and hopeful, chattering along as if I've responded in any kind of normal way. I feel terrible that she believes I'm a real customer.

26

"That's not really the kind of thing I'm good at," I tell her.

"Birthday parties aren't something you're good at?" Her eyes laugh but she's not making fun of me. There are some things you don't tell people right away. They'll get sad and that sadness turns to pity and then the pity stands between you like a lake you can't row across. So I don't tell her that, in fourteen years, I've only had one birthday party. Some charity donated it but because I didn't have any friends my age, we just invited the hospital staff to Chuck E. Cheese.

Instead I smile and say, "No, I mean art classes. My stuff never comes out the way I see it in my head."

The lady scoffs at that. "Well, good. That would be so boring. That's part of what I love most about creating pottery—the way the final product always surprises me." With her chin, she points at one of the craft-paper-covered tables. Piles of peach-colored clay sit there wetly in earthen bowls. "Why don't you give it a try? You might amaze yourself."

She seems so positive, so certain, that it feels rude to ask if I can just stay on the bench instead. I only have a few minutes left anyway. When I sit at the table, she introduces herself, as if I have earned the right to know. "My name is Manuela. This is my studio. I would have put my name on it but that was too many *M*s."

Even though it's a joke I can tell she tells often, I laugh. "My name is Cara. It's a really lovely studio. But I don't have any money—"

Manuela cuts me off. "It only costs money if we fire a piece in the kiln. The kiln is an oven that burns very hot and transforms our pliable sculpture into finished works of art. Otherwise, you can use the clay again and again. It's good for the clay actually—to be handled."

So I perch on the stool and lower my hands into one of the bowls. The clay feels cool and soft. I wonder whether Manuela feels bad for me. Or maybe she's telling the truth and other people have worked this particular ball of clay. They've formed it into shapes and stretched it between their fingers. While I experiment—bouncing it and pressing it against the table—she turns on music. It's piano music, more like tinkering, and it makes me feel like I'm in a movie with my own soundtrack. In that movie, I am a girl who goes out on her own all the time. She's an artist who sculpts figures that stand on podiums in galleries.

For a few minutes, I worry only about working the stubby segments of my clay into graceful limbs. I use one of the sharp little tools on the table to carve out a long nose and a tangle of antlers. Manuela walks by and leans over to see.

"It's not a bowl," I apologize.

"Do you know they've recovered similar figures in prehistoric caves?" I don't know if that's a compliment, but Manuela says, "Isn't that fascinating? In every age, we try to create the image of the other figures that share our earth. That's what almost everyone does when they first sit down in the studio. Although your antlers are particularly outstanding."

The deer gazes up at me. In the movie, he might come to life and leap out of my hand. Instead the bells on the door clatter. It startles me and my first thought is that Mama has somehow found me. But it's a tiny elderly woman, slipping in from the cold. I glance up and see her as I'm cleaning up the space I've taken at the table.

"Anya! How are you?" Manuela swoops over to greet the elderly woman entering the studio. "Where's Joseph tonight? Shall I put on some tea?" I watch Manuela fuss over the older woman and understand that the fussing is part of her job too.

When she sees me at the sink, washing the mud off my hands, she says, "So soon, chica? Maybe because it's a school night? We have open studio hours on Saturday mornings and Sunday between three and seven. Bring your friends. Or make some here!"

I know she means that I'll have the chance to meet people, but for an insane second, I imagine that Manuela intends for me to create a network of ceramic deer and live among them, cavorting in a pottery forest. I would finally be the least fragile of my friends.

"I'll be back," I promise before heading out the door. But probably I won't be. I can practically hear Mama: *Everyone uses the same clay. Do you know how many germs must be lurking in that stuff?*

The streets are fully dark, so I walk faster. My calves scream every last step up the hill and my chest aches from walking faster than I'm used to. I was wrong to push myself like this. This is what I realize after attempting a sprint in the final press up the hill. After my chest feels like it's splitting open while I wheeze up the empty driveway. After I rush around the house, flicking on lights, I kick off my shoes and lie down on the couch, wrapping a blanket around my shoulders so my skin doesn't feel cold to the touch. For a while I lie there panting. *You made it*, I congratulate myself. *But just barely—you can't go taking risks like that for no reason.* And then I focus on deep calming breaths so that my heart's pounding subsides by the time Mama comes home and gets out her stethoscope.

I'm almost back to normal—well, my version of normal—when she actually gets back, a half hour later than expected.

"Cara, sweetheart—I hope you're not sleeping on the couch," she says. "Honey, that's terrible for the alignment of your back. You know that."

"I'm sorry, Mama. I must have just dozed." I watch her carefully, waiting for her to notice something out of place, some minuscule detail that I forgot. I realize my nails look like I've been clawing through cement. No amount of rubbing gets the clay out.

"Of course you dozed! Because you needed to rest! Just like I told you." She sits on the arm of the sofa and brushes my hair from my face. "I'm glad you dozed. Even on the couch."

Mama sighs. "I'm sorry I was in such a mood when I left. We talked it over at group. I just worry so much. These teachers—I'm glad they see you at your best. But they can't possibly imagine what it's like to see your child's eyes roll back in her head or watch her choke on a feeding tube."

"I'm sorry, Mama." This time I mean it.

"No, honey, I'm sorry. Listen, I admire how determined you are to still do well in school, despite all your challenges. I should celebrate that more. We should celebrate more in general." She giggles a little and it sounds so unfamiliar to me that I fight past the weighted blanket to sit up and see her more clearly.

Mama looks pretty. That's the only way to describe it. She's wearing mascara and she's clipped back her hair in a silver barrette instead of her usual no-nonsense bun. But it's more than just makeup. I notice this intangible quality—a lightness—to her.

"I learned so much tonight, honey." Mama leans forward to tell me. "Really inspiring group session. It's just amazing how the medical world keeps making such progress so quickly. I left that meeting tonight absolutely energized. We have to stay on top of things, Cara. Let's not let the Mr. Brinkses of the world get us down. At this very minute, some scientist is bent over a microscope discovering an effective treatment for your immune disorders. It's coming. In the meantime, we have to keep your body as healthy as possible."

We've seen a lot of doctors. We've sought second, third, and fourth opinions. But Mama sounds breathless with hope. She looks young with it. So I nod. It's all she needs to start chattering again. "I've signed up for a few workshops. And we might even have the opportunity to take part in a health study or two. There's a physician in the group—very advanced ideas. Understands the need to balance pharmaceutical with holistic treatments. Our kind of doc."

"I thought it was a group just for parents?"

"He stopped by at the end. He had some info to share and he was looking for a few patients who might qualify for a clinical trial. He's received funding from Stanford and from Harvard Medical School—I'm telling you, Cara, I heard him speak and it was like an angel whispered in my ear. I've always thought, you and me, we have to just keep knocking on doors—to find the right answers, to try the right medicines. At some point, we're going to unlock whatever code has your health in its strongbox. Maybe this is it. Maybe Dr. Eric can figure out that combination."

"Dr. Eric?"

My mom shifts a little and tucks a strand of her hair behind her ear. "Long Greek name. He said *Dr. Eric* would be easier to pronounce. I thought it was very down to earth. You know how these doctors sometimes are—stuffy dictators who think they know more than the people dealing with illness every day. But Dr. Eric wasn't like that all. He truly listens." She stands up then and begins straightening the pillows. The lightness around her dissipates. I can almost see it float away. "But I didn't realize how late the meeting ran. We really need to get you to bed. And I haven't forgotten about the breathing treatment." I groan and she holds up her hand. "Cara, we've talked about this. We don't want to play around with that congestion. Especially since Dr. Eric might be able to fit us in for a consultation next week."

Later, after I brush my teeth and wash my face, I try again to scrub the clay from my nails. She will notice eventually and I still haven't come up with a viable explanation.

"How's your pain level?" Mom asks when I climb into bed.

I'd been so nervous about being caught I hadn't considered my pain level. "Three," I say so that she won't guess how much I overexerted myself. Truthfully, my legs hurt in kind of a good way. A useful way. They feel like they have accomplished something.

They haven't, I remind myself. No homework done. No library card. My little deer has probably already been reduced to a lump of clay again. I lie back on the bed and try not to stiffen as Mama fastens the elastic bands of the mask around my face. They pull the corners of my eyes into a squint and pinch the bridge of my nose. "Stop fighting it, Cara," I hear Mama say. When I try to breathe deeply, I smell scorched rubber and menthol.

I think of the walk into town—how the cold wind burned my nostrils and made my chest ache. Mama turns on the machine and the room fills with its rush and wheeze. I keep the corner of the bedsheet between my fingers and rub it, trying to distract myself from the noise and the pressure. Mama shuts the light and I pretend it's not cotton in my hand but clay. I remember what it felt like to sit on the stool in the studio and coax a shape from nothing. In my mind, I send myself back to that warm studio. I try to replace the machine's beeping with the memory of the clay bells. And then I understand: I do have something to show for the evening's adventure. I have a secret from Mama, maybe the first I've ever kept.

CHAPTER FIVE

When I arrive at school without my completed assignments the next morning, no sirens go off when I walk through the classroom doors. No one says anything. So I pay close attention and nod during lectures and smile at the right moments and jot down notes as if there is the slightest chance I will glance back at them later.

Each day feels a little bit like progress. My arrivals make fewer ripples each day because they count as less newsworthy. I figure out tricks—I set the alarm on my phone for 4:00 a.m. and slip off the breathing machine mask so that the angry lines on my face have a chance to fade before school.

I stop getting lost so often between classes and even start sharing those little inside jokes that exist by default—like the way Mrs. Fontana seems to end all her sentences with "and so on and so forth," so that if you look around the math classroom, you can watch students mouth the words at their desks. I learn from listening to conversations that Tuesday nights are teen nights at the coffee shop in town and I groan right along with everyone else when Mr. Brinks throws in a pirate pun during morning announcements. I even line up with the rest of the ninth grade at lunch for chicken fingers, which I am sure aren't free of antibiotics but actually taste delicious. I stand up when the bell rings, and relearn how to turn the dial of my locker correctly. I pay attention and work productively in groups.

But all of it exhausts me. I have to work hard to seem cheerful and alert. I don't want to give Mama any reason to keep me home. Some mornings, she clucks over my blood pressure or insists that I have a fever. But no matter what, I give her a pain number of two—nothing higher than that. Nothing worth staying home over. At school, I make myself walk briskly, the way I did on my way home from the library. The way the sea of other legs around me moves. I push myself to keep up but it feels as if there's maple syrup running through my veins.

Each day until about noon, I feel foggy from my morning meds. My head starts to pound around two o'clock and I start counting down the minutes until I can rest. So I try to make the most of those two good hours between twelve and two. I force myself to say hi to at least three people. I make sure to walk past Mr. Brinks's office, just to prove that I'm in school.

One time I recognize Science Kid from the library. I spot him sitting in one of the chairs in the office, the ones usually reserved for kids in trouble. Science Kid holds his head in his hands while the secretaries fret over him. I turn my head away quickly and let the hallway current carry me on.

Each afternoon, on my way out to Mama's car, I think up three safe things to tell her about the school day—Kevin Pike's crazy T-shirt or the therapy dog they had holding court in the library. Something light and without controversy. I try to keep chirping news the entire ride home so she doesn't get it in her head to worry so much. Once we're home, I sit with a textbook at the kitchen table and let my eyes rest. I don't ever actually complete homework. I don't ever have the energy to study.

Mr. Brinks told me that I couldn't afford to miss another day of school and so I make certain to show up. But I can't handle all of it. I don't really understand how some kids do.

Mama keeps recording her daily videos and she spends a whole episode showing me slaving away at Algebra II homework, even though I'm just doodling in my notebook and shading in squares of graph paper.

I don't throw away my failing grades or anything. I immediately fold the papers, before any of my classmates can see, and slip them into the folder in my backpack. Mr. Cohen tells me to get my European history test signed at home and I nod solemnly.

I have eight consecutive school days of waking up and moving myself along with the current carrying me from home to school and class to class and then back home again. I wouldn't say I have friends, but there are people at whom I consistently smile.

The folder of failure gets heftier and I know teachers will

release interim reports soon; maybe because I see the end in sight, I try to push myself as far as possible. On the Tuesday before Thanksgiving, I tell Mama I have a research paper for biology, even though I don't.

"I'm supposed to pick a pioneer of science," I tell her.

"Well, you can use the computer, right?"

"Dr. Presley actually said not to. She wants us to learn how to use other sources."

"What kind of sources? When Dr. Presley does research, I bet she uses Google and Wikipedia."

I shake my head, composing a silent prayer that Mama won't send an email complaining about the double standard of scientific research at school. My voice doesn't even falter when I tell her, "Those are exactly the sites she wants us to avoid. She says the public library has an incredible research section." The Libby Gilfeather in my head raises her eyebrows. Since when have I learned to lie so well?

Mama sighs heavily. "We'll go later on in the week."

"Well—"

"Cara, please don't tell me you've left this until the last minute. You know how I feel about manufactured emergencies."

"Of course not. It's just that I'm feeling pretty good today. I thought I'd capitalize on the unexpected energy." Really I just want to walk down the street, stop, and get a cup of hot cocoa. On my own. I have a five-dollar bill creased in my pocket and a mental list of about two dozen acquaintances I'd probably be able to have an awkward conversation with.

I think Mama can tell how much I want it. And I am showing unexpected energy. She reaches for her jacket and keys and says, "Well, how can I argue with that?"

"You can just drop me off there. I can text you when I'm ready." Mama's arm stops in her sleeve. The keys jangle against the counter. I freeze. I've pressed it too far. "If you want—I know you haven't recorded tonight's video. My priorities shouldn't always trump yours, Mama."

She actually seems to consider it. "I appreciate you acknowledging that, Cara." She checks the clock. I see her eyes skitter to the kitchen chart, where all my daily numbers are recorded. Lately, they've stayed pretty steady—either because this careful schedule benefits my body or because I've deliberately scored my pain so low.

"Okay," she says. I can hardly believe I hear the word. "I don't see why not. I'll wrap up my shopping at the natural foods market on Stelton Avenue. That should give you enough time to get some research done."

"Like an hour?" I try to sound breezy, as if it hardly matters.

"Yeah. I can spend an hour shopping for produce." There's a smile in Mama's voice.

The concern doesn't completely go away, though. When we pull up to the front of the library, she says, "Text me if you start to feel at all fatigued. Don't wait until your blood pressure drops."

"Of course." I nod. "But I feel really good." Despite the low-key guilt hammering my heart. "Thanks, Mama," I tell her, as if that makes up for lying.

The enclosed glass in the front of the building looks like a tall lantern on the shelf of Main Street. After I step inside, I drink from the water fountain, mostly to prove I can but also because my afternoon pills dry out my mouth so much. I make a quick circle around the reference section and then head right back out the exit, feeling the librarian's eyes on me as I leave. *Relax*, I remind myself. It's not like I'm about to sit in the corner on some dude's lap, petting his face and twirling his hair. And there is no way that I am the first teenager to use the public library as an alibi.

I'm going to the coffee shop across the street. It hardly counts as an unforgivable act of defiance. I don't even order anything caffeinated—just herbal tea. "For here or to go?" the barista asks. I look around the little café. In my head, I imagined it full of my classmates from school. I thought I'd breeze in and find a table of girls I recognized and settle in for a lifetime of friendship. They would have sophisticated names like Cameron and Zoe. Later on, we'd laugh at what a big deal it was for me to be out by myself.

But I don't see any teenagers. There's a group of bearded guys in the corner, clutching iPads and swearing at each other. There are some moms with baby strollers and one little old lady reading a catalog of flower seeds.

And there's the guy behind the counter. He must see that I'm flustered because he rolls his eyes at the bearded bros. "Gamers. Whatever, right?"

I hand him the five-dollar bill and wave away the change as if I make such exchanges all the time. Then I ask, "Hey. What's your name?" As soon as the words fly out of my mouth, I know they're weird. I want them back.

But the barista just smiles and points to the name embroidered on his green apron: Ivan.

"Oh, right." I touch the place on my chest where my name would be on an apron and tell him, "I'm Cara Jean. Thank you again." I gulp at my tea to have something to do and immediately scald my tongue. But it's still something, I tell myself—some connection to the outside world. I bought a beverage. I made conversation. Sort of.

Two doors down, Mud Matters beckons but I know that time-wise, it's too risky to duck in. And I feel guilty that I spent five dollars on tea and don't have any more money to qualify as an actual paying customer. I can see through the window that it's bustling with some kind of class. Little girls in scouting uniforms look like they're earning their pottery merit badge under Manuela's watchful gaze. I wave hello and add it to the tally I'm keeping in my head: another connection.

Because Manuela waves back. And then she points to the display window. There, on the top shelf, sits my little deer. I see now that his antlers are disproportionately large. They look like two enormous candlesticks balanced on his head. But his surface is glossy and he looks sturdy and sound. The rest of his form can carry his burden. He has become permanent.

I can hardly look away from him long enough to mouth *Thank you* to Manuela, but she has moved on to the troop of Brownies. At the library, the librarian sees my Styrofoam cup and promptly kicks me out, so I sit on the bench right outside and sip carefully. When I finish, I chuck the cup in the trash and keep sitting, breathing in the cold air and congratulating myself on another minor adventure.

When Mom comes barreling around the circle in front of the building, she looks surprised to see me waiting. Surprised and then concerned. When she asks me which biologist I chose to research, I make up a name, Ivan Nastovsky, and provide so much detail that I worry. I've become a good liar.

Poor Mama, with all her kindness and trust in me, has no idea.

In school that Wednesday, it looks like lots of my classmates started Thanksgiving break half a day early. But I get there, right on time, and see Mr. Brinks notice me across the slightly emptier hallway.

"How's it going, Cara Jean?" he asks. He looks pleased he remembered my name.

I tell him I'm great, and move on before he can ask me anything else.

At home we start prepping Thursday's meal. Mama and I sit on stools in the kitchen. She has me peeling potatoes and she keeps snapping pictures of the pile growing taller. At four, the doorbell rings and we both freeze. It's always this way, ever since I remember. Mama hates when people show up on our doorstep unannounced.

"Cara Jean," she says, "go upstairs for a minute."

"Why?"

"Just go on. Now." She barks the last part and it gets me hustling off the stool and up the stairs. I sit at the top of the steps and try to listen. I used to think my father might show up. Days when I felt so sick, when we'd go weeks with only Mama and me in the house and we'd only leave to shuttle back and forth from the hospital for treatments . . . on those days, I'd think, *Doesn't he have to check on me?*

"Oh, thank you, that's so generous," I hear Mama say to someone at the front door. She's using her YouTube voice. "It's just my little girl and me this year, but we will put it to good use. We always do. Please pass along our thanks to the rest of your congregation."

I hear murmured voices and the clank of the screen door stretched open. "Oh, that's so kind of you, but my daughter's simply too ill for us to venture out. Her immune system is compromised, so the slightest germ . . . Well, you know, God has his plan." The door slams and she calls out, "Thank you again! God bless!"

I hear Mama moving around, but she doesn't call me downstairs. I finally wander back to the kitchen and find her putting away bags of groceries in the pantry while an enormous turkey sits stranded in the sink.

"Will you look at all this, Cara Jean?" She gestures to the cans of green beans and cranberry sauce on the counter, the boxes of stuffing and instant mashed potatoes. "The sweetest folks from St. Luke's Episcopal Church just came by. I don't know how they got our name but they wanted to make sure we had a Thanksgiving supper."

"Wow." I'm not sure what else to say.

"I know. So many blessings."

"But, Mama, you said I was too sick to go out." I want to point out that we also have plenty of food. I've been peeling potatoes for hours. The giant turkey might feed us for the duration of the winter.

"Cara Jean, people like to feel like they are helping. It does no harm. It enhances their holiday."

"But—"

"Do you want to go over to some family's house? Total strangers? Sit around someone else's dining room table so they can tell themselves they answered their charitable call?"

"No," I answer automatically. Honestly.

"Well then. It doesn't cost us anything to show appreciation. And we'll freeze the leftovers." Mama claps her hands together. "Now back to those potatoes!" She kisses the back of my head and then pulls out her phone. It must be time to record a little segment. I keep my head down and out of camera range.

"Happy Thanksgiving, wellness warriors! We've got an attitude of gratitude in our household today. Thanks to a local church group, Cara Jean and I will be feasting tomorrow on a variety of traditional recipes. How about you all list your favorite holiday recipes in the comments? And let's have some straight talk—we can't always afford organic in our household—who else out there is with me on that? Sometimes free-range nutrition stretches outside a single mama's budget but we work with what we have and we make healthy choices when we can. And that's all you can do with the best you've got. Happy Thanksgiving from my girl and me, wellness warriors! We are so thankful for you!"

I turn in early that night, and Mama thanks me for that too.

"I'm impressed with the choices you're making, Cara Jean," she says.

"Mama, I haven't been coughing."

"As much," she corrects me. "You haven't been coughing as much."

"Maybe I could skip a night of the breathing machine?"

"What happens when we take our healthy days for granted, Cara Jean?"

My shoulders slump. "Okay."

"I'd like the answer, please."

I recite it for her: "We lose our healthy days."

"That's right. I know how hard it is. You know I do."

Mama rarely talks about her own bout with cancer. It's mostly too painful for her to remember. It ended her skating career, for one thing. I know she suspects it could be hereditary in some way. And I've heard her ask my doctors if the chemotherapy she received could have somehow sat dormant in her body and triggered my disorder now. I've heard one doctor say, "Absolutely not." And another say it was "medically impossible."

But nothing convinces Mama. Nothing stops her from blaming herself.

CHAPTER SIX

On Sunday night, Mama discovers an email from the school in her spam filter that informs her I'm failing three classes.

Any other mother would rage. And Mama *does* rage . . . just not at me.

"First of all," she says, "there is absolutely no way you can be failing. Cara Jean. You are an intelligent young woman, with plenty of innate ability. You have some disadvantages and I truly wish your teachers could be more understanding of those."

My mom sounds like she is speaking from some place far away or underwater. I can't tear my eyes away from the computer screen. I feel nauseous and shaky. I think of the folder with my tests and quizzes. I close my eyes and picture the numbers circled in red at the top: 48, 39, even a 17. But those were just quizzes; they are supposed to help you refocus your efforts. And I've been sitting through every minute of every class lately. Almost all my teachers count class participation. How can I show up to school and do worse than I was when I stayed home sick for months at a time?

"I don't understand." I keep whispering it. But I do understand. I expected it, after all. It just feels different to see it made official. "Mama, I'm really sorry."

"Stop that right now. You have nothing to be sorry for. To think of what you have suffered, what I, as your mother, have watched you suffer. These are paper pushers, not educators. Bureaucrats. You are legally entitled to certain accommodations, Cara Jean, and they are not providing them. Instead that Brinks character has you terrified of missing school due to your medically recognized condition. That is illegal. I know my rights. And as your mother, I know your rights too."

The next afternoon, Mama plays Mr. Brinks footage of me working at home. I sit beside her in the conference room, cringing. Mama's tinny voice blares out of her phone ("Hello, wellness warriors!") and Mr. Brinks raises his eyebrows.

"What a lovely hobby, Mrs. Wakely, but I'm not quite sure how that's relevant to Cara's academic difficulties." We sit around a table with a guidance counselor, who I don't recognize; Mrs. Fontana, my math teacher; and Mr. Cohen, who teaches

European history. Dr. Presley couldn't make it, but I am failing biology too. Apparently she left notes.

"It's Ms. Wakely, thank you, and I'm showing you video of my child studying about as much as she can, despite extraordinary extenuating circumstances."

"But I can't grade video," Mrs. Fontana says first, and then adds quickly, "As much as I'd like to." She smiles at me, as if that makes this whole meeting any less excruciating.

"You can see our difficulty here?" Mr. Brinks holds up his hands. "We know that Cara has experienced health challenges, although we have little documentation of the specifics of her condition. However, we see the lethargy. Cara often struggles to get through a typical day of a Middlefield High School student. She appears to be in significant pain. I'm no professional, but Cara looks very thin. She looks pale and gaunt, as well as jaundiced."

"She is jaundiced because her kidneys don't currently function properly. And her pain level sometimes interferes with her appetite," my mom explains carefully. "At times, she experiences brain fog and has difficulty focusing. Cara has been in remission for several years from childhood cancer, but the medications that keep her well also have significant side effects. *That* is her condition." Mama highlights his choice of words with venom in her voice. She reaches for my hand and grips it, hard. "She is a survivor."

With that, the mysterious school counselor leaps into the conversation. "Of course she is, Ms. Wakely. We just want to support Cara. And just like her body has needed time to heal, perhaps academically, Cara needs some time to catch up with her peers."

"But I'm fourteen." That's dumb of me to say; they know how old I am. "I'm running out of time to catch up."

The counselor nods and smiles. "It must feel that way, but we all have our own timelines."

"But not really," I say. "Not for homework." The two teachers shift uncomfortably in their seats. I slide my eyes to Mama and glimpse the slightest lift at the corners of her lips. She gives my hand another squeeze.

"What do you mean by that, Cara?" The counselor leans forward, his pen poised on his clipboard.

"Well, when Mr. Brinks and I met last time, he said that if I missed another day of school, I would have to repeat the year. And so I've been pushing myself really hard. But sometimes . . ." I hang my head. "Sometimes that's just when my body gives out." I take a deep breath and meet the eyes of the counselor. "So when you talk about timelines, it just makes me wonder: Is it possible for me to have a different timeline for some assignments or the occasional test, until my body gets more used to being in high school?"

"What does that even mean—more used to being in high school?" Mr. Brinks looks like a kettle about to whistle.

"I think I understand." Mrs. Fontana speaks up then. "I have a son who is a sophomore at another school. But it was an adjustment—switching classes, the early mornings, and we didn't have the added complication of health issues."

I nod gratefully at Mrs. Fontana. "That's a lot of it. I'm just so tired when I get home."

Mr. Cohen clears his throat. "I can make allowances for homework." Mrs. Fontana nods beside him. My mom exhales. She reaches under the table to squeeze my knee. Mr. Cohen adds, "But I am concerned about the midterm exam."

"That's right," Mr. Brinks says. "We have midterm exams, which are cumulative assessments of a student's progress in each course. These are critical. Cara, your teachers have shared your recent record of dramatically low test scores. So obviously we're concerned about your ability to prepare for midterms. Which are a requirement."

"But let me just chime in to say that we haven't even discussed extra help," Mrs. Fontana volunteers. "Dr. Presley also asked that I pass that message along—we are always available before school, after school . . ."

My mom looks around the table, nodding. "We appreciate that you are all available for extra help. That's difficult for Cara, due to the fatigue she experiences. But in an effort to be better partners in this process, I think we should try."

I nod vigorously. "Of course," I say. "Anything that will help."

The counselor nods along with me. "Well, I have to say, I am really heartened by how productive this meeting has been. Good job, all of us. I think I speak for the full school administration when I thank you, Cara, for your transparency and self-care in this process. Let's meet again after midterms and assess how we can continue to provide appropriate support." As he wraps up his closing speech, the counselor looks to Mr. Brinks.

Mr. Brinks doesn't look as optimistic. "Well, we have a plan," he says. "Let's hope to follow it."

"Wonderful." My mother's voice drips sweetly. "When we have that meeting, may I ask that Dr. Dunkirk be present?" Dr. Dunkirk is the principal. The best part of hearing Mama request his presence at the next meeting is watching the sly look pass between Mrs. Fontana and Mr. Cohen. Mama continues to lay it on. "I'm sure Dr. Dunkirk is a very busy man, but at this point, I believe we need his support."

"Of course." Mr. Brinks chokes out the words. "As long as his schedule permits."

As long as his schedule permits," Mama mimics Mr. Brinks in the car on the way home. I laugh because she's mocking him for my benefit but my head pounds. Every time the car hits a bump, a wave of nausea crashes over me. When I think of all the studying I need to do at home, the waves rise higher. The problem with Mama's game of us versus them is that she doesn't have to face Mr. Brinks and the faculty every day at school. She can afford to be mean-spirited. She's graduated high school already.

"You made me so proud in there, Cara Jean." Mama pats my leg and pain reverberates throughout my body. "The way you gave it right back to them. Pointed out their arbitrary timelines? I'm so proud of your self-advocacy and grit."

"Thanks." But I grimace and give myself away.

"That meeting took a lot out of you."

Everything takes a lot out of me. Later on, upstairs in my room, I crawl into bed before seven thirty. Mama made me drink some Gatorade with my afternoon meds but I still feel my mattress pitch like a raft beneath me. My mouth tastes sour and my throat burns from swallowing bile. I remind myself I'm supposed to be studying.

I can hear Mama downstairs and hope she's not treating her

subscribers to her impersonation of Mr. Brinks. I can't make out exact words but her voice rises and falls and vibrates along my nerves. She comes up an hour later with a tray of rice and bananas and turns on the humidifier in the corner and the salt lamp on my bedside table.

"There's my wellness warrior," she says softly.

My hand pushes the tray away instinctively and Mama says, "Cara Jean, you have to eat."

"Could I please just sleep?" My eyes fill and I bury my face in the pillow. "I really feel terrible. Like an eight, Mama." I give up the number without her even asking.

"It's probably the stress. Today's meeting triggered my anxiety. I'm sure it was just as uncomfortable for you."

I want to tell Mama I am far more than uncomfortable. The vein at my temple pulses and I wonder if it can simply snap like a rubber band pulled too taut. Mama brushes my cheek with her hand. "I worry what will happen if you show up tomorrow without preparing properly for class. You might need to show them how committed you are."

"Mama—I can't." It hurts to sit up, to see even the low glow of the salt lamp. *What happened to putting my health first?* I want to ask. But I can't pronounce words that complex. Instead I just sob and pull a pillow over my face to muffle my tears. I barely feel her draw the sheet up to my chin. I don't notice when she slips out of the room.

For the next two weeks, I try. I can barely get through homework after my afternoon meds but now I try to work through lunch.

I set my alarm even earlier to meet Mrs. Fontana for extra help.

Still, the only subject I'm not failing is Japanese.

Mama brings up homeschooling one night after dinner, when I'm trying to get homework done.

"No," I tell her. "Absolutely not."

"Cara Jean, it's something we need to consider." I consider how closed off my life is already. I spend more time talking to Libby Gilfeather in my head than I do any real person at school.

"I've found a lot of resources. I can get certified relatively easily. Then we can make our own schedule. Goodness, you already do most of your homework on the computer. Maybe that's how it should be. When you have good days, we'll plow through material. I know how bright you are. But when you have bad days or bad nights like last Monday, well then, we'd have the autonomy to let you rest and heal."

I wouldn't have autonomy. I would be even less independent. Already there are some days in which I only speak to my mother. I think about sitting on the bench in town. Sitting in the cold night and waiting for Mama to pick me up. I like to feel the air wide around me. Without school, I'll never have a chance to breathe.

But that's exactly what Mama calls her plan: breathing room. "It just buys us some space, where you can finish things in your own good time." Mama taps her finger against the folder sitting on the table between us. "These scores don't reflect your abilities, Cara Jean."

"I'm really trying."

"I know." Mama stares at me, her gaze unwavering.

The realization slams into me like a minivan, all no-nonsense and brutal. "You think I'm stupid."

"I do not."

"You don't think I can do this."

"Do what?"

"School. All of this." I gesture at the computer and my books spread out in front of me.

Mama measures her words in tiny teaspoons. "I think you work very hard to catch up but that sometimes you underestimate your own health challenges." She sits down heavily at the counter. "And I wish I could provide more. Some families would be able to hire tutors. I just don't have the budget for that, Cara Jean. It's all I can do to keep up with the co-pays and the costs of all of these medications. I'm sorry—you've landed in some crappy luck for a kid. First cancer and then all the complications afterward. Having an underemployed single parent just tops it all off, doesn't it?"

It's not a charitable thought, but I hate it when Mama does this. She takes something that causes me pain and twists it around, aiming its blade at her instead. I don't feel any better, but I have to stop my wallowing to comfort her. "That's not true, Mama. You do the best you can." The words come out automatically, but tonight my heart's not in it. I try to put on the strong voice I used in the teacher meeting, the voice she claimed to be so proud of, when I say, "In three weeks, I'll take those midterms and I plan to do really well on them. I'm going to surprise you and Mr. Brinks and whichever teachers have already written me out of their gradebooks." Plenty of perfectly lackluster kids pass the ninth grade. I see them every day at the sophomore lockers. "If I can't pass my midterms, we can talk about homeschooling." I regret the promise as soon as I make it.

I set my alarm even earlier—not just to free up my face from the breathing machine. I discover how much easier it is to understand my reading assignments before all my morning medicines deliver their pharmaceutical fog. Three times a week, I wake up in time to get dressed and downstairs before Mama can even question bringing me for extra help before first period. Some mornings I even fill out the chart on the kitchen walls with my numbers myself.

Instead of my usual orbit around the school cafeteria, in search of an elusive friendly table, I sneak bites of my bag lunch in the library. I sit near the smart kids and listen in on their study sessions. Because I have to sit out of gym anyway, Coach Epps lets me sign out to math wing. Mrs. Fontana keeps a folder of extra worksheets on her desk just for me.

I try to accomplish as much as possible before 4:00 p.m. Like a house on a timer, my body starts powering down. I save my Japanese and English Lit homework for those hours at the kitchen computer. Those grades hover at solid Cs and so I have a little room in case our internet goes out or Mama demands I lie down with a warm compress across my eyes.

Any morning I'm tempted to snooze my alarm, any time I consider skipping extra help, I visualize what my days would be like without school, without my modest ventures into the world of the healthy.

I hurt all the time. The breathing machine does nothing to help me; it just interferes with the few hours of sleep I can afford.

And then I get really sick. Not my usual sick, but one of those viruses that lights a furnace in your chest. My entire body aches and my hacking cough scrapes the back of my throat. On the

Monday morning before my math exam, Mrs. Fontana tries to make me go home.

"Hey, Cara," she asks, "are you okay?" We're balancing equations but I feel dizzy and feverish. I'm thirsty but it hurts too much to swallow.

I keep working at the problem. Mrs. Fontana splays her hand over the worksheet page. "Cara, look at me."

My eyes water. She probably sees them as tears but my whole face feels wet and hot.

"It's just seasonal allergies," I say. I direct my coughs into the crook of my elbow so that Mrs. Fontana doesn't absorb my germs. For the rest of the day, I keep my head down even more than normal. I bumble my way through classes. At home, Mama keeps pressing her hand to her lips in the way she does when she's worried.

"You know, Cara Jean, these tests aren't anything."

"My midterms?" my voice croaks. The midterms are everything.

"I'm sure they give makeups if you need to take a day tomorrow."

Everyone knows that the makeups are harder. The teachers are contractually obligated to ensure that. "I don't need makeups. I feel okay: Pain level two. Fatigue level three."

"Yeah? Those numbers seem low to me. Let's plan on going to bed early tonight."

Mama's so proud that I'm not waiting for makeups that she records a vlog about it. "Good afternoon, wellness warriors! It's revenge of the nerds here in our home, as Cara Jean crams for her all-important midterm exams. Today we're highlighting Cara Jean's hard work and determination. She's kept that nose in a book for weeks lately. As a mom, here's how I try to provide extra sustenance to feed her belly and her brain."

Mama hauls a tray of sliced apples dipped in sunflower butter from the fridge. "Clean protein helps memory retention and concentration. But this snack won't weigh down your little scholar and put her in a carb stupor." Mama turns on her megawatt smile. "And how about the taste, Cara Jean?"

She nods for me to taste, so I reach to take one. The smell of the sunflower seeds hits me before I take a bite. I need to gulp to work it down. For a second, I almost vomit on Mama's video. "Yum!" I enunciate my words carefully. "Thanks for the study break snack!"

We Wakely women are both good actresses. Mama acts like she wants me to do well on my midterms. And I act like I believe her.

I turn in for the night a little past 8:00 p.m. I unwrap the second to last of the four DayQuil capsules that I found in the first aid kit under her sink. I take it with my nighttime medications and wash all of it down with a cup of almond milk. Upstairs, in the dark, I try to shut my eyes and rest. My heart races, though. My palms sweat. My blood moves too quickly through my veins. I can barely tolerate the pressure that the breathing machine puts on my face.

I do not sleep. I keep the breathing machine on until I hear Mama climb up the staircase and even a little while longer after that just to be safe. I hold a blanket to my face to stifle my coughs and review equations in my head. Mama made me leave all my textbooks downstairs. When it seems quiet enough, I unfold the tiny kites of paper in my jean pockets and use the light on my cell phone to review some of the worksheets that Mrs. Fontana and I completed in our sessions.

My eyes droop and my heartbeat slows back to its usual pace. It's lonely to imagine I'm the only one awake.

And then the sky lightens and leaves me wishing for eight more hours to study. Additional extra help sessions. Even just a few more minutes to rest.

In the bathroom, I brace myself against the sink and force myself to look up at the mirror. My fingers reflexively go up to my lips. For a second, I look just like Mama—worried.

Red veins stand out in the whites of my eyes. Each time I cough, I see more red. My lips are chapped and peeling from only breathing through my mouth. When I shower, I inhale as much steam as I can. I take the last of the DayQuil capsules right before breakfast. I don't log in my own numbers, because my hands are too shaky. I tell Mama two for pain and fatigue and four for sleep and appetite. She refuses to put them up.

"We don't lie to ourselves on the wellness chart, Cara Jean. You don't look well at all." She's aiming to pick a fight just to distract me. I chug my green smoothie and hold out my hands for more pills. I will not be baited.

With my tongue, I touch the inside of my cheek. It's so hot inside my mouth. I know a thermometer would register the kind of fever that would send Mama scurrying to draw a cold bath. Once, in our old apartment, my fever ran so high and my mom dunked me so insistently in the tub that I clawed out two of the tiles in my shock and delirium. They stayed like that—like two broken teeth reminding us how frightening illness could be. Or its remedy.

I can't afford a scene like that this morning. I keep quiet as if I'm just centering myself. At school we'll take two exams today and two exams tomorrow. After math this morning, I'll have two hours to review my notes for English Lit. But I'm passing that class already. Tomorrow I'll sit for biology and history.

And then I'll come home, crawl up the steps, and fold myself into my bed, with its cotton comforter. I'll ask Mama for an icepack and keep it under my pillow to cool my cheek. It doesn't help any to dream about that now.

We all sit in the gym to take our exams. On those rickety folding metal chairs with the built-in desks. For some of us, just sitting in those contraptions for two straight hours qualifies as enough of a challenge. High school isn't designed for the chronically ill.

High school was invented for Libby Gilfeather. When I arrive, she has already staked out her seat in the first row and calmly flips through index cards as the rest of us mill around in a panic. I try to slide into my desk with the same confidence. Instead I almost topple over.

Within a few minutes, I stop longing to be Libby and instead marvel at all the math I actually know. My body feels like it's collapsing around me—my pulse races, my nose runs, my vision blurs, but the numbers on the pages in front of me make sense.

Mrs. Fontana circulates around the rows, checking in on her students. She hovers over me. "Cara, you okay?" Her voice soothes, like a cool sheet.

"I am." I sound as surprised as my math teacher looks. I keep thinking about that Celine Dion song: "It's All Coming Back to Me Now." I hear the chorus playing over and over and keep my head bent to the desk, plowing through each math problem, one by one. All the rules I worked so hard to remember surface in my brain.

The clock at the front of the gym counts down. Other kids look up at it and frantically pick up their pace. I am feeling a different kind of time at my back. My throat feels like it's lined with razors. My temperature climbs. When I shift in my seat, the folding chair seems to sway. I can't see straight. All those numbers on the exam pages begin to swim. I'm working through the last section of the exam when they vanish altogether. I clutch at the desk and feel myself give out and pitch forward. The last thing I see is the wood grain of the gym floor as it rushes up to meet my face.

CHAPTER SEVEN

From some far-off place, I hear a lot of scuffling. A girl screams. Maybe a few different girls scream. Someone tugs my legs out from the folding chairs and helps me stretch out on the floor. I feel pressure on my neck and understand, in a vague way, that someone is taking my pulse. I hear the crackle of a walkie-talkie and the scrape of chairs. Very close to my ear, Mrs. Fontana coos with concern.

I wonder what happens to my exam—if my score gets disqualified. What happens to all the exams? I feel myself jostled and believe my classmates are lifting me—the way the team lifts up the quarterback after the game is won. They thought I was so insignificant, but I alone have put a stop to the math exam.

Later on in the hospital I find out the exams continued on after the paramedics loaded me on the gurney. Mr. Brinks doesn't give many details. Apparently, he had to ride with me in the ambulance and now he sits in a plastic chair in the makeshift room in the ER, texting back and forth with the school secretaries.

"Cara, please don't worry about your exams right now," he tells me, sounding more sincere than I've ever heard him. His tie looks damp and rumpled and I hope I didn't puke on it.

"I'm trying to connect with your mom. We'll get her here as soon as possible." I know he's trying to help because he doesn't promise that with any visible dread.

"I'm sorry for all this trouble." I mean the earlier meeting—Mama's demands to meet with his boss, even the accounting for all my absences in the computer system.

"No, no. We were all just so afraid."

I spend the afternoon lying in a hospital bed, while people stop by and worry. The doctors and nurses. Sometimes they pull the curtain around my bed for privacy. Sometimes I duck my head so my hair hangs in a curtain around my face: even more privacy. Eventually they summon a social worker, since no one can reach my mother.

"Do you know where your mother works, Cara?" The social worker looks like the librarian, but with different glasses.

"My mom doesn't work." I stop myself from adding that I am her full-time job.

The social worker looks down at Mr. Brinks. "Do you often have difficulty reaching Mrs. Wakely?"

61

"Ms. Wakely. And absolutely not. I consider this very uncharacteristic."

"Well, we're going to admit her. And we'll need some information about Cara's health history. Do you have access to her health records?"

Mr. Brinks nods and stands. "Of course. Let me connect you with our school nurse." They both head out of my curtained compartment and leave me to wonder where Mama could be and if she ever managed to submit the school physical form.

An orderly arrives to unlock the brakes on my bed. "Hey there, sweetie pie. My name is Omar and I will be your pilot this morning. Please fasten your seat belt now. You're headed up to pediatrics." I laugh even though it hurts my throat.

"Will someone tell my . . ." I start to ask, but I can't get it all out.

"Someone will tell your dad."

The pain in my throat migrates down. "That's not my dad. That's the vice principal at my school."

"No worries. They'll tell him too." Omar pushes me through the hall, hamming it up. "Make way, please. Sick kid on board!" The crowded corridors of the ER clear a path for my bed to pass through.

Omar hits the button for the sixth floor and I feel the elevator rise. My guts lurch and I clutch at the bed's metal railing. "You okay? Don't go hurling in the elevator. They gotta pay me extra if you hurl in the elevator."

I try to nod but my head hurts too much to move it. I feel around for my phone, checking for the time. I must be late for my medicine. "My phone?" I ask, rubbing my temples.

"You kids are crazy with those things, going into withdrawal without it."

I shake my head and wince. "No—"

"They probably have a bag with all your personal effects. Your clothes too. 'Cause you didn't wear a hospital gown to school, right?"

"Of course not."

"Well, I don't know. You teenagers got all kinds of weird styles going on. Yesterday it was facial tattoos. Maybe today it's hospital gowns." I laugh in spite of all the muscles pleading with me to stay still.

Omar leans forward and pushes the bed out of the elevator. We pass by a small waiting room with a rainbow mural on the wall and I struggle to sit up. I'm almost positive that I saw Science Kid sitting there with a clipboard. Maybe I've started hallucinating.

"What time is it?" I ask.

"You got someplace to be, fashionista?" But Omar tells me anyway. "It's two thirty."

It doesn't make sense to me that Mama hasn't answered her phone. And it makes less sense that Science Kid would be here at the hospital instead of taking his English exam. Omar navigates the bed around one last corner and parks me in the hospital room. He points to the open bed by the window. "No roommate yet. Do you want the window seat?"

"No thanks." It seems greedy to request a particular bed, the way Mama always asks for a booth at the Olive Garden.

"Okay, this is where I leave you. The less knowledgeable professionals will now take over."

I must look crestfallen. Omar locks my bed into place and straightens out my IV. He even untangles strands of my hair from the plastic tubing. "It's going to be fine, fashionista. Make sure to order the pudding if they give you the chance." And then he dances from the room, leaving me to wait in the sterile emptiness for what comes next.

What comes next is Mama. I can hear her from the moment the elevator doors open down the hall. I listen and follow her procession to the nurse's station. "Excuse me, you're holding my daughter here. You have Cara Jean Wakely on this unit?"

The nurses respond in soft murmurs but Mama is having none of it. Her voice carries clearly to my room. "Well, given I did not provide permission for you to treat her, you are holding her. Have you stabilized her? I don't see how it's possible to provide adequate care if you don't have the context of her full medical history." More hushed responses. "That man does not speak for my child. That man's complete lack of empathy led directly to my daughter's collapse."

Her last zinger rings out just as Mr. Brinks steps into my hospital room. We both look at each other—two mirror reflections of awkward horror.

"Well," he says, "it seems we've managed to reach your mother."

"I'm sorry," I apologize preemptively.

But the vice principal shakes his head. "No need." He steps closer to my bedside and tells me in a low voice, "Please listen to whatever advice the medical team provides, Cara. We will figure the rest out." He backs his way out of the door, fortifying himself before turning to face Mama's direction. "Ms. Wakely. Let me start by saying we are so relieved that Cara is relatively okay.

Please let me know how the school can provide support for you both. Her welfare is our first concern."

"Now." Mama's shriek reaches each ear on the unit. "Maybe it's your first concern *now*. I hold you personally responsible for her condition." I watch Mr. Brinks accept her torrent. "Do you have any idea how she's been punishing herself these past few weeks?"

"Mama." My voice emerges as a whisper. "Mama, please," I call out more loudly, and watch Brinks step aside. Finally my mother looks past the vice principal and sees me in the bed.

"Oh my goodness—Cara Jean!" She rushes in, scared and angry all at once. "What in the world happened? The school secretary claimed you lost consciousness. How are you now? What's your pain level? What kind of medications have they given you?" She beelines right to me, but doesn't bend to hug me or anything tender like that. Instead she examines the intravenous bag hanging beside me. She grabs the chart off the foot of my bed.

"Looks like they're just running fluids, but you've got a heart monitor on. Did you have palpitations? Any facial paralysis? Honey, do you feel disoriented at all?" Mama hands flutter around me. She straightens the hospital sheet out across my chest and peers toward the door. "Has a doctor even seen you since you got up to the unit?"

"I just got here," I say. And then, "*You* just got here." It comes out like an accusation but I mean it as a question. My whole life, I've felt tethered to Mama. I couldn't shake her off if I tried.

"My phone died." Mama sighs at another life detail failing us. "I charged it just this morning. You saw me with it plugged into the car. I can't figure out this technology. But you know this is why I hate the thought of leaving you at school every day. It terrifies me. Here you're having a medical episode and I'm just blithely running errands."

"The exam was going well."

Mama stares at me, dumbfounded. "Cara Jean, you ended up in an ambulance."

"I mean I knew the math."

"We're not discussing this right now."

"Could you just call and confirm that they'll count the work I did do? I know I missed the English exam but I'm already passing English. Mr. Brinks said—"

"We are absolutely not discussing Mr. Brinks."

"How about we discuss Cara's lab results?" Just about filling the doorway, the woman in the white jacket is the tallest woman I've ever seen. "I'm Dr. Abidi; I'm the pediatric attending today. How are you feeling, Cara?"

"Much better, thank you," I answer automatically.

Dr. Abidi sits on the edge of my bed. Her legs stretch out toward the movable tray in the corner. She has a single black braid hanging down her back. It reminds me of Manuela from the pottery studio. "What happened today?" She asks the question quietly, as if the answer might be private.

"I don't know." The doctor looks at me steadily. I hear Mama take a breath, ready to launch into a litany of my symptoms, but Dr. Abidi holds up her hand.

"Just Cara for now, please. I know you've had a lot of health issues. But let's just talk about today right now. What was different today?"

"I had my math midterm. It's pretty important." Dr. Abidi nods. "That I pass. It was important that I pass."

"Okay, so . . ." She leads me forward ever so slightly.

"So I maybe haven't been sleeping very much. At all." Mama opens her mouth to object. "I pretended to go to bed but stayed up studying."

"All night?"

"Pretty much. I think I have a cold."

"A cold?"

"Or the flu. I ran a fever. But I couldn't stay home sick."

"Most kids want to stay home sick. Especially on exam days."

I shake my head. "Yesterday I started taking some cold medicine. To help with my sore throat." I keep my eyes down but see Mama's chin tilt, listening even more closely.

"What kind of cold medicine?"

"DayQuil? I found it in my mom's medicine cabinet."

"How much DayQuil?" Dr. Abidi flips a notepad out of her pocket.

"I don't know. Four?"

"Four? Four at once?"

"No." I shake my head. "Of course not. Between last night and this morning."

Dr. Abidi jots down a note. "Okay. That's still a higher dose than I might recommend. DayQuil is an antihistamine, so that might account for the racing pulse, the shortness of breath. Cara, do you often self-medicate?"

"No. Never. I just wanted to get through these two days of exams. It was just cold medicine. I had a cold."

"And, Ms. Wakely, did you know about this?" Dr. Abidi looks up.

Mama snaps to attention. "Not at all. I run a very regimented household in terms of our health. I don't know where she would get—"

"I found it in your bathroom."

"Then I don't even know how old that medication was." Mama's voice catches a steel edge. "And I'm shocked to hear about the sleeping. This kind of deceit is completely uncharacteristic, Doctor. I can only say, on Cara's behalf, that the pressure that school has put on her has been extraordinary. It doesn't completely surprise me that it could result in my daughter compromising her own health. However, I'm disappointed in her and very sorry for all this trouble."

"We're not talking about trouble," Dr. Abidi answers. "And we cannot attribute all of Cara's symptoms to taking a few DayQuil. She is severely anemic. Underweight. Our bloodwork also shows an electrolyte imbalance and elevated white cell count. Her sodium levels are off the charts. That alone could have caused her collapse. The teacher who was with her said there was a history of cancer?"

"That's the vice principal at her school. The one who's put such pressure on her. It's been devastating to have to stand by and watch."

"But the cancer?" Dr. Abidi asks.

"She's been in remission for about four years. Renal carcinoma—a Wilms' tumor."

"I see. Okay, that background helps us understand these numbers. We tried to gather some information from the school nurse, but they considered Cara's medical records incomplete. So without you here, we were working at a disadvantage."

"I've sent the school the records—several times. We recently moved and her former school was flooded in Hurricane Michael."

"Oh goodness, that's challenging. Maybe her pediatrician's office?"

"That whole area was hit very hard."

"Right. Well." Dr. Abidi pats the mattress. "Let's keep working to piece together an accurate history. That's going to continue to be important to keep Cara well. At the very least, I'd like a list of her current medications."

Mama reaches down then, to take hold of my hand. "Aside from prescribed supplements, our approach is mostly holistic. She and I stick to a whole-grain diet. We avoid mass-produced meats and refined sugar."

I swing my head up, but Mama's eyes stay steady on the doctor. She squeezes my hand, ever so slightly.

Dr. Abidi gazes down at me. "I'd never dissuade you from a nutritious diet, but some of these labs concern me. We're looking at irregularities. Cara, is there anything else you need to share with us? We just want to help."

I feel another squeeze from Mama. "No. Except that I feel much better now."

"Well. I'm glad to hear that. We're going to keep you here overnight, however. Just to monitor the situation a bit more closely. Cara, I'm going to issue orders for bed rest for now— that's how important it is that you slow down and let your body recover from today's events. Ms. Wakely, your daughter did speak with a social worker earlier today." Dr. Abidi flips through the chart. "Dr. Hoffman. She'd like to follow up with you and then we'd like permission to reach out to the counselor at school. So that we're all working in tandem. We'll also need a full list of any vitamins and supplements she's been taking. You can even just snap a photo of each label with your phone. That will give us some vital information to sort through these odd test results."

"Thank you, Doctor. Thank you for all of your help. We so appreciate the great help you've given Cara. Not everyone has been so understanding. As a single mother with my own health challenges, it can feel very hopeless at times."

Dr. Abidi nods. "Of course."

As soon as she leaves, Mama moves to shut the door. She doesn't need to squeeze my hand. I know I'm supposed to whisper.

"I'm really sorry, Mama."

"I don't even know what to say. The choices you've recently made frighten me. And now we have this doctor, who doesn't know you at all. She doesn't understand everything we have suffered in the past few years. But she gets to judge me."

"She wasn't judging—"

"For God's sake, Cara, she referred us to a social worker," Mama hisses. "Do you know what that means? Because I had cold medicine in my own home!" She paces in front of my hospital bed with her arms folded across her chest. Each time she crosses the room, she checks some part of the apparatus. She traces her finger along the screen of the heart monitor. She pokes the IV bag. "I have half a mind to sign you out and get you to a doctor we can actually trust. But you have no idea what kind of chaos that would set off. I finally felt like I might have found us a solution. And yet, here we are, because you panicked over a math test. Haven't I always taken care of us, Cara?" The question hangs there. All my monitors beep in response.

70 "Maybe they'll let me go home tomorrow?" I try to lift my voice

as if that's something I want. Tomorrow, Libby Gilfeather will sit in the front row of the gym again. She'll take her exams without incident. She won't even notice how much of ninth grade has already passed me by.

A nurse brings a tray of lunch—just broth and saltines. Mama asks for something more substantial but the nurse says, "Doctor says we need to reintroduce solid foods slowly." I look longingly at the stacked cart of trays. Other patients have followed Omar's advice and ordered pudding.

"My daughter's hungry. That can't be part of her treatment plan."

The nurse gives Mama a sympathetic look. "Doctor's orders. But you might want to grab a bite to eat in the cafeteria. Ground floor. They'll pack it up to go for you. You know, so that you can come right back." The nurse winks. "They've got some gourmet grilled cheese down there. I'll be down the hall, making the rest of my deliveries. No one's going to nab me for sandwich conspiracy."

I watch the nurse scoot out the door and tell Mama, "People are really kind here."

"Well, they should be. They're going to bill our insurance enough to warrant saintliness." Mama rummages through her purse. "Does a grilled cheese sound good? Whole-grain bread? Maybe some avocado if they have it?"

I nod eagerly. "And maybe something sweet?"

But Mama points at the IV drip. "That's basically sugar water. They have no clue how that's going to throw off your system. We're lucky if you don't have a hyperglycemic reaction." She pauses. "What do you want?"

"The orderly recommended the pudding."

"And they call this a health care facility. I'll see if they have sugar-free."

"Thanks, Mama."

She nods. "I'll be right back up. I cannot stress this enough, Cara Jean. If the social worker comes back, a nurse, even Dr. Abidi, you don't say a word without me in this room with you. Do you understand me?"

"Yes, Mama."

"People seem kind on the surface, but everyone has an agenda."

These are the first waking minutes I've been alone all day and I spend them considering my own agenda. If the social worker stops by, I could ask her about my midterms. Maybe there's a state rule or a student support service. A hospitalization has to count the way a doctor's note would and Mr. Brinks rode with me in the ambulance, after all.

In my head, I think of questions to ask Dr. Abidi. Without Mama next to me, tugging me into silence. I would ask her about how tired I get and all my headaches. I'd ask her if she's seen kids like me get better. It occurs to me that Mama and I always talk about methods of managing my symptoms, ways to prevent them from worsening. It's like we can't even conceive of a scenario in which I am totally well.

But no one comes into my room. Not the careful doctor. Not the kind nurse. Not the concerned social worker. I lie there in the bed with all the intricate machines and wait for Mama to return and decide what we'll do next.

CHAPTER EIGHT

After Dr. Abidi clears me, the hospital starts the discharge process at one the following afternoon, while my classmates sit in the rickety desks filling in the history multiple choice questions.

The nurse discharging me says, "Dr. Abidi recommends we continue bed rest for at least three days."

"Can I go back to school?"

"Not in a bed." The nurse's voice sounds like an eye roll. Mama stands by, nodding along. "She wants you to schedule a follow-up visit on Monday morning." The nurse hands a small card to my mom. "She's happy to see you at her office. When you call to make an appointment, let the receptionist know that Cara is a patient from the hospital. In the meantime, Dr. Abidi has prescribed an antibiotic and advised Gatorade and Ensure to help with hydration and hyperalimentation." This time she gives Mama a slightly wider piece of paper. "You can stop at the pharmacy and fill this here in the hospital. You can find the other products at any large grocery chain. Do you have any questions?"

Mama says, "I'd like a copy of her chart."

"Why?" The nurse looks back up from her clipboard.

"My child's medical records. I don't need to justify the request."

"Well, it's going to take a few minutes."

My mom shrugs. "No problem. I can only imagine how busy you are." She tries a smile. "How long have you worked pediatrics? I worked coronary care myself."

"Almost fifteen years."

"At the same hospital? No kidding. That's an incredible achievement."

The nurse's face visibly relaxes. "Thanks. How about you? You're a nurse?"

"A long time ago, but then I gained a kid and lost a husband. No real loss, if I'm honest. I don't have a whole lot left for other patients. But I really admire those of you who take such great care of other people's kids."

Mama's new best friend nods and smiles. "Let me make you that copy."

"We really appreciate it. I'm sure you're busy."

"Oh, it's no trouble."

I shake my head at my mom. She always does this. Mama

charms people in every doctor's office, in every waiting room. "What?" She splays out her hands, all innocence.

When Dr. Abidi pokes her head in the doorway, Mama barely glances at her, however. Even when the doctor says, "I'm so glad I caught you two. My charge nurse is making copies of Cara's chart. Are we going to start keeping better records now?"

Mama's smile pulls tightly across her face. "Oh, I'm a stickler for records." An image of our dining room table, piled high with filled folders, flashes through my mind. "Especially since I've learned how careless agencies are with them."

"Right. That flood." Dr. Abidi turns her attention to me. "How are you feeling, Cara?"

"Terrific." I give the same thumbs-up I trot out for Mama's subscribers.

"That's good to hear. No more over-the-counter medicines, all right? When you come in to my office, let's bring all the supplements you're currently taking. We can take stock and see what we might need to switch out. And let's get a wheelchair for you for the trip downstairs. You still need to take it easy."

"I can walk. Really."

But Mama has already commandeered one from the hallway. "Cara Jean, you have to listen to Dr. Abidi. Thank you, Doctor."

Her nurse friend stops by to hand over a manila folder with a copy of my chart. "We'll call an orderly to push you."

But when he arrives, Mama refuses to budge from her station behind the chair. She hands him her bag and he looks thrilled to carry some lady's purse. I slump forward in my chair, sorry for him, sorry for me. Sorry for the spectacle that our procession creates through the pediatric unit.

"Cara, honey, how are you doing?" Mama's voice issues its question over my head.

"Just fine, Mama."

She parks me beside the giant Christmas tree. I have to crane my neck to see the star perched on top. I wonder idly where they get a tree so tall and wonder if they transport from the farm on top of an ambulance. Each ornament is the size of a large grapefruit, and in them I can see my reflection—red and round. Embarrassed by all the fuss.

"I've got to pull the car around. This kind man will stay with you until I get back. If you feel faint or dizzy, just give a wave. Isn't that right, sir? Thank you so much for staying with her. It's tricky for us to manage, two ladies on our own."

"Of course, ma'am."

Mama sprints off with her keys, like the lead actress in a hospital soap opera.

"Sorry about my mom." I mean: *Sorry for the drama.*

"She's just a mom," the bored orderly grunts.

I miss Omar. Omar would have some jokes about this. The lobby where we wait has windows on all sides—the namesake atrium for the hospital. The sun streams through the glass and dapples the blue carpet with light. It looks warm and all but I know outside there's a chill. Sometimes I think Mama is like that too.

When we get home, Mama calls the school and tells the secretary that I'll be staying home at least until early next week. Mama's tone sounds all business when she tackles the subject of my midterms. "I'd like to set up a meeting with the principal, please, to discuss the best way for Cara to finish her exams. But at this time her health complications prevent me from scheduling anything on my calendar just yet. We've seen what happens when we place unreasonable pressure on her and the doctors say we are at a critical point in her recovery."

She brushes her hands after that call. "Did you hear me handle that?"

"Thank you." I mean it and promise myself I'll be a little more cooperative. "You must be tired, Mama," I tell her. "You barely slept last night."

"How could I sleep?" She shrugs and sorts pills into my plastic organizer. She hands me three of them and I wrinkle my nose. But I know she hasn't forgotten all of Dr. Abidi's warnings about supplements. Mama's a nurse, after all. "And speaking of sleep—" She nods for me to swallow the pills with the Gatorade we just picked up. "You, darling, belong upstairs. Bed rest, please."

"Maybe I could just rest on the sofa downstairs."

"That's not a bed," Mama says. "Let me help you upstairs." But I can walk on my own and Mama lets me. She follows me up, carrying the toolbox from under the sink. "No studying either. At some point, we need to discuss how you lied to me, Cara Jean."

"What are you doing?" I hear hostility surface in my voice and remind myself again how grateful I should be.

Mama attacks the door hinges with a screwdriver. "We'll find a way for you to earn your door back. But you just got home from the hospital. I can't risk you slipping into a coma because you've been hiding bad choices from me."

"Mama, please! I promise—"

"Absolutely not. I'm aware that you're too ill to have this conversation. For now, I don't want to hear another word."

There's nothing else to say. I feel a twinge of satisfaction watching Mama struggle under the burden of the thing and listening to her bang her way down the hall. The doorway yawns. The blinds are already lowered like eyelids on the windows.

By now, Libby Gilfeather has aced her exams. Science Kid, the library lunch crew—all my classmates probably tumble out of the school, celebrating the upcoming break. Until I sat next to the tree in the hospital lobby, it hadn't even occurred to me that we were verging on Christmas break. I try to imagine the squares of the calendar and count out the days before the whole school is closed for winter break. I'm confused and tired and confused about being tired. I've been sleeping almost constantly since yesterday morning. But even as I try to sort myself out, the familiar fog rolls in, weighing on me like a heavy quilt, blanketing me into sleep.

I wake briefly to see two figures in the doorway. At first I think I'm back in the hospital, but then I remember that my mother took down my door. My mouth feels full of cotton. "Go back to sleep, Cara Jean." Mama's voice seems strong and certain. It takes me a minute but I finally pinpoint it as happy. At first my heart lurches, thinking the broad-shouldered figure beside hers must be my dad's.

Of course that's not so. I wake up hours later in the dark and I hear them talking and laughing. No matter how young you are when he leaves, I think you must recognize the sound of your father's voice. Even if it's just the familiar way it vibrates in your chest. But when I hear this man, I don't feel anything like that. His voice creaks and pitches up and down like an elevator in an old building.

I pull a sweatshirt around my shoulders and make sure to hold the banister on the way down the stairs. Even then, Mama calls out "Cara Jean!" in a sharp voice and snaps her head up with alarm. She and a man in a white doctor's lab coat are huddled at the kitchen computer station. There is a picture of me sleeping on the screen and for a panicked second I believe maybe she's installed a video monitor in my bedroom, like the lack of door didn't count as a safety precaution enough.

But then I notice the tubes and metal rails and realize it's a photo of me in the hospital. I shouldn't be surprised; Mama probably recorded an episode in my hospital room. After all, she tries to help other families like ours. I remind myself that it only feels weird because I didn't know.

Just like our current scenario: standing in the kitchen in my pajamas, facing a strange man in a lab coat. "Cara Jean—" Mama has recovered from her initial shock. "I'm glad to see you awake, although I wish you'd have called from upstairs. Honey, I'm happy to bring you anything you need." Behind her, Lab Coat minimizes desktop windows. He clicks and saves. "How's your appetite?" my mom says as she stands up and moves to the stove. "We've got some pasta on the stove here. How does that sound?"

"I'm not really feeling hungry."

"We just want to see you keep getting stronger." Lab Coat sounds like an oatmeal commercial. He stands up too and awkwardly holds the back of the chair in front of him. I stare at him, waiting.

"Cara." Mama uses her calming voice. "I've told you about Dr. Eric. He was so kind to come over to our home to check on you in person."

"And eat pasta."

"Cara!" Mama's voice swings sharp again.

But the man just chortles, "Well, of course. I couldn't turn down your mom's cooking. And you know it's good that she got herself a hot meal too." Dr. Eric leans forward as if confiding in me. "I have a sneaking suspicion that your mom spends so much time looking out for you that she doesn't always look out for herself." He has black hair, speckled with silver, wrapped into a messy bun at the back of his head. His eyes are light blue—a bright blue. Beneath the lab coat, he wears a blue turtleneck sweater. Some lady probably picked it out for him and told him it matched his eyes.

I wonder what kind of doctor wears turtleneck sweaters. And long hair, for that matter. I tell him, "My mom and I look out for each other." But when I reach for the bowl that Mama passes me, my hospital bracelet slides down my wrist. I feel exposed and ashamed.

"Dr. Eric has been kind enough to look at your chart."

I nod and take a bite, mostly so that I don't have to thank him. I don't quite understand why Dr. Eric has my hackles up. When Mama shoots me a look, I can hear her unspoken words in my head: *People just want to help.*

I concentrate on my dinner and try to spear a piece of rigatoni on each tine of my fork. Dr. Eric sits across from me at the table. "Cara, you're very unwell. At the same time, you're so fortunate. Thank goodness your mother has a medical background. Even her experiences, recovering from cancer—she's uniquely equipped to challenge the medical establishment on your behalf. Otherwise, I shudder about what your quality of life would be like. It probably doesn't always feel like it, but you a very lucky girl."

My head keeps up the nodding but I glance at the computer.

Dr. Eric leans forward and taps the table next to my food. "That's going to be the last gluten for a while. We've been talking about revamping your diet."

Mama and I have revamped my diet every year or so. I chew my pasta more slowly, savoring it while I can, wondering if it's rude to ask to go back to bed.

"Has your mother told you much about me?" Dr. Eric smiles. His teeth look so white I wonder if they're veneers.

My eyes travel to Mama, looking for her cue. She dries her hands on a dish towel and joins us at the table. "Oh, I was so excited after we met—Cara will tell you—I felt that you'd been guided to me by God. I truly felt the intercession of an angel." Mama wipes at her eyes.

"Aha!" Dr. Eric claps his hands and Mama looks as startled as I feel. "Well, that explains it, then! Cara, I'm going to be honest with you. I can only be honest—it's truly a flaw in my character. But I have sensed a wariness from you." Dr. Eric nods, looking back and forth between my mother and me. "And I have to admit to feeling a little bit—a tiny bit—hurt." Mama's hand flutters to her mouth. "Not insulted," he rushes to explain, "because I can tell your mother has raised you to be a polite and respectful young lady. But just a little stung. You know. Because I'm used to people trusting me." He straightens the lapels of his white lab coat. "But hearing that glowing description from your mom? Well, I completely understand the wariness. The two of you have been searching for answers for a long time, haven't you?"

Dr. Eric waits until I nod before continuing. "And people have always let the two of you down. Especially doctors." He smiles up at Mama. She closes her eyes and presses her lips together as if it physically hurts her to nod. "Your mom is mistaken." Mama's eyes snap open. "I'm no miracle worker. No one in medicine is. But I'm very good. And we're going to get to the bottom of what's making you sick. Do you hear me? The two of you aren't alone in this anymore." With that, Dr. Eric reaches over the table and covers my hand with his own. I stay perfectly still and tell myself that my fever must be back. But really I think it's my skin crawling.

"Do you want to get better, Cara?" he asks.

Mama abruptly stands up and starts fussing with the dishes, "Of course we want her to get better."

"Forgive me, Shaylene. You do so much. But I have the distinct sense that Cara would like to speak for herself." He looks back at me. "Isn't that right?"

My skin crawls a little less. It isn't often that someone understands me like this.

"Yes," I say. "And yes. I want to get better."

"Why?"

I feel my eyebrows rise.

Dr. Eric notices too. "Oh, I know. No one wants to be sick. But what is your specific vision of wellness? You need to visualize it, Cara. What do you want to will into existence? Because that reality is attached to your health."

"I want to go to school." It's all I'm thinking about, really.

Dr. Eric nods. "Okay. An education. That's admirable."

"Not just an education." I've said more than I mean to. But there's no going back now. "I don't want to be homeschooled. I want to attend classes. Regularly. I want to have friends. Real friends. I've never even gone to a slumber party. And there's a pottery studio in town. I want to take classes there. I think I'd be good at it."

Mama looks flabbergasted. "Pottery? What do you know about pottery?"

"I just saw it from the car one day." My heart skips and I work to keep my voice even. "I looked it up online."

"Well, I think that all sounds tremendous," Dr. Eric proclaims. "That a beautiful vision, Cara. Let's work together to make it come into existence, shall we? But sleepovers and pottery classes, that's a tall order for such a sick young lady. Do you see that? Most doctors would tell you to focus on pain management, to be grateful that you're cancer-free."

Yes. I know that. My cheeks burn. I feel greedy and ashamed.

Dr. Eric holds up one finger. "But! Shaylene, I want you both to hear this. I think that is a perfectly reasonable set of requests. Do you hear me, Cara? Perfectly reasonable." He grins at me and I let myself smile back. I'm so tired. With everything that has derailed in the past few days, maybe I wasn't seeing him clearly at first.

Dr. Eric stands up and reaches to the counter for the folder I recognize as my file. "I'm going to review all this. We'll look to switch to a fairly cutting-edge protocol, post-pharmaceutical—medications those companies aren't even releasing to the public yet. Because those companies are corrupt. They have built themselves a fortune by exploiting struggling families like your own."

I'm not quite certain what I'm supposed to say.

I settle on "thank you."

It feels good to have a doctor who understands what I want—and who might even ignore my mother in order for me to get it.

CHAPTER NINE

Dr. Eric wasn't kidding when he said that making a commitment to good health would be expensive.

A few days later, Mama and I pore over the printed estimated cost of treatment. I've already had blood drawn. He has brought over a collapsible treadmill and timed my attempts to run. Dr. Eric now knows I can barely jog, that I've never had a period, and that my lymph nodes seem to swell each evening. He's seen the faint scars on my belly from feeding tubes and the raised welt in the crook of my elbow, where Mama says an IV once got infected.

It turns out that daily monitoring, "developing a pharmaceutical protocol," and possible plasma transfusions might run more than thirty thousand dollars. And then there's my spleen. I've tended to think of the organs in my body as necessary components—you keep them or you get a transplant. But Dr. Eric says my spleen actually interferes with my health, because my antibodies have been targeting my blood platelets, compromising my immune system.

Mama keeps tracing her fingers along the numbers. "How much will insurance pay?" I ask.

"Not a cent." Mama shakes her head and bites her lip. "Dr. Eric's practice centers on alternative medicine."

"But we've tried everything else. We need an alternative."

"They don't care. Insurance companies punish people for venturing out of the bounds of traditional treatment. All those kickbacks come before patient care." Mama sighs. "But I've been working on something. Come here." She steers me over to the kitchen computer. "We can make changes if you're not comfortable. But this is the general idea. I think it will help." She seems to reconsider her words. "Actually, I think it's our only shot."

She types in a web address and clicks open some windows. Up comes the same photo from the other night: me in the hospital bed last week, looking particularly pathetic. I feel just as exposed, seeing it a second time. Mama might think I have grown used to photos like this. I've probably seen more pictures of me in the hospital than I have regular baby photos. My baby album looks like a medical scrapbook. Sometimes I wonder why Mama even kept those: little me, swamped in tubing in the metal grated hospital cribs. Tiny me, toddling along a sterile corridor, dragging a giant IV along with me. I guess she thought any childhood is worth remembering.

Above the recent picture scrolls a banner that reads: *Caring for Cara*. And then there's a measuring bar with a goal amount highlighted. It reads *$50,000*. Below my photo, a paragraph describes our need.

> Cara Jean Wakely has spent most of her life in and out of hospitals, first defeating the monster of childhood cancer and then battling the daily struggle of chronic illness. Like any teenager, Cara has hopes and dreams. She envisions a future free from debilitating symptoms and possible organ failure. However, relentless pain and medical challenges interfere with her ability to regularly attend school and plan for the future. Cara's mom, Shaylene, is a single mother forced to give up a promising career in the health care industry in order to serve as primary caretaker for Cara. Facing mounting medical bills and imminent bankruptcy, this courageous family appreciates any financial support you can spare.
>
> *Thank you for your support,*
>
> *Layla McKinnon*
> *(on behalf of Cara and her mom)*

"Who's Layla McKinnon?" I ask. My eyes keep scanning the rest of the writing, trying to process it.

"Should I put more in about your symptoms? Would you feel comfortable with more photos? I do feel strongly that we have to show the worst of it. That way people will see our need as genuine."

"Mama, who's Layla McKinnon?"

My mother turns back to the computer and starts to pull up more images. "She's a friend from my parent support group. She helped me with the wording."

"It sounds like Dr. Eric helped with the wording."

"Well, he didn't," Mama snaps. "That would be unprofessional."

I shrug. "Okay."

"Okay? About the fundraiser? You feel fine with the content?" Mama looks so hopeful.

"Sure." It surprises me a little that she thinks I'd object. She would never let me stop her. I feel certain of that. When Mama lands on a project, the only thing you can really do is stand back and let her plow through.

"Will people at school see it?"

"Possibly. But I suspect not. The site is really geared to adults. You need a credit card to make a donation."

I don't even know that people at school would recognize me. They probably remember me as that girl who fell down in the middle of the math midterm.

"Are we going to meet with Mr. Brinks again?"

"The vice principal?" Mama asks because she is stalling. I can tell. "I've scheduled a meeting with the principal and that guidance counselor instead. That should be more helpful."

"Without me?"

Mama rubs circles on my back. "You remember what Dr. Eric says—we just want you to keep on getting stronger. No distractions from that." She points back at the computer screen. "Layla McKinnon says that this happens to be the best time of year to create a charitable website. People look to give between Thanksgiving and Christmas. And they want to record a donation before January first because of taxes."

"Mama, it has to be almost Christmas now. What date is it— the twenty-second?"

She smiles and pats my hand. "It's the twenty-third."

I feel like the worst daughter in the world. *All she does for me* . . .

"Mama, I haven't even gotten you a present."

"Oh, Cara Jean, you dear girl—that part of the holidays doesn't matter to me. With your hospitalization, honestly I didn't even have the energy to put up a tree this year. Your good health would be the best present I could ask for."

But I can't give her that either. "Can you drive me to town? Just for an hour? Maybe two hours? You can go do the food shopping or maybe research fundraising at the library."

Mama laughs. "What? You're giving me homework now? Where do you need to go? You know, Cara Jean, I've kept Christmas super small this year. We just don't have anything extra in our budget."

"I know that." But I also know she managed to pull something together. We'll wake up Christmas morning and listen to the gospel choir sing carols on TV. She'll make baked apples and I'll open gifts and no matter how many times I ooh and aah over them, Mama will look a little teary and tell me she wishes she could buy everything I've wished for. "Please, Mama. This is so important to me."

"Is it going to cost me money?"

"No way—that wouldn't be any kind of Christmas present."

Mama hems and haws. "What if you're not up for this? We can't have another emergency, Cara Jean. Especially when I'm not there to help. What if something happens to you? After the last time? People will think I am a terrible mother."

"You can drop me off at the coffee shop and then pick me up right there two hours later. Two hours. I'll take all my medicine now and pack a thermos with some green tea in case I get a chill."

"Well, let's hold off on the big blue pill. That one sometimes makes you drowsy. I want to make sure you're alert enough to call me for help if you need it."

"Of course. That sounds like a plan."

"Is your cell phone charged?"

"Fully."

"I can just go with you—wherever it is, Cara Jean. I already appreciate the sweet thought behind your intention."

I don't mean to look over at the laptop. It's not like I'm threatening Mama or bribing her or something disrespectful like that. But it works all the same. She follows my eyes to the charity page and seems to consider for a minute. "All right, then. Two hours. I hope we don't get lost in a sea of last-minute shoppers."

It takes me a few minutes to gather myself together. I haven't brushed my hair in days. Upstairs I change into a slightly less worn-out pair of leggings and a fluffy sweater that I hope indicates *festive ski style* rather than *Goodwill donation*. I grab a ten-dollar bill from the top drawer of my dresser and then two more singles. I turn back and put on lip gloss.

At the top of the steps, I feel myself get a little dizzy, but that could just as easily stem from excitement. I haven't left the house since the day I came home from the hospital. I must still be recovering from that virus because the days since have blurred together more than usual. Mostly I've moved from my bed to the sofa, talking only to Mama or Dr. Eric when he stops by.

I make my way downstairs and see Mama back at the computer. She rests her cheek on her hand. Then she reaches over and hits a button. "Well, there we go," she tells me. Two hours of freedom for my permission. I'm sure she doesn't mean for it to feel like a transaction either. "We just went live."

On Main Street, the township has hung holly wreathes from every lamppost. A nativity stands in the front lawn of the Catholic church, with statues kneeling around the empty manger. Holiday lights hang from most of the storefront windows. I try to avoid the blinking ones in the hope I might dodge a headache. The sidewalks bustle with people but mostly they carry takeout rather than wrapped packages. It looks like a Domino's commercial version of *A Christmas Carol*.

"My word, everybody's out and about tonight." Mama pulls the car up to the curb in front of the coffee shop. "Right here? You know that coffee drinks would probably irritate your delicate digestive tract, right?"

"Mama, you're sussing out clues. You better watch out or I'll tell Santa."

"Okay, okay. Target beckons me. We each have two hours. Don't make me worry."

I stand outside the coffee shop, shivering in the cold until I can see the very last twinkle of her taillights disappear around the corner. Mud Matters is one of the busiest places on the block. I'm happy for Manuela even though it stresses me out—I don't have the time to wait on line for a seat at the craft table. She's done up the front window to look like a ceramic toy factory and it looks magical—with a delicate dollhouse and train set, even a jack-in-the-box with a metal spring connecting his glossy head to the rest of the sculpture. And just when I think she must have tossed out my little deer, I spot him standing on one of the train's flatbed cars, right between an expertly sculpted giraffe and an elephant.

Inside, Manuela notices me right away. "It's my little fawn! I knew you'd come back. Did you see that your tiny friend has joined the circus?"

It feels like I've taken a sip of tea from the thermos that's still closed in my hand. Warmth spreads throughout my chest. My eyes even sting as if I might cry, that's how good it feels to be welcomed. "I did see that deer! Thank you for firing it. This whole place looks like a wonderland." And it does. She's set up a table in the back with cocoa and cookies, and tiny twinkle lights twist around every possible surface—none of them blinking. It's bustling with activity and Manuela must have been rushing around to help everyone. Her two braids hang loosely from their red ribbons.

"I brought money this time." I try to say it quietly. "How much do you charge per piece?"

"Oh, honey, you just make it and we figure it out. What do you want to make?"

"A gift for my mom."

"Oh, wonderful! We specialize in gifts for moms. What do you think? A little pinch pot? A bowl? Maybe a beaded necklace?"

"What about a vase?"

"Perfect! It will be the gift that keeps giving because you will need to occasionally fill it with flowers. But listen—"

"It's very expensive?"

"No. It's quite challenging. If you took my ceramics class, which you should, it's lesson three or four. You have talent but we still have to harness that talent. How much time do we have?"

"I have two hours. And twelve dollars."

Manuela considers these constraints. Then she snaps her fingers. "Do you know that I am a genius? Seriously. I don't want to intimidate you but truly I am a genius. I have a bunch of sample vases. I love being at the wheel and I need to practice, you know—I can't allow my clients to develop more skills than I have. But that leaves me no time to paint anything. Honestly, the painting part of the process? It sometimes bores me. The color doesn't change the shape. I am a potter because my hands love the mud. They enjoy the shaping. I think you are that way too.

"So I propose this. Maybe you make me one more little deer. I have an empty train car in my display and the deer really need to match. And then you paint one of my spare vases. You pick your mother's favorite colors; I can teach you how to make a lovely ombre effect. Then the gifts abound! What do you say? Can we make an exchange?"

"Thank you. Seriously." I don't totally understand how Manuela's business doesn't go under, weighed down by the cost of her own generosity.

"Let's not be too serious. I will tell you the one thing I am serious about—it's my only lecture for you. Are you listening, little fawn?" I nod, hanging on her every word. "Everything you put out into the world comes back to you. I believe that to be true." She goes to the back shelves, checking in on her other customers as she walks by.

I set the first deer in front of me so I can study it while I sculpt his companion. I make another male, with narrow antlers and an alert stance. As I am remembering how to shape the legs correctly, Manuela comes by to drop off a vase for me to paint.

"What do you think of this one? It's graceful, right? I think it's just the right height to set on a kitchen table. With carnations or roses? Maybe a sunflower every now and then?"

"It's perfect. I'm going to paint it with sunset colors." She helps me assemble a palette of red, oranges, yellows, and golds.

And deep blues. "Don't underestimate the power of navy blue. It's the evening sky bearing down on us. Or maybe you're painting a sunrise and that blue is a remnant of the night." Manuela helps me blend the shades together so the gradient looks like a natural progression. "So possible grim news for Santa's elves . . . are you ready? Don't panic." For a second I worry that the vase will cost more than twelve dollars. I'm sure it does. Maybe Manuela thinks I'm one of those kids with a credit card in her pocket for emergencies.

But that's not it. "It takes me eight hours to glaze a vase." My brush pauses midair. "However, that will turn out to be just fine. Because I'm going to load the kiln one more time tonight and then reopen the studio bright and early to unload."

She looks so happy to solve the timing dilemma. But my face must give something away. "I know it's a busy time. Are you traveling tomorrow? Maybe you live too far away to stop by?"

"No—walking distance."

"Fantastic! Problem solved." She looks so relieved.

"Well, no. Not really. Walking distance for other people isn't always walkable for me."

"Yeah? It's true—you took a long time between visits. That deer felt lonely but we had faith. Are you okay?"

"Yes. But thank you. I will figure it out. Even if I pick it up after and it's a New Year's present." Manuela's nose wrinkles. She does not approve of this plan. "Really, you've already done so much to help me. I'm so grateful. For this whole place, really." I unzip the front pocket of my backpack and press the bills toward her.

"Don't be ridiculous. Keep your money. I've got myself a brand-new deer."

"You seriously have to let people pay for things. Do you even charge for the cocoa?"

Manuela looks at me as if I've lost my mind. "Charging for hot chocolate would be Christmas sacrilege. But listen, people give me all kinds of business advice. I know I need to do better. One thing I'm trying is to build my mailing list. That way I can send out coupons and promotions, a calendar of events. Let me get the clipboard so you can sign up?"

I write my name below the others very carefully, then my address, working hard to remember this latest zip code. I use a Sharpie and write my initials on the bottom of the vase. I even touch the top of the new deer's little head for good luck. I clean up my workspace with a smile plastered on my face the whole time. It's not Manuela's problem that I messed up Christmas. I make sure to look cheerful.

The smile wavers when Mama picks me up. She pulls in front of the coffee shop ten minutes early and finds me sitting on the curb. I wasn't trying to get run over or anything. I just figured that bringing in my own personal thermos of tea inside would count as poor coffee shop form. "Cara Jean, cold cement could give you a chill!"

"Really? I have to be afraid of pavement now?" My life and all its limitations can be so frustrating. A migraine starts ricocheting between my temples.

"Hey. What has gotten into you?"

"Nothing." I see Mama examining me, trying to figure out where I am hiding a gift for her. I want to dive out of the car and cry on her shoulder all at once. Then I begin sniffling. "I just messed it up. That's all. I had these plans and it turns out I don't know anything. I can't even accomplish the simplest task." The tears come hot and fast and make everything that much worse.

"Cara Jane, I didn't request any kind of present from you."

"I know that, Mama."

"Well, I don't see what calls for you to be so angry at me. You asked to come to town. I drove you to town."

"I know that, Mama." I take deep breaths and try to summon the calm I felt in the studio.

"I've never behaved in such a manner as to lead you to believe that material things are important to me. I try to be the best parent possible, to meet all of our needs. We have a hard row ahead of us but we have a whole lot of love in our home. You know the holidays stress people out. They do whole psychological studies on that. But our little family doesn't really have the luxury to indulge in that kind of stress. Our trials have taught us what really matters."

"Mama! Stop talking to me like I'm one of your subscribers."

As soon as the words tumble out, I want to catch them. The minivan's windows have frosted with cold but the temperature drops inside the vehicle too. I press my lips together, trying to word it correctly in my head. But there's no right way to tell your mom you're tired of hearing how bravely she's faced the grueling task of raising you.

We ride in silence. We enter the house without speaking. Mama and I have never come home from a funeral before but I imagine it would feel like this: climbing the stairs with my shoulders bowed, burdened by grief and guilt. I sit on the edge of my bed and kick off my boots. I remember Manuela's philosophy about everything we put out into the world. She would consider this a Christmas sin. I might as well have spit in Mama's cocoa.

I take the trip down the stairs just as slowly, taking the time to practice my speech. She sits in the kitchen with the laptop. Her back's to me as I speak. "Mama, that was completely uncalled for." My voice starts out small, but it grows stronger as I speak. "I'm very sorry. You don't ask me for gifts ever. But you take really good care of me. I was hoping to do something special for you."

Mama doesn't speak or turn around. So I keep talking. "And I think your channel is a really good thing—it benefits people. And I appreciate all of our subscribers. They're like an extended family you built up . . ." I babble on until Mama lifts her hand. She points to the computer screen in front of her.

"Cara Jane, would you just look at that?"

My eyes follow her shaky finger to the donation bar of the Caring for Cara website. The color green marks part of the previously blank thermometer. We've raised four thousand dollars in the past three hours.

CHAPTER TEN

"Four thousand dollars," Mama says breathlessly as a new message appears and the green graphic creeps up farther.

"Four thousand twenty-five," I correct her. The number on the screen rises. Somewhere, someone just sent us money. "This has to be a joke, right?" Who are these people just sitting around their homes on a cold winter weeknight, sending out money to complete strangers? Who has that much extra in their lives?

A series of messages unfurls along the donation thermometer. *Stay strong, Cara! Feel better soon! Merry Christmas, Cara and Shaylene!* Some of the people promise to pray for us. Some beseech us to turn to Jesus. My favorite one simply says: *We are with you.* I don't recognize any of the names listed.

Mama and I sit in our kitchen and watch the list of names continue to grow. The donation thermometer inches up. I admit it feels good to see that big green number rise. It feels like total strangers have wrapped a warm blanket around my shoulders. Mama sniffles. She reaches to the counter and pulls a box of Kleenex to her lap.

"You okay?" I ask, wondering if we are still technically fighting.

"People are very kind." She dabs at her eyes with the tissues.

It seems strange to sit and watch the screen, as if that counts as holding my hand out and asking for donations. Instead of just waiting, I busy myself around the kitchen. I pull out a can of soup from the cupboard and start chopping vegetables for a salad. In the refrigerator, I find dough for breadsticks.

Mama looks over. "Maybe no gluten, Cara Jean. You know how it contributes to inflammation in your system." Sometimes I just want something simple and normal like bread warm from the oven, with real butter melting. I put the canister of dough back in the fridge and wonder when Mama meant to eat it. Maybe when I'm at school, she devours a feast of carbs and makes generally unhealthy choices.

For now, she is hypnotized by the computer screen. Every once in a while, she gasps or clucks. I make a game out of guessing the amounts people have donated according to the noises Mama's makes in response. When I serve up supper, she doesn't even move to the table to eat. She holds the bowl of soup on her lap and periodically waves her spoon at me, instructing. "We need to record an episode about this. Let this be a lesson to us both—we need to ask for help more. That's not a skill I've taught you but it's so crucial, especially considering our situation."

It turns out that the universe delivers all kinds of miracles. For one, when I wake up to warm up my shoulder wrap in the microwave, I see a delicate frost icing the trees' wintry branches. It looks like the whole street has been draped in the most intricate lace. And just a few hours later, before the lazy late-December sun has fully risen, I hear the rumbling motor of a car pulling into the driveway and boots thumping across the front porch. I listen to the car's engine idle and don't check at first—I figure Mama has had my prescriptions delivered from the pharmacy.

But then my brain wakes and brightens and I remember that donation campaign. For the briefest minute, I imagine the website has delivered sacks of money right to our front stoop, like a cartoon solution for all of our problems. Of course that's not how it works. But what do I know? No one's ever given me almost five thousand dollars before.

It turns out that it's an even more magical delivery. I slip down the stairs and softly open the front door, taking care not to let the metal latch bang open and wake Mama. That's when I see it. I know immediately Manuela delivered it. The cylinder-shaped package is wrapped in the same brown craft paper that lines the tables in the pottery studio and I recognize the bow—it's tied from the same kind of thick red ribbon that Manuel wears in her hair.

The note taped to it reads: *Merry Christmas! Sometimes Santa needs a bit of help.* And I have to sit back on the steps at first, cold as they are, because I don't want the sound of my sobs to wake up Mama. I realize then that Manuela isn't building up a mailing list of the addresses of wayward and sickly teens. She planned to deliver Mama's present all along.

Some people move through the world and make their whole existence a gift to others. As soon as I feel well enough, I aim to be one of those people.

The cold draft chases me inside and I scurry to the den to leave Mama's vase under our little tree.

When Mama stumbles downstairs around ten, bleary-eyed, with a quilt wrapped around her shoulders, she looks panicked at the thought that I've been left uncared for this long. "You let me keep sleeping. My goodness. How are you? Give me some numbers?" She pulls the quilt tightly and swoops toward my clipboard. "Cara Jean, seriously!" She taps the blank spaces on my chart. "You took your temperature and that's it."

"I feel fine, Mama. I already did meds but taking my own blood pressure stresses me out; that has to be counterproductive. Look how gorgeous the yard looks."

She barely looks. "How's your pain level? Fatigue?"

"How's yours?" I nod to the computer. "You had quite the late night."

"Sweet Mary and Joseph—Cara Jean, have you checked the current total yet?"

"No."

Mama waves me off and goes to the computer. After the screen lights up, she thumps her hand on her chest and points to the ceiling. "Hallelujah—seventy thousand three hundred and twenty-three dollars." She gives a little whoop and twirls in front of the computer. "Cara Jean—is this real life?"

I lower myself gently into a kitchen chair. "Seems like it, Mama."

She clicks through the site and a bunch of charts and graphs appear on the screen. "All I keep thinking is, why didn't we pursue this kind of support sooner? All those Christmases we struggled . . ." Mama trails off.

"People have been generous with us." I hesitate, unsure if I should list the ways: the car, my clothes, even our Thanksgiving dinner. "Right?"

"You're sweet," Mama says quickly. "Let me tell you though, there's something different about cash donations. It's giving you a choice to decide your own needs. Honestly, it means we might grab a little bit of our freedom back. Do you see that? These are people who believe in your recovery, Cara. Don't you feel empowered?"

The question sits between us. I do not pick it up.

"What are we doing today?" I ask. Mama shoots me a quizzical look, as if she has completely forgotten the day itself. "For Christmas Eve?"

"Well, I think we should plan some merriment! I have some phone calls to make first." She turns away to start digging through the fridge. "Dr. Eric might stop by—your numbers have me a little concerned. I know that the local Baptist church planned to stop by and check on us. And then I think we should treat ourselves a bit—let's go out to dinner."

"Really?" Mama and I never go out to eat. For one thing, I can rarely eat much off the menu. For another, we could buy a week of groceries for what most nice restaurants charge for dinner.

"Yes. Really. We'll have a lovely and restful day after Dr. Eric checks in."

"Doesn't Dr. Eric have a family of his own? You know, to spend Christmas Eve with?"

"I'm sure he does, but thank goodness for his dedication. The blessings that have recently landed on our doorstep!" Mama says in wonder, and I can't help smiling to myself, thinking of the wrapped package that Manuela delivered this morning.

Mama nudges my hand open and deposits two pills in my palm. "Make sure to hydrate. And we don't really know if Dr. Eric has family waiting for him. Maybe he'd like to join us for dinner."

Apparently Dr. Eric doesn't have family nearby, and that's how we end up sitting across from him in a booth at the local Chinese place on Christmas Eve. It's early—not even 5:00 p.m.—but he has hospital rounds or some other virtuous duty demanding his presence after six.

Mama finds all his jokes hilarious and listens rapturously to his seemingly endless repertoire of heroic doctor stories. We hear about his time in Guinea, distributing mosquito nets and combating malaria. We hear how he combed the streets of downtown Cleveland in a harm reduction van, providing clean needles to addicts as long as they'd also accept a peanut butter and jelly sandwich.

He allows my mother to order for the table and she beams when he praises her for ordering brown rice and steamed chicken and vegetables without any MSG. He requests sesame sauce on the side. Mama asks him his thoughts on acupuncture.

It's like I'm not there. Which is actually okay. I'm happy not to be the focus of attention.

And it's amusing to see my mother flirt.

As Dr. Eric expounds on the merits of Eastern medicine in our local strip mall Chinese food place, I wonder how we might look to other diners. Do they see us together and believe we are a family? Do they know we've chosen Chinese food because my mom thinks it's the best option for a ketogenic and gluten-free diet?

"Wouldn't it be nice to go out for Italian once in a while?" I ask. "I mean, if we're going to splurge with the money that strangers donated to fund my health care?"

My mother's spoon pauses on the way up to her mouth. "Cara Jean—what has gotten into you? I'm so sorry, Eric. Lately, her moods have swung uncontrollably. I simply cannot keep up."

I stare at them, across the table, suddenly legitimately fearful that they have read my mind. The maroon carpet at my feet ripples. The walls look like they're breathing. There is no place left to retreat.

"No, that's quite all right. Is that how you feel, Cara? I'm happy to pick up the check for dinner." Dr. Eric leans in, his face moonlike and shiny. He tilts his head and I worry that his moving lips might slide off his face. "Cara? Can you hear me?"

Mama's tone shifts to alarm. "Is she slurring her words? I think she might be slurring her words?"

I realize my mouth is open, and when I try to help close it with my hand, I come away with strings of drool. "Am I talking out loud?" My voice sounds distant and hollow, as if I've fallen down a well. "Can you hear what I'm thinking?"

"You okay, Cara? She's not okay," Dr. Eric declares. He flicks on the penlight attached to his key chain and shines it directly at my eyes.

"Hey. Hurts my blinkers."

"Oh good Lord." My mother sloshes past her soup in order to squeeze my arm.

"Her pupils are dilated. What did she take? Cara Jean, what did you take?"

"I took the green pill. And the big blue pill." I catch a flash of disapproval zinging from Dr. Eric's eyes to my mom's.

"Names, please. Names of medications would be helpful." The diners around us who might think we are one big family now believe we are one big family with serious issues.

Our waitress arrives, harried and concerned. "All okay? She okay?"

"May I have some more crunchy noodles?" I hold up the empty bowl, daring Mama to stop me.

"Please lower your voices," Mama seethes to Dr. Eric and me as the waitress leaves on her mission. "I can provide you with a list of names. She takes mostly supplements. I would never expect my child to know the complex pronunciations of pharmaceuticals, Dr. Eric. She is not the one with a background in health services, after all."

Dr. Eric holds up his hands: two meaty starfish squirming in front of his dark shirt. "Just here to help." He speaks slowly to me.

"Cara, can you hear us?" But he does not give me time to answer before asking, "How's her pulse?"

"Slightly slow," my mom answers sharply. "Maybe it's a stroke? Cara Jean, are you experiencing any strange smells? Any numbness?"

"It's not a stroke. She's overmedicated, Shaylene. Look at her. Cara, you took a green pill and a blue pill? Is that what I heard you say?" I watch Dr. Eric's starfish hands float across the screen of his phone. His fingertip traces lines of pills organized by color.

"Oh no," I say.

"No—you didn't take those pills?" Dr. Eric asks.

The waitress returns with the noodles and we all pause in silence for their delivery.

She sets the bowl on the table in front of me. "All okay here?" Her voice sounds desperate for it to be okay.

Mama's voice sounds that way too. "Everything's fine."

I look at the bowl of noodles and decide they count as my reward. And that obviously I need to convince Mama and Dr. Eric that considering it is Christmas Eve, we should embrace a more all-is-calm, all-is-bright sensibility. So I announce very slowly, clearly, and carefully: "Everything is okay. These will be very merry noodles."

Dr. Eric exhales. "All right, Cara." He says to our waitress, "Thank you very much." The waitress scurries away quickly. "So you took a green pill? And a blue pill?"

"Oh no." The noodle breaks into pieces in my mouth and each piece tastes like the best crispy noodle I've ever devoured.

"Oh no what?" Mama's and Dr. Eric's heads loom and demand.

"Two," I say between crunches.

"Right. Two," Dr. Eric says. "You took both the green pill and also the big blue pill."

"No, both. Twice." I swallow the shards of noodle in my mouth. My memory is crystal clear now. I see myself standing at the kitchen counter, with the morning light filtering through frosted trees. I take both pills at the counter while I put the kettle on. And then again after Mama woke up, when she called my coloring sallow and handed me the two pills and a glass of water. "I took both those pills twice."

CHAPTER ELEVEN

Somehow they bundle me out to the car, along with our entrées packed up in white cartons of non-MSG goodness. I know this because it feels as if I blink and I am sitting at China Moon Chef, glaring back at my mom over a flickering paper lantern. Blink again and I am sitting at my own kitchen table, with my coat still on, eating from one of the cartons with a plastic fork.

I am aware of my own slurping and that the inside of my mouth feels like someone has swabbed out all its moisture with a Q-tip. I am also aware of Mama and Dr. Eric arguing in the next room. They are arguing about me.

"She is fourteen years old." That is Dr. Eric, informing the woman who gave birth to me how long ago that was.

"True. And for most of those fourteen years, she has dealt with chronic illness. I'm not just a single parent; I'm the only parent. Cara Jean needs to take ownership over her health. Otherwise it all falls on me. And I struggle with my own pain and the nerve damage." My mother's voice trembles. "You have no idea how much all of this wears a person down."

"It's not that I'm not sympathetic to that," I hear Dr. Eric say unsympathetically. "But listen, we can both agree that serious medications like those require basic monitoring, can we not?" His voice drops to a murmur and I hear my mother sniffle. While I dig through the soggy paper bag for those crunchy noodles, I hear only snippets: "overdose," "compromise," "public scene." Then I hear Dr. Eric unleash the unthinkable phrase "child protective services" and my mother immediately wails, the way a wolf pup instinctively howls at the first full moon.

"I don't want to tell you how to parent," Dr. Eric announces, while advising my mom about how to properly parent. "But other people might, particularly those who are now financially invested in Cara's recovery."

"What exactly does that mean?" Mama's voice has been sharpened by alertness. I give up on the crunchy noodles and find a spicy chicken dish with water chestnuts and those baby ears of corn. For a moment or two I feel really sad about eating baby corn, as if it's an act of special cruelty. I picture a mature, maternal ear of corn, unfurling its husks in grief. *Poor corn*, I think to myself, and immediately get the giggles.

While I'm apologetically considering the relationships of vegetables, Dr. Eric spells our new dynamic out for Mama. "It means that everyone who donated money to that campaign is going to feel connected to Cara's recovery. That's terrific. That's what we want, after all. But they are also going to feel involved in your choices. Imagine what would have happened if we needed to call an ambulance. And then they did a full panel of drug tests. Or pumped her stomach. Are you legally required to inform Cara's father about medical treatments?"

My fork halts on the way to my mouth, hovers and waits for her answer. "Absolutely not. I've already told you; I am an only parent."

"Not anymore. Ninety percent of those donors will have opinions about Cara's treatment. Just wait. You cannot provide them with an excuse to interfere. You've done the right thing. She doesn't need to be in inpatient care. She needs an individualized treatment plan. But, Shaylene, you must let me actually treat her. You have worked so hard and taken her so far. Let someone help you. I understand what a quagmire insurance companies create with billing and reimbursements. No one wants to see the two of you sunk in that swamp. Keep up the fundraising campaign— give yourself some freedom from that. I'll charge you at cost. Really restoring her health is all the payment I need."

Mama responds with a predictable wail and I hear the murmur of Dr. Eric's sympathy.

She trots out one of her recent favorite mantras: "As soon as I accept one miracle, the universe delivers another. I don't know what to say."

"Just say you trust me." Something settles in the pit of my stomach—a hard knot of fear. It all sounds so serious. I want to remind my mom that we're supposed to be lighthearted today—listening to the gospel choir sing carols and curling up on the sofa in front of *It's a Wonderful Life*.

But I hear in the next room, "Of course I trust you. We both trust you." I hear Mama solemnly promise this to the man we met a few weeks ago. I would call out in protest but my mouth is full of rice and I've forgotten how to chew.

"Well, that's wonderful news. I'm going to make sure our patient is stable before I head out."

All at once, I realize that the ball of pain in my belly might not be fear or anxiety. Dr. Eric finds me doubled over the kitchen sink, hurling up a decidedly unmerry amount of Chinese takeout. "It's probably the best immediate development we could hope for," he tells Mama on his way out the door. "It'll help to clear out her system. Plenty of fluids, plenty of rest. And cut her some slack—it's Christmas." He smiles over me indulgently as if I broke into the liquor cabinet or something equally rebellious.

"I'm so sorry, Mama." Her expression makes it clear I need to apologize. Braced over the kitchen sink, I've ruined Christmas Eve.

"Let's get you to the sofa." Her voice sounds weary as she hooks one arm around my waist and leads me to the living room. "I'll get you a basin. How are you feeling? You do seem more clear-eyed."

My throat feels sore from vomiting. "I guess I chased off Dr. Eric."

"He has rounds tonight. We just invited him along to dinner

out of simple, human kindness, you know, Cara Jean. There was no need to go to these lengths for the sake of attention."

"I didn't mean . . ." I give up and allow myself to trail off. What's the point of arguing?

Mama continues to fuss over me. She brings over a cool cloth and lays it across my brow. I grapple my way to a sitting position and watch the room pitch to the left. "I'll clean up the kitchen, Mama."

"Nonsense." She laughs ruefully. "Try to sleep it off. There's a church group planning to swing by, so I need to clean up a bit."

"On Christmas Eve?"

"They want to deliver a meal. Try not to worry," she says wryly. "I won't tell them about your preference for chow mein noodles."

She props me up and flicks on the television set, and just when I believe she might never forgive me, Mama makes sure to put on the classic movie channel, with the volume down low. Behind the TV set, the ice melting off our backyard trees streaks the windows. She really seems to feel like I took the wrong meds on purpose. Briefly, I wonder if maybe I had acted out some small kernel of rage and resentment. But then I dismiss that too.

I hear the doorbell ring and expect it to be like that time the group sent over Thanksgiving supper: a quick delivery with me hiding upstairs. I fight to stay awake in case Mama decides to send me running up the steps at the last minute. Even if she ordered it, I couldn't run, however. My body feels hollowed out and empty. For some reason, Mama invites the group into the house and they stand uncomfortably in the living room, gazing at me like I'm Jesus in the manger.

"Merry Christmas," I croak.

"Hush now, Cara Jean. It's important that you rest." Mama sounds decidedly less ambivalent and more devoted in front of our guests. She moves to lead them straight past me through and into the kitchen.

I think I am hallucinating when I see him, trailing at the end of the procession, the last of the three wise men peering down at me. It's Science Kid—that boy from the library. I've seen him at the hospital too. Today he wears a red cable-knit sweater and green argyle socks. Each time he takes a step past me, I glimpse his fancy socks peeking out from his dress pants. They mesmerize me—those diamonds running up his calves. His pants are too short and I figure he grew a lot this past year and his mom still made him wear his good clothes because of the holiday.

Science Kid glances back at me and I see real worry in his eyes. There's probably puke crusting my hair or smeared on my shirt. Mama slides the heavy wooden door closed between the living room and kitchen. Science Kid becomes more and more narrow a sliver until finally he disappears.

I hear Mama tell them how blessed we feel because of their visit. "Cara Jean's really struggling today, but she feels your blessings and the grace of the Lord during this season." On the television in front of me, Tiny Tim hobbles across his humble kitchen on his crutches, as Scrooge and I look on. I hear the synchronized voices of our visitors reciting a prayer in our kitchen and then, to my absolute horror, I listen as Mama informs them about the Caring for Cara campaign. She goes on and on, describing all the aspects of my treatment the financial donations will provide, and I cringe at the idea of these charitable people seeing us as grubbing or ungrateful. "It's miraculous—just like your donations and even the sheer fact that I have another Christmas with my baby girl. That alone is proof of God's grace."

"Amen," I murmur. And then my heart jumps up my throat to see the heavy wooden door ease open.

"You okay?" Science Kid peeks through the slim opening. I feel like he should probably use his powers of observation to draw a different conclusion. "I thought I heard you say something— Cara, right?" I can't tell if he knows I said *Amen* and means to call me out for mocking religion. Or maybe I'm still slurring words and it sounded like something less sarcastic. I stay silent, so he tries again. "Should I get your mom?"

My head shakes vigorously, instinctively. Science Kid steps fully into the room. The door stays open behind him like the eye of a hall monitor. "We go to school together," he says. For the second time in a single day, I wonder if my thoughts are spooling on the outside of my head. "You've missed a lot of classes."

I remember worrying about that once. Science Kid chews his lip and continues. "My mom is talking to your mom about maybe setting up some tutoring sessions." I wonder why his mom needs tutoring. "I hope you'll allow me to help you; I'm a very capable student, with fantastic study skills. And in order to qualify for the National Honor Society, I have to perform a certain number of hours of community service."

My body feels like a lump of soft eggs, a blob congealed on the sofa. But my face still hardens, hearing his offer. "No thanks." I make sure to pronounce that clearly. I remember how smug Science Kid was in defining a library for me. In the library. Over in the next room, my mom has already sold my dignity for a frozen turkey, going on and on about my illness, in hopes of translating the church group's charity work into financial support. I don't need to provide Science Kid with another reason to feel superior.

"Listen. There's no reason to feel embarrassed."

"Nobody feels embarrassed," I respond as I roll the cuff of my sweatshirt up over a splotch of vomit.

"Okay, well, I do." Science Kid steps forward. "You sure seem like you have enough to worry about. What should you care whether I qualify for the National Honor Society?" I shake my head slowly. "Right. You don't. But you care about your schoolwork. You were sick as a dog—worse than this even—and you still showed up to take the math exam. That's some badass scholastic behavior."

"You know about my math exam?"

"Everybody knows about your math exam. Your head made this sound when it hit the gym floor. CRACK! And then I craned my head to see, even though they tell you to look at your own paper and whatnot. But that noise—CRACK!" This time he claps his hand on his thigh. "Then I see you, faceup on the floor, surrounded by pages of math problems. Unreal. You know how people always moan and groan. *Oh no! This test is gonna be the death of me! This test is gonna kill me!* And they're exaggerating. Well, you were not exaggerating. And we're not going to even approach the fact that you were deliriously belting out Celine Dion as they loaded you onto the ambulance."

I force myself to fully sit up. "Wait. Are you for real?"

Science Kid laughs. It's a sweet giggle, high-pitched and impish. "Is it all coming back to you now?" He sings it just like Celine does in the song.

"That's what made you want to help me?"

"Nope. That's what made me want to know you. The honor society made me want to help you." He steps forward and sort of perches on the arm of the sofa. "And I can help. That's the thing. You shouldn't just dismiss me because of any preconceived notions. I'm good at explaining things. Except maybe at the library."

I figure that counts as close to an apology as Science Kid will offer. "My mom probably won't go for it."

"We're not dating. We're studying Algebra Two."

I command the blob of myself to sink into the couch cushions and disappear. I shut my eyes, but when I open them, Science Kid still sits there, peering down at me. "I didn't mean that." My voice steadies as I use it. "Mama has really set ideas about schoolwork. She thinks I work too hard. She makes me stop studying so that I can make better choices for my health." I say it expecting Science Kid to declare that Mama is awesome and ask if she could talk to his mom and convince her that studying didn't qualify as the most important activity for adolescents. But he doesn't say that at all.

He just nods. "Maybe you need to work smarter and not harder."

"Maybe," I allow.

"Listen. My mom will make it happen. No one denies Giselle Barnes. Especially if it involves her boy's application to the National Honor Society, even tangentially. Just wait. Your mom will walk us out the door, saying, *I don't know how we could ever thank you.* You know, that's what people say in these kinds of scenarios." He gestures toward the kitchen. "And my mom will act like the thought just occurred to her. *Just because you asked*, she'll say. *My Xavier is a phenomenal student* . . . and she will have us scheduled for tutoring in a manner of seconds."

"Okay. You have a lot of faith in your mother's power of persuasion."

Xavier pushes his glasses back up his nose and grins down at me. We hear the volume of the chatter rise slightly and then the door opens more widely. The church ladies spill into the living room.

"Oh, she's awake. Hello there, Cara! Happy Christmas Eve to you, sweetheart. Xavier, tell me you didn't wake this poor girl up." The woman I presume is Giselle Barnes does, in fact, seem like a powerful force. For one thing, she could star in a Hollywood movie, or at least a Lifetime series. She stands about six feet tall and wears her hair natural so she stands even taller. Her gold leather boots match her gold leather gloves. When she speaks, her gloved hand whips through the air, like a highlighter underlines all the important words.

Mama hangs back behind the group, her eyes flashing their warning signals. I know how to translate that look: hold myself together and refrain from puking on the church ladies. Mrs. Barnes says, "This boy has gone girl crazy on me, let me tell you." At that, Xavier springs up and puts distance between us faster than you can say teenage non-romance. Mama lunges to take his spot and reaches for my hand.

"We were just talking about the possibility of my tutoring your daughter, Mrs. Wakely," Xavier says.

Mama smiles and gives me a squeeze. "That's so sweet. But as you can see, Cara Jean's not feeling up to studying just yet."

"Well, when she does, the offer stands. We have some classes together and I'm happy to help." Xavier speaks confidently and the church ladies coo their approval.

Mrs. Barnes claps her yellow leather gloves together. "It's wonderful to see you two young people connect. But this is sacred time, y'all. This is family time, so ladies—and gentleman—" She squeezes Xavier's shoulder. "We should leave these Wakely women to enjoy a peaceful evening celebrating the birthday of the Lord Savior Jesus Christ."

"I'm sure Cara and I both enjoyed the company. More than you can imagine. The battle sometimes gets lonely—well, you know that." Mrs. Barnes nods in agreement. "And of course we are grateful for your generosity. You ladies thought of everything. We have more than we can possibly need. Isn't God great? If we are ever in the position to be of help, I'd love to do so. Maybe Xavier needs help getting to his treatments? We'd be happy to provide rides."

Science Kid studiously avoids my gaze. His mom answers, "That's so sweet of you, but I couldn't add to your plate. But you know, think about his tutoring offer." Mrs. Barnes drops her voice low, but we can all hear her clear as day. "Kids need to feel like they're worth something. I believe in living a life of service to the world. It lifts you up. And this would lift Xavier up in more ways than one—tutoring Cara would help him qualify for a scholarship."

"Would it, now?" Mama asks.

"Oh yes. The school has nominated Xavier for his academic excellence."

The other church ladies squeal and laugh. "You are proud, Giselle."

"I am. I can't help but talk this child up. So let's plan something soon after the holidays." Mrs. Barnes pushes her cell phone into Mama's hand. "Put in your phone number." To my amazement, Mama accepts the device and starts typing. "In the meantime,

Cara Jean, you take care of yourself. Feel better. Enjoy a fabulous meal. These are the best cooks in the state of Ohio."

"Cooks?" one of the church ladies says incredulously. "Girl, we are *chefs*, thank you." I can't remember the last time so many people have laughed together in our house.

My face aches from smiling. Mama hands back the phone and noticeably freezes when Mrs. Barnes goes to dial it. "I don't hear it ringing. Do you hear it ringing?" She looks down at the phone's screen. "Oh, you left off the last digit. Thank goodness we checked."

"Yes," Mama says, taking back the phone to fix it.

"Thank goodness," I add. Xavier wriggles his eyebrows at me and I have the sudden sense that he understands everything.

That, if true, is the real Christmas miracle.

CHAPTER TWELVE

It turns out that Xavier Barnes understands almost everything. Quadratic equations, mitosis and meiosis, iambic pentameter, dramatic irony. Working with Xavier is like watching the *Jeopardy!* Tournament of Champions except the only person winning any Daily Doubles is a skinny Black kid who gnaws on the eraser end of his pencil and never phrases his answer in the form of a question.

Xavier phrases everything in the form of an answer. And while I absolutely believe that he offered to help me in order to earn community service hours for his National Honor Society

119

application, I also believe he genuinely enjoys answering questions. Xavier considers himself very knowledgeable about most things.

He is not so proficient at small talk, though. Mrs. Barnes called on three occasions to set up a study session and you would have thought that with all the time it took to arrange a meeting, Xavier might have developed a little more finesse in his game. He rings the doorbell instead of texting me to say he's at my house. He brings a bag of books that he needs my frail self's help to carry in through the door, and after we've been reviewing the plot of *Antigone* for a good half an hour, he trots out this line: "You can call me X, you know. I mean eventually, I might be."

"You might be what?"

"Never mind."

And let's face it, it's not like I'm so used to sitting in my living room with a boy, even Science Kid, studying, while my mom researches recipes for keto-friendly stir-fry dishes in the kitchen. At first I just feel unduly dense or worry that my afternoon brain fog is rolling in. "Sorry. I don't get it."

Xavier squirms and chews on his eraser with more gusto. "Just let it go."

"No, really. C'mon. I want to understand." Doesn't he realize, this person who knows everything, how little experience I have sitting next to someone on the sofa and conjuring up cute things to say?

But Xavier openly groans. "No. I meant like ex-boyfriend, you know? You don't call me your ex now, but maybe someday you might."

"You're going to skip right to ex?" My voice sounds more hurt than I mean it to.

"What? No. It was just a joke, Cara Jean. Because of my name." Xavier rubs his temples with his hands. "Let's just focus on this uplifting story of this imprisoned girl who hangs herself."

"Spoiler alert. Jeez."

"Cara Jean. Are you for real right now? It's a Greek tragedy. Did you think she would move to Seattle and open up a coffee shop?"

"You can call me Cara. My mom is really the only one who calls me Cara Jean."

"All right." He makes it clear that the extra syllable doesn't really matter much to him. "It seems like it's gotten a little hard for you to focus. Break time. Let's stand up and do some jumping jacks."

"Wait. What are you doing?" I look up to see that Xavier is completely serious right now, hopping up off the couch and squatting to stretch out his hamstrings.

"C'mon, move it. Before I change my mind and decide that we should do burpees instead."

"You're not supposed to tutor me in gym," I remind him. "Besides, I have a note, excusing me from PE."

"Yeah, yeah. I have that same note, brainiac. That doesn't doom you to sit on a couch and let your body atrophy, though. And it doesn't negate the benefits that physical activity has on your cognitive ability. Let's go: ten jumping jacks."

I groan as I stand and face Xavier. We try to jump and clap together but I land just a little late on each beat, so it sounds like he is exercising with an echo.

"You do this terribly," he says. "How do you feel, though?" I do not admit to feeling a little winded. Nor do I say I feel silly, even though I do. Xavier prompts me, "Don't you feel more alert?"

"A little," I admit grudgingly. "Now what do we do?"

"We sit back down. It's just a quick break to wake up our brains and get our neurons firing again."

"That's how you study?"

"Sometimes. Especially on rough days when I have trouble concentrating."

I cannot imagine Xavier having trouble concentrating. "When do you have rough days?"

But Xavier holds one finger up to his lips, shushing me. "I hear your mom. Maybe she's calling you from the kitchen?"

I listen closely to a familiar tone in Mama's voice and hear the sounds of cupboards opening and closing and small kitchen appliances. "Nah. She's probably recording a video."

"What kind of video?"

For some reason, I find it more embarrassing to tell Xavier about the wellness warriors channel than to attempt jumping jacks in front of him. I take a deep breath. "My mom has a channel. She uses it to educate other families who have kids with chronic illnesses. It sounds like she's demonstrating a recipe for today's episode."

Xavier seems to consider this. "Huh. Well, that's cool. What's the channel called?"

"Cara's Wellness Warriors," I mutter.

"What?" he asks. So I repeat it louder. "Okay, yeah. That sounds like basic white lady stuff, but you know, good for her."

I laugh. "What does that mean?"

"You know what that means. I bet she talks about essential oils a lot. And chemical-free cleaning products."

"She does, actually." I can't help but laugh with him.

"Do you make guest appearances?"

"It is occasionally required of me."

"Well, I didn't know I was in the presence of a real-life YouTube star."

"Shut up. She started it when I was like six years old."

"That's wild. You have an online record of your childhood."

I'd never thought of it that way. "Mostly just a lot of hospitals," I say, then wince because that sounds like a play for sympathy. "I guess that's just what's most memorable, though. How about you?" I ask it like it's a casual question, remembering him perched on the plastic chair in the ER that day, his face etched in pain.

"What about me?" Xavier shuffles through the books. "We should really start outlining this essay."

"I saw you in the hospital one day."

"What?" He sounds shocked and makes a big show of creasing open the paperback copy of *The Theban Plays*. "So the essay's whole topic focuses on dramatic irony."

"I know I did."

"Doubt it. Oh, maybe I was there doing volunteer work."

"No way. You were hooked up. Getting a transfusion or something."

"Blood drive maybe." Xavier taps the spine of the book against the table. I stare at him but his eyes are focused on some spot behind my head.

We work for a little more than two hours and break four times for jumping jacks. "You're getting better at them," Xavier tells me, and I laugh and tell him he's a terrible liar.

"I'll text you to set up another study session." He sounds very professional. "You should finish the first draft of this essay and then we can proofread it together."

"You're giving me homework."

"What did you think—this was some kind of Slacker Academy? We've got to get you ready for those exams so that you don't need to rely on musical interludes to distract from your abysmal performance."

"I was acing that exam."

"It's all coming back to me now," Xavier sings at me, and loads up his bags. He leaves one full set of books with me. When his mom honks the horn to let us know she's waiting in the driveway, he motions for me to stay on the couch.

When Mama shuts the door, she leans back against it, as if warding off an intruder.

"Okay. Give some numbers—honest numbers, please."

"Mama, I feel okay." I close my eyes and imagine every muscle in my body pink with fresh oxygen and measurably stronger. I have made a friend.

Xavier Barnes isn't my only visitor. But Dr. Eric comes and goes at odd hours, sometimes two or three times a day. He records a lot of data and usually has some kind of new supplement for me to try. He and Mama also spend a lot of time camped out in front of the computer, charting my progress and keeping a watchful eye on the Caring for Cara campaign.

There are even tinier changes. Mama's bought name-brand shampoo and conditioner and blow-dries her hair each morning. Once in a while my phone pings—a link or ridiculous literary meme from Xavier, an automatic advertisement from Mud Matters.

And then there is the vase. When she opened it on Christmas

morning, Mama fussed the way I had hoped she would. She barraged me with questions about how I made it—so much that I ended up admitting that Manuela had actually sculpted it. "I chose the paint colors and painted it the way I thought you'd like best."

"I don't understand—why would she do that? Is this someone you know?" Mama's face clouded. "Is this Manuela a friend from school?"

"No, she's older." And because I realized that might sound worse, I added, "She owns the studio."

"Oh, that's a marketing trick." Mama waved her hand. "She's overselling her product. I respect that kind of go-getting attitude. It's working, right? This is the place where you want to take classes?" Mama viewed most things as a possible scam. But that morning she held up the vase in the light. "It is absolutely gorgeous, Cara Jean. I love the colors you chose, and you used such a steady hand to paint it."

The day after Christmas, she moved the vase from under the tree to its current place of prominence on the kitchen table. And when she ran out to the pharmacy, she returned with a bundle of flowers. I don't think I had ever witnessed Mama buying herself flowers. "Eight dollars," she said. "Don't they make the rest of the house seem so happy and lovely?"

It was one more change—not a seismic shift but a slight calibration.

When Mama and Dr. Eric share the plan with me for Mama's next episode, I focus on the petals of those flowers. They want to present Caring for Cara on the wellness warriors channel. They explain it's a natural development, combining both these streams of support.

"The hallmark of our channel has always been honesty, Cara Jean," Mama reminds me.

"Okay," I say. "But why are you asking me?"

"Well, honey, we're a team." I want to point out that it seems like the team has been reconfigured. Instead I wait and see what comes next.

Dr. Eric steps up to the plate. "You probably haven't noticed your extreme mood swings lately. Please don't take it as a criticism, Cara; it's not meant that way at all. It's a biologically natural reaction to the inordinate amount of stress your body has been under, not to mention the factor of the unreasonable academic pressures your school has placed on your shoulders. And then there's the difficult brain chemistry of adolescence, even in the most typical scenario. All this comes down to . . . these mood swings aren't your fault."

Mama gazes at her own hands while I listen to what an awful kid I am. Dr. Eric keeps going. "We'd like to post an update to the wellness warriors. We'd like to see you take an active role."

"That makes sense," I say. Mama looks up so quickly. Her reaction surprises me. It's not like she's ever allowed me to boycott before. "I mean, as long as I'm feeling up to it."

"Even if you aren't," Mama says, "that's okay too. We can only ask you to be yourself."

"Okay."

Relief washes over my mom's face. Maybe Dr. Eric is right. Maybe I've become the most unpleasant version of myself possible. "That's just wonderful, Cara Jean. I appreciate that so much.

I'm aiming to post in the next two days. Dr. Eric is just helping me plan it out a little bit on something called a storyboard."

"Your videos are great, Mama," I assure her. "All your subscribers trust you because you're so genuine."

We don't talk about the video again until she wakes me up in the middle of the night to film part of it. Mama had insisted on breathing treatments before bed, but she used an eyedropper to add one of Dr. Eric's tinctures to the reservoir. She said that the peppermint oil would help clear my lungs. It burned though, and after the second time I woke up clutching my face, I left the mask sitting on the bedside table.

When Mama shakes me awake from a dead sleep, my first thought is that she's caught me without the mask on. "I'm so sorry," I tell her as my eyes adjust to the suddenly bright light.

But she only asks "How are you feeling?" as if it's perfectly routine to wake me in the dead of night to check.

"Horrible." As the word emerges, I realize it's true. "I'm in so much pain." I barely recognize the whimper in my voice.

"What hurts, Cara Jean?" Mama asks so gently. "I'll heat up your lavender pad if you think that might help."

I brace myself in order to nod. The bones in my face feel like they've hardened and might shatter if I move too quickly. "Everything hurts." The space around my eye sockets burns and the light sears my eyes. I grope toward the bedside table to switch off my lamp but the room doesn't dim the way I expect it to. That's when I notice it. There's a spotlight clamped onto the camera that Mama has positioned in the corner on a tripod.

"Mama, what are you recording?"

"Don't worry about that now. Just focus on some deep breathing."

It hurts more to squint but I do it anyway and see the smolder of the power button's red light. "It's recording right now!" It comes out like a shriek.

Mama smooths the weighted blanket across my chest and speaks calmly, firmly. "Cara Jean, we agreed we'd be recording an episode soon. You reacted with such grace about that. I was just setting up the camera. And thank goodness I was or who knows how long you might have lain alone in this room suffering?"

She keeps talking. "I think you're experiencing an allergic reaction. I'm going to get you some antihistamine, to help counter that. My kit's in my bedroom. I need you to lie back and continue to breathe deeply so that I can leave the room for a moment. I will duck down the hall and be right back."

Mama's nurse voice has kicked in and that's how I know she's scared also. Eyes closed, I stay as still as possible and count the seconds until I feel her return to my bedside. "Don't get lazy now; give me some more of that deep breathing," she orders, and I hear her unzip the case where she keeps the medication I'm not allowed to touch. The plastic bottles clack against each other and the pills rattle while she searches.

"Okay, let's try this. Can you swallow a sip of water? And then I'm going to give you a muscle relaxant, all right, Cara Jean?" I can't nod but I part my lips to take the first capsule and then lean forward to drink. "All right, Cara Jean. I'm going to give you something for the pain, but I need you to listen to me. Are you listening to me?"

I am trying not to writhe because any movement intensifies the pain. I can't nod, so I whisper, "Yes." It comes out the way my voice might if I were a ghost haunting my mom, after all her caretaking failed.

"Do not swallow this pill. I'm going to put it under your tongue. You need to just leave it there and let it dissolve. Do not chew it or suck on it. I know how much you're hurting and I know you want the pain to stop. In order for the medicine to work, we have to follow the directions just right, do you understand me?"

"Yes," I hiss again.

Mama's hand taps the side of my face, so I open my mouth and lift my tongue to its roof. She places the pill in my mouth carefully, like it's a religious ritual. It feels a little bigger than a Tic Tac and more porous somehow. "There we go. Now just let your mouth close naturally. Lay your shoulders back on the pillows. Let's take some deep breaths together." Every time I inhale, my face feels like it might split into pieces. "As you breathe, you're getting oxygen to your blood cells and they are carrying that medicine around your body. You're probably going to feel a little bit woozy—that's fine. That will mean that the medicine is working. When you feel tired, just let yourself rest."

"I want a pillow on my face." My eyelids feel heavy and my sinuses still ache. It takes great effort to pronounce the sentence clearly.

"What?" Mama sounds alarmed. "Cara Jean, what do you mean?"

"The soft pillow. On my face." I imagine it will feel like a cool cloud, muffling all my screaming pain receptors. I try to shift my body to free up one of the pillows beneath me but the weighted blanket keeps me trapped and sluggish.

There is a long pause. I can feel Mama thinking. "I want to keep you propped up, just in case you vomit. Do you understand?" And then because I don't answer immediately, she repeats, "DO YOU UNDERSTAND?"

"Soft pillow." My ghost voice is insistent.

Mama sighs. "All right. I hear you. I'll be right back." I know she stands because the bed bounces up slightly when she gets up. I hear her footsteps retreat and return and she leans over to tuck her own pillow under my arm. "I don't like the idea of you blocking your airway with that," she tells me as I draw the pillow up over my face. "You might sleep a bit harder than usual. You might not feel like yourself. How about we just cover your eyes? That seems to be where your pain is concentrated."

I don't have the energy to argue. Instead I lean back and let Mama settle the pillow over the top of my head. The tight mask of pain over my skull has loosened to a dull throb. Every now and then, my skin tingles. Maybe that means the medicine's working. I visualize that feeling as a silver thread and try to follow it to a place of numbness.

"I'll leave your door open," my mother reassures me. I can't manage the effort it would take to point out that she confiscated my door weeks ago. "Call me if you need me." And then she hesitates for a second. She hovers. For some reason I think she's about to apologize for the door, for the tincture, for speaking so sternly while I cried out in such pain. But she only says, "I'll be right down the hall." The whole room seems to exhale as she leaves.

I force my leaden eyelids up just enough to see her retreat. I swivel my head slightly toward the corner to see that the red light of the video camera still glows. Then I lower the pillow just slightly, to shroud my whole face, so that at least I can sleep knowing that I'm not being recorded.

CHAPTER THIRTEEN

"Okay, Cara, let's try it one more time. Remember, don't let yourself trail off. Stay with your point and finish strong. You're just speaking to our viewers. They've practically watched you grow up. No need to feel self-conscious."

Except I can barely hold my head straight in order to look directly at the camera. When I speak, I hear my own voice, but it sounds like it's on a delay. My lips tingle and my tongue feels too large for my mouth. "Just act natural," Mama reminds me. Strands of drool keep spooling at the corners of my mouth.

"Hello, wellness . . . warriors. I want to thank you for all your well wishes during this holiday season."

"Okay! That's a great start." Mama flicks off the camera. "I'm going to give you a note, okay? For some reason, and I don't why, you keep pronouncing it *howl-a-day*. Usually, I don't think we should be picky about saying just the right thing. But some people see Christmas as a very holy time. I wouldn't want them to think we were making fun. Does that make sense?"

Not much makes sense. I feel as if my brain has been replaced with a puddle of syrup. My thoughts pour so slowly. "I feel sticky," I announce to my mom.

She only says, "I don't know what that means." Then she lifts the video camera back up to record me again.

"I'm Cara Jean and I'm thanking all the wellness warriors for their thoughts and prayers this winter." Mama flashes a thumbs-up. "Last month challenged Mama and me. School officials bullied me for my illness and I ended up in the hospital. My doctor is still doing lots of tests. We're looking for a combination of medications to help." I stare at Mama, losing the thought, and then add, "Me live my life," as soon as I remember the rest of the sentence. I stop again, thinking Mama will shut off the camera, but she waves me to keep going.

"This month has been different. I've read all your inspiring comments. And a kind, kind friend of my mom—" Mama stabs toward me with her index finger. "And a friend of me too," I correct myself, "has created a fundraising page for us. To help with medical expenses that will help me have a better life." I remember Mama's vase and Xavier's bag of books in the living room. "This is already the best year so far. Thank you for your help."

I look up and wait for Mama to shut the camera off. She doesn't. "How do you feel, Cara Jean?" she calls out.

"Really tired."

"But otherwise?"

"Slow today."

"How about spiritually? Are you determined?"

"Yes."

"Then say that." She pauses and nods to me. "How do you feel, Cara Jean?"

"I feel determined," I proclaim in the best wellness warrior voice I have.

"Fan-tas-tic." Mama draws out the three syllables of the word. "Congratulations, baby girl. I know this was a tough task to confront this morning, but you stuck with it and fought through your lethargy."

"Can I see the video?" I straighten the wool cap on my head and wish Mama had let me take the time to brush out the tangles in my hair.

"Oh, sweetheart, I've just gathered all the raw footage we need. It will take me some time to edit it to the version we'll post on the site."

But it actually doesn't take that long. It's up a few hours later.

I know this because I see it on the computer when Mama's in the other room on the phone, probably talking to Dr. Eric. It transitions from the collage of my baby pictures to snapshots of me slipping through various stages of consciousness, with that Jonas Brothers song about diabetes as the soundtrack. Once in a while, a key lyric unfurls across the screen and underscores a picture of me looking pathetic in a hospital bed.

The line *waiting on a cure, but none of them are sure* frames the still shot of our collection of pill bottles, the labels blurred out to protect my privacy. Then there's a photo of Dr. Eric taking my blood pressure. You can't really see his face, just the lapels of his white lab coat and the stethoscope around his neck.

Next, Mama has included photos I have no memory of her taking. In most of them, I lie with my eyes closed. In a couple, my eyes stare glassily into space. In maybe the most unsettling moment, the camera zeroes in on my mother leaning over my bedside. I recognize the sweater she wore the previous night. In the video, Mama looks up, pretends to suddenly notice the camera, and then directly addresses the audience. "Shhhh," she says. "Cara Jean is finally resting. Let's talk in the kitchen."

Then the camera cuts to my mom perched on one of our kitchen stools. She sits posed between an open shoebox packed with medications and a stack of paperwork, mostly envelopes stamped with the words MEDICAL BILLING. "I have to be honest, fellow wellness warriors. It's been a devastating winter. Cara's symptoms are worsening, despite medical intervention and round-the-clock care. It's hard not to feel helpless or to worry that I'm failing her. She's a teenager now—smart as a whip and so sad when her sickness keeps her from attending school. Cara has ambitions and dreams; I remember what that was like." Mama's brave and tragic smile slips through her cloudy expression. "Even still." Mama tilts her chin up. "We do have a glimmer of hope. We've recently found a new doctor who has developed a treatment protocol specifically for Cara. He is brilliant and at the forefront of immune-deficiency research. We are so, so lucky that he's taken an interest in her case. His time, expertise, and access to medicine all cost money, though. Just like all the other expenses that pile up when you have a sick child. We are also lucky that a good friend took it upon herself to create a fundraising campaign to benefit Cara Jean over the holidays. Our Caring for Cara campaign has already far surpassed my wildest dreams. People have been so generous. Unfortunately, it's also already been surpassed by the costs of Cara Jean's treatment. For so long, your emotional support and well wishes have nurtured and inspired us, wellness warriors. So much so that it's difficult for me to ask for anything else. But if you ever wondered about a tangible way you could ease our burden, just a little, well, here it is. Please feel free to click on the link below only if you are able. And don't worry—Cara Jean and I will continue to provide content about family, faith, and facing chronic illness together. No matter what. In the words of Cara Jean herself—" The camera cuts to another scene of me, disheveled and almost delirious. "I feel determined!" I bellow.

And that's it: about four minutes of Mama starring as the patron saint of long-suffering caretakers. A few glimpses of me that will lead viewers to believe I'm either rapidly declining or sniffing glue. Then the Jonas Brothers' diabetes music swells again. As the song continues, the URL of the fundraising website flashes across the page. Maybe not flashes. It's more like it reaches out on-screen like an outstretched hand.

I click over to it—and that's when I see the fundraising goal has changed.

I see how much my health is worth.

Three hundred thousand dollars.

CHAPTER FOURTEEN

The following morning, I try to put my exorbitant price tag out of my mind as I get ready for tutoring.

Xavier Barnes is taking the time to come to my house and help with my schoolwork, so at least I can make an effort to look decent. I put on matching sweats. Then I think maybe that's too matchy-matchy, so I change into leggings and this teal velour tunic with a wide boatneck. But the wide boatneck shows my shoulders and I don't want to worry about leaning forward and inadvertently baring too much. Jeans seem like a good idea— still informal, but you can't mistake them for pajamas. I switch to a pair with ripped knees and a flannel shirt. Xavier's mom was so put together though, with her gold accessories and gorgeous coat. If that's his standard of femininity, he might see my grunge look as an indication that I don't take our study sessions seriously.

I settle on leggings and a flowered sweatshirt, with lace trim. Then I look in the mirror and wish I could switch versions of my face. My eyes still look bloodshot from my clash with the breathing machine the other night and somehow I've managed to lose more weight in the few days since Christmas.

I end up feeling ridiculous for putting in so much effort when Xavier greets me with "Wow, you look terrible." Had I chosen the grunge look, at least I could have told him that terrible was the intended effect. Instead I tug awkwardly at my flowered sweatshirt and remind myself that Xavier Barnes wears cable-knit sweaters and oddly flashy argyle socks. He's super skinny and not at all tall. When he's deeply thinking, he blinks his eyes and wrinkles his nose in a way that looks like the mole from *The Wind in the Willows*. He lectures and sometimes drones and laughs at his own jokes.

I make myself open the door wider and let him in out of the cold. "My stylist is also on winter break," I tell him. Because Xavier Barnes is a complete geek, he responds by giving me finger guns.

"I don't mean your outfit. Your sweatshirt is very . . . botanical," Xavier offers. "But are you feeling okay?"

I've waited a long time to have a friend. I don't want to waste that time talking about how sick I am. So I tell Science Kid that I'm just fine and turn away to shut down that subject.

We set up inside and he asks if I have my first draft done. I whip it out of my folder. "Get ready," I warn him.

"Oh yeah."

"Yes. I present to you the most extensive and informative first draft ever composed on the play *Antigone*."

Xavier cackles. "You're so sure about that? No one else has written anything of merit about this ancient Greek drama?"

I smack my hand down on the paper. "Not this much merit." We both crack up. And then we tackle the essay. Xavier shows me a trick he does to build transitions between paragraphs and I show him the way I write conclusions so they don't sound redundant.

When we're done with English, Xavier says, "All right, brainiac. We need to switch gears and start factoring for x in these math problems."

I sigh deeply.

"Don't act tired," Xavier warns. "If you're going to act tired, we're going to do push-ups."

"Jumping jacks."

"No way. We already mastered jumping jacks. I gotta throw something new in your fitness direction. Just wait—by the time I'm done, they'll give you credit for all your missed gym classes too."

If Xavier requires me to complete a push-up, I might vomit all down my sleeve again. I must look over at him with such a panicked expression.

He reaches his hand and sets it gently on my arm. "Cara, are you sure you're okay? You look like you're in a lot of pain."

I swallow the lump in my throat rather than answer him. It feels like we're sitting in a snow globe. It's very quiet. We're surrounded by tiny specks—the secrets we haven't yet told each other. But all it would take is one good shake and I might tell Xavier everything.

"Thanks," I say, and mean it. I reach for my Algebra II book and open to the correct chapter. "I'm just not up for push-ups."

That's when Xavier Barnes flexes his scrawny arms. "Well, see? That's unfortunate. Because I wore this sweater vest to show off my guns."

I laugh so hard that Mama comes running into my room with her magic medication bag and the stethoscope. That only makes me laugh harder, so I achieve guffaw levels of hysterics.

"This doesn't seem like schoolwork, you two," Mama says. Then she tells me to calm down.

Xavier speaks because he isn't as paralyzed by laughter as I am. "My apologies, Mrs. Wakely. We didn't mean to goof off."

"I know it's winter break and study sessions shouldn't be so serious, but my goodness that scared me." Mama reaches over to squeeze my hand and then she sneaks her grasp over to check to make sure my pulse is not racing. "I'm sure Cara Jean told you that we had quite a scare the other night."

"We were just talking about that, Mama," I say, hoping she'll reverse course and go back to tracking new donations in the kitchen.

"Cara Jean experienced an allergic reaction," Mama tells Xavier. "Just the thought of seeing her experience that again—that's why I barreled my way in here. My apologies, Xavier. I certainly can't help you two with your math studies. But the way she clawed at herself . . ." With two fingers under my chin, Mama tips my face up and traces the scratch marks across my cheeks. "Will you look at those? Unbelievable."

"Mama, please." I wrinkle my nose and brush her hands away from my face.

"She hates when I fuss."

"Then maybe you should try not to fuss, Mrs. Wakely." He grins at her until she can't help but smile back.

Mama slinks back into the kitchen and promises to bring out snacks for us to enjoy on our next break.

Xavier whistles low and taps his pencil against the coffee table once she's gone. "Wow. Sounds like you had a really rough night," he says. I start copying down math problems and solving equations. "You don't want to talk about it?"

Now it's my turn to grin. "What gives you that impression?" And then I go back to work.

"What are you allergic to?"

I glance up at him and sigh, blowing my bangs away from my eyes. "Almost everything, apparently." And then because I don't want to intrigue Xavier with a new mystery to solve, I add, "This was just a new medication."

"It sounds like it didn't help." I feel Xavier's eyes on me. "What did your doctor say?" He's treading carefully, but there's not much more I want to say about the other night. For a second, when Xavier brings him up, the image of Dr. Eric looms in the corner of my vision. I remember his points about my mood swings and my prognosis, and how it seems that Mama and I have never treated my disease aggressively. Dr. Eric has a lot to say. But none of it seems like details I'm supposed to share with Xavier Barnes. I stay quiet, keep concentrating on math problems because there's a set way to solve those.

He goes on. "I was thinking, and actually you might have seen me at the hospital. You know, like you said. I go pretty often."

"To donate blood?"

"No. Sometimes I go to get transfusions, though. People donate blood to me." I nod like I know what he's talking about. Xavier keeps pausing. If I interrupt him or provide a distraction, he might never return to the topic. Instead I just wait. It's up to him to shake the snow globe. He asks me, "Do you know what sickle cell is?" In his expert Xavier way, he assumes I don't and plows through with the definition. "It's a genetic disease that affects red blood cells. You know how blood cells are round? Some of mine are shaped differently—crescent-shaped—and so when those cells move through my body vessels, they have the potential to get all caught up on each other and kind of clog up blood vessels. That can cause episodes of pain and stiffness. So I'm absent a lot too." Xavier says it casually, but it doesn't sound like a casual revelation.

"I'm really sorry." I almost clamp my hand over my mouth when I hear myself speak. I hate when people say that to me. "How long have you had it?"

"Ehhh. My whole life. Most hospitals screen African American babies for it, so my parents knew. I started having pain crises when I was about two years old."

I think of his mom commanding Mama to program her correct number into her phone. It's hard to picture Mrs. Barnes slowing down for anything. "Do they have it? Because it's genetic."

"Nope. They're carriers. We think my great-uncle had it." Xavier shifts over on the couch and turns back to the math book. "Listen, it's not this huge thing. I just wanted you to know I get it—you know, some of what you're going through. If I seem nosy about medical stuff, that's the reason. I just want to understand."

"You're going to cure me, Science Kid?"

"I mean, if I accidentally discover something on the way to curing myself, I won't throw it down the drain."

"Well, then thank you. That's the sweetest thing I've ever heard."

"All right. That's enough of that. You need to learn how to do some math. Make sure you can contribute something to this relationship." We settle in and start mapping out equations, and I try not to get sidetracked by the fact that a boy referred to our relationship.

That's what it feels like, though. Not a capital-R *Relationship*. But I *relate* to him.

"Do you take a lot of medications?" I ask a little while later, as we snack on the apple slices that Mama brought in.

"Not really. Certain foods help because they fight inflammation. I have to hydrate. That's super important."

I sigh. "Same." I look over at him. "Is that why you're so small?"

"Jeez, Cara Jean—aiming for the jugular. I am currently in between growth spurts, thank you." Xavier takes the opportunity to flex again in his sweater vest. "But yeah, probably."

"And there's no cure?"

"I haven't found it yet. Don't rush me." But then Xavier gets serious. "It's mostly something you manage. My parents made sure that I understood what was happening in my body, even when I was little. That helped make the flare-ups a little less scary. It gets hard that you can't really predict a crisis. You do what you can to prevent them, but at the same, you have to live your life, right? Stress triggers it. Winter triggers it."

"Do you have a fundraising campaign?"

Xavier crunches through his apple. "A what?"

"You know, to pay for your medical expenses."

"No, Cara. I have insurance. Don't you and your mom have medical insurance?"

Somehow I've said something wrong and my voice scurries to try to make it right. "Of course we do. But you know how those companies are. The coverage is terrible. The co-pays and then this new doctor who my mom really loves, he's great, I guess, but he must be out of network." I echo all the terms I've heard Mama use on her channel. But Xavier still looks troubled. "You know what?" I say, gesturing to the stack of books on the coffee table. "Let's not talk so much about being sick. Let's talk about being smart."

My tutoring session ends without any more conversation about diagnoses or disorders. Xavier doesn't seem to mind but I still feel awful about cutting him off. I decide to text him. *Thank you for the tutoring session*, I say, in a truly spectacular act of groundbreaking communication. I follow it up with *And the chat.* Then I hide my phone under my pillow and force myself to go downstairs so I don't just sit and wait for him to text back.

Mama is on the phone. She's pacing around the kitchen, occasionally stopping at the counter to jot down notes in one of her little memo books. I overhear snippets: "Yes. I do understand. I very much appreciate that." And then: "We feel so welcomed. Everyone has rallied around us and shown us such care and support, especially during this holiday season." I reach over to grab her pen and scrawl across a page of her notebook: *Who is it?* But Mama just shakes her head and holds one finger up over her mouth to tell me to stay quiet.

"Well, I'm not sure about that." Mama walks toward the dining room and speaks more softly into the phone. I sit at the kitchen table and pretend to read my biology book but really I am full-on straining to hear her conversation. "Please understand," I hear Mama say, "Cara Jean is a very sick young lady. She has good days and bad days. We're happy to provide photos and some old family videos but we would find a camera crew completely overwhelming right now."

I can hardly believe what I'm hearing. I've never known Mama to turn down a photo op. And a camera crew? I remember when I was really little and all of our neighbors chipped in to send us to Disney World. Someone from the charity came along to take video and by the end of the trip I called him Uncle Allen. That's how much Mama loves camera crews.

"Absolutely. And I do have some additional footage. I did my best to keep the fundraising video brief, but it seems so important to tell our story." I hear Mama pause and listen, then rush to say, "Oh, I appreciate that. That's high praise from a professional such as yourself. I will send you what I have. You let me know what works and if there's anything else you need. This kind of exposure is such a gift for our cause. I know that."

Mama hangs up the phone and does a happy little spin. "Cara Jean, do you have any idea who I was just talking to?"

I'm not supposed to know, so I shake my head.

"That was Fox Channel Seven News. Cleveland affiliate. They intend to do a segment about the Caring for Cara campaign." Mama sounds breathless and bubbly. "Can you believe that?" I shake my head, trying to make sense of everything she's telling me and everything else I overheard.

"Cara Jean, we're going to be on television!"

CHAPTER FIFTEEN

When Xavier Barnes texts me back, he has no clue he is writing a future media darling. I go back upstairs to escape Mama and her manic planning and find his message waiting. *No problem. I am happy to help and chat.* **And then:** *What do you do for fun?*

I am so glad I have recently cultivated an interesting hobby if only so that I can write back and say, with complete sincerity, *Lately I have been into pottery. There's a place in town. My friend owns it.*

Xavier writes back, *Mud Matters?*

"Yes!" I say out loud. And then I type, *Yes! That's the place.*

I see the three dots blink on the screen and know that Xavier is thinking. Xavier is probably always thinking. But right at this moment, Xavier is thinking about what to say to me. *We should go sometime.* I feel both exhilarated and a little bit ill.

The three dots blink again and for one awful minute I think maybe he changed his mind. It's a tiny second but long enough for me to realize that I want him to like me, even if I don't know how I feel back. Then the follow-up message materializes. *We should celebrate after your makeup exams.* And I understand that Xavier Barnes is dialing it back. He is being careful with us.

I start to answer: *We should celebrate sooner than that.* But that doesn't sound like me at all. I erase it and instead write, *Sounds like a plan.*

When Mama calls me downstairs, I leave my phone under my pillow again. Not because I'm slowing my roll with Science Kid but because I know she'll have something to say every time I look down at my phone. I want to keep this for myself as much as I can.

In the kitchen, she is sitting at the table with her arms folded across her chest. Not a good sign. "That's great about the news story, Mama. Thank you again for putting together that amazing video. Look at the momentum it's gaining."

But Mama will not be distracted. She nods toward the pill case in the center of the table. "Well, I don't know what the point of going to all that trouble is if I can't rely on you to take a pill on time." The compartment labeled TH for Thursday is open and there's still a handful of pills in the pocket. More pills than there are supposed to be. I can see that much from here.

"Oh." My mind races to find the thing to say that will make her the least angry. "I thought—"

"Don't think. There is a chart." She points to the whiteboard behind her. "It's a simple matter of following the chart."

"The chart keeps changing, though. It's kind of hard to keep up." I almost remind her what happened the last time I accidentally doubled up on my meds, how she and Dr. Eric had to carry me out of China Moon Chef. Mama's grim expression tells me it wouldn't be helpful to trot that tidbit out. I default to my old standby: "I'm really sorry, Mama. Maybe my brain's a little foggy today."

"You seemed alert enough to chatter through your tutoring session. Maybe that's all just too much of a distraction, Cara Jean. The schoolwork, this boy coming over—"

"It's not, Mama. I'm so sorry. I got all excited about the news story and what it might mean."

She presses her hands to her eyes. "Cara, I can't do this by myself."

"Should I take all three pills now?" I expect her to say *Of course not*. Three pills will knock me out. Even I know that. It's not even six o'clock. I'll be lucky if I can stay awake for *Wheel of Fortune*.

But Mama answers, "Yes." I reach for the pill container in the center of the table and wait for her to stop me. I fumble getting them out. She still just stares. I tip the three capsules into my hand and reach for my bottle of water. I move deliberately—not slowly enough to set her off, but not too quickly either. Mama doesn't say a word. She glares at me the way she glares at Mr. Brinks during our meeting at the high school—as if we are no longer on the same team.

I toss the three pills into my mouth at once. I take a gulp of water, swallow, and then open my mouth and lift up my tongue. 147

Neither of us speaks but I feel a slight thrill of victory when she looks down at the kitchen table first.

I turn on my heel and retreat back upstairs. I complete my bedtime routine as if it's after ten already and force myself to drink some water too. I prepare to be hit by the soft wall of sleep that I know is coming.

I check my phone and see that Xavier has texted back—just a smiling emoji. I picture myself as an astronaut, trying to complete a mission before the oxygen in my tank runs out. What would a normal person write? But then Xavier doesn't need me to be completely normal. I go with as much honesty as is reasonable. *Suddenly feeling worn out. Going to power down on all fronts.* The three dots blink, but I turn the phone off before reading his response. Slide it into my desk drawer. Mission accomplished. I've got to get back to the shuttle.

CHAPTER SIXTEEN

Having a friend means that when I turn on my phone, there exists the possibility that I have a message waiting. It's just a thumbs-up emoji, indicating that my previous text was read, understood, and perhaps appreciated. Even still, it registers with a frizzle of electricity. Last night I was not as alone as I felt. Xavier Barnes was thinking about me.

Mama is in a good mood when I go down for breakfast. She's humming as she's buzzing around the kitchen. She looks stunning. Her hair is something to behold. She has managed to achieve a style on her own that most country-and-western singers need a full entourage of hair and makeup artists to craft. And then there is the business suit. It's pink tweed and has a slight fringe on the sleeves and the lapel, but a tasteful fringe. Mama looks like Weather Girl Barbie.

Dr. Eric shows up and tells me my color's improved. Then he goes with Mama to the local Fox station for her interview. Mama's in such a good mood she tells me if I'm truly feeling better, I can go to the pottery place later on.

I tell myself to wait until 9:30 a.m. to write to Xavier. First, I make a kale smoothie and parcel out the morning's vitamins. I log on to the school portal to see if there are any messages from my teachers. Just one from Mr. Durand to let me know he received the *Antigone* paper. *Looking forward to reading this. Hope you're having a good break.*

Am I having a good break? On the morning news, the hosts discuss resolutions. People like Libby Gilfeather are probably sleeping in, thankful for a vacation from the constant grind in high school. And I bet Mr. Brinks would say I've been on vacation all year.

But chronic illness doesn't feel like that. I never get a day off. Every morning I wake up and spend the first few minutes trying to gauge exactly how much suffering I'll face that day. At night, I take stock of the events I've missed, the ways I've fallen short. That's my own grind.

I wonder if that's how Xavier experiences his days or if there's ever a morning when he thinks of something else before the shape of his blood cells. At nine fifteen I give up waiting patiently. His thumbs-up requires a response.

150   *Change of plans*, I write. *Let's celebrate early.*

What are we celebrating? Last night I cried enough to soak through a down pillow. I want to celebrate that today is not last night. But maybe that's sort of grim to send to Xavier Barnes before 10:00 a.m.

My Antigone paper is in. I consider my response carefully and decide I like it. It refers to our shared goal of my academic makeup work. I hit send.

Almost instantly, he replies: *Old news.* Xavier Barnes is messing with me.

There's only one play here, I figure. So I aim for authenticity.

I drank my kale allotment. My mom said yes already. While the blue dots blink, I remind myself that regardless of what this boy says, I can go to the pottery studio on my own. I'll catch up with Manuela and thank her for delivering Mama's vase. Maybe I will sculpt another woodland creature. That will still guarantee that today is a better day than most.

You are such a party animal. Let's study some first. Xavier and I set tutoring for 2:00 p.m. We have this really awkward moment because at first we plan to study at noon and then he writes back and says his mom wants to confirm that my mom will be home. Then I have to admit that I don't actually know when Mama's due home and now Mrs. Barnes probably thinks I'm planning to seduce her son.

When Mama and Dr. Eric pull into the driveway, I send Xavier a text and he confirms that he'll head over at two. Then I settle in on the sofa, take a few deep cleansing breaths, and try to focus on acting with a greater generosity of spirit. When she walks in the door, I ask, "How did it go, Mama?" and try not to notice that her mascara has smeared all over her face.

She looks to Dr. Eric before she answers. "Really well. I think it went really well." He nods and moves to put the kettle on. "I just get so emotional. But everyone was so kind there. My goodness, they all say that they are praying for you, Cara Jean. There was a lot of love and care in the room. A lot of support." She calls over to Dr. Eric, "Wouldn't you agree?"

Dr. Eric stands in our kitchen, his hands in his pockets. "Your mother was phenomenal. She spoke very eloquently. She's a born star, really. But your privacy is paramount, Cara. If anyone calls, if someone ever stops by the house, or even shows up at school, please do not speak to them without your mother present, all right? You are a mature and sensitive young woman, but you are a legal minor. In situations like these, it's best to operate with a spokesperson."

"Eric!" Mama seems surprised, as if she hasn't told me the same things herself. "For goodness' sake. Who is going to come out to the house?"

"We just don't know, Shaylene. Now that you've opened yourselves up to the public, people are going to feel a certain amount of ownership over your lives and your choices. I've seen it happen before. All that concern comes from a good place, but you are two women on your own. Forgive me for worrying. Of course, I don't mean to be patronizing."

"Don't worry," I say to both of them. "I wouldn't want to answer anyone's questions about my illness. I just want to focus on feeling better and going back to school." Mama sips her tea. I figure she's feeling triumphant and it's a point worth pressing. "Do you think you'll set up an appointment with Mr. Brinks soon? To figure out my makeup exams?"

"Sweetheart, just you wait. Once this news story airs, Mr. Brinks will fall all over himself to try and help us."

Later, when we meet up, Xavier furrows his brow when I tell him about that last comment.

"What could that possibly mean?" he asks.

"No clue. She was all fired up though, with her mascara running in rivers down her cheeks."

"I don't get it. Brinks seems like a stand-up guy." He shrugs and turns his attention back to his cup of hot cocoa. We move from the coffee shop up the street.

"Careful, you'll lose your nomination for the National Honor Society."

"Due to my unwavering respect for the vice principal?" Xavier asks, laughing.

"Due to your lack of critical thinking."

"No way. I critically think all over the place. Brinks looks out for me. You just have to communicate. And he needs everything documented, but that's state mandated."

"What does that mean?"

"Well, you know—it doesn't matter how many doctor's notes you get. If you miss a certain number of days of school, you repeat the year. But listen, Brinks will work with you. There are some days I can barely move but at least if I get there, he'll find a way to count my attendance. He seems better than most. There are kids in my support group who've had to switch to be homeschooled."

"My mom keeps threatening that."

153

"My worst nightmare."

"It would be, right? A nightmare?" I want to ask Xavier: *What if it wasn't? What if we just did this—learned on our own, without anyone glaring over our shoulders?*

"All the time I'd lose in labs alone, it would derail any chance of a premed program."

So that's probably a no, then. Sometimes I forget. When Xavier and I study, he's just logging in community service hours. I'm the one who's actually learning.

But at the pottery studio, the playing field evens out a little. First of all, when we walk through the door, Manuela reacts as if we're artistic luminaries. "My darling fawn, my Christmas angel, how are you?" She swoops in and gathers me into an embrace. When she sees Xavier, Manuela whips her head around so quickly, one of her glossy braids slaps my face. "Who is this gentleman you've brought to me?"

"Before I even introduce him, I wanted to thank you for bringing by Mama's present. You have no idea—" I try to tell her. "It meant so much to me."

"And so you have brought me a handsome young man in appreciation? I will accept that offering. Mr. Suave Young Man, you would not believe the magical powers this girl has. She waves her hands over clay and then beautiful creatures appear as if from the misty forest. I have never seen such delicately crafted antlers on deer."

"Antlers, huh?" Xavier grins and stares. I watch him try to make sense of Manuela but she acts like a lab experiment, erupting in friendliness. There's no containing her.

"Pick out a table for working. Let me get you some clay."

Manuela finally takes a break from practically singing to us and spins away with a flourish.

"Wow." Xavier turns to watch her go. Then he turns back to me and says, "You surprise me, Cara Wakely. To think I was walking the same school corridors as an antler-sculpting savant. I had no idea about the unexpected depths of your talents."

"I didn't want to intimidate you." I settle onto a stool and motion for him to sit down too. "Isn't this place amazing?"

"I thought it was for little kids."

"I know." Right then, the door rings and a gaggle of kindergartners stumbles in. Behind them, a harried mom carries a sheet cake and a bunch of balloons.

Xavier buries his face in his hands. But when he lifts his head, he's laughing. "Okay. That's also fun though, right? I mean, who doesn't love a birthday party?"

Manuela clearly loves a birthday party. We hear her whoop wildly from the back room and soon see her sashay out with two large slabs of gray clay that she sets on our table. "Let's chat later. This incoming princess needs her party." She heads over to the front of the studio. "Hello, my exquisite darlings! Are you feeling artistic today?"

"Do you remember how birthday parties were like playdates to the extreme? You had to plan something different than everyone else in the class. You'd go roller-skating or bowling or to the trampoline park. Birthday parties, man. Playdates that ended in ice cream cake. How could anything in adolescence live up to that?" Xavier grins and watches the pottery party kids clamoring around their table.

"I didn't go to many birthday parties. We moved around a lot; I never knew anyone well enough to score an invite."

"Gosh, Cara. That's tragic right there. We always went all out for my birthday. Still do." I think of Xavier Barnes's mom in her white Mercedes and her trendy accessories. Something tells me each year there are a lot of layers to Xavier's ice cream cake.

"I guess your parents spoil you?" I realize I've spent all this time feeling self-conscious about my clothes and my bony clavicle and drawn face. It never occurred to me that our house might seem tiny to Xavier Barnes. Or that he might have noticed our shabby, donated furniture.

"Well, I'm all they've got. And you know that kids with sickle cell have a lower life expectancy."

The air feels like it leaves the room. I look up, expecting the party balloons to have deflated. "I wondered about that. The other day you talked about uncertain tomorrows."

"Yeah. It's no big thing. Besides, the medical community makes strides every day." He shrugs and smiles wryly at me. "I didn't mean for us to compete in the adversity Olympics. We don't need to spend this whole time talking about being patients."

I let myself exhale. "All right." I smile back at him. "Let's pretend to be artists."

Xavier tentatively kneads the clay in front of him. "I will wait for your direction on that endeavor. I am *terrible* at art."

"That can't be true. You're not terrible at anything."

Xavier laughs. "Now I know you're lying."

"Look," I say, "I have a confession to make." He looks solemnly at me. "I can really only make antlers."

A look of relief washes over his face. Then he shrugs and says, "I mean, maybe in our lifetime, the world will experience a shortage of antlers. It will recognize what an extraordinary resource you are."

I decide to make a bowl and Xavier decides to make a pencil cup.

I say, "You know what I appreciate about you, X? You completely embrace your geekiness. There's no halfway, this-is-an-ironic-kind-of-geekiness. You are apologetically, full-on nerd."

"Of course I am. Why would anyone ever apologize for being himself? Or herself? Besides, of all people, you should be grateful for my geekiness. After you ace those makeup exams, you'll need to make me thank-you antlers or something."

"Yes. That is factual. But first I have to convince my mom to schedule my makeup exams."

"Why would you have to convince her?" Xavier's first pencil cup collapses on the table in front of him.

"She just keeps putting it off. She and Brinks get on like cats and dogs and she thinks tests take too much out of me." And then because I see his wrinkled brow again, I say, "She's just not really supportive of that stuff."

"That stuff, meaning your future? Listen, I know it's been the two of you on your own for a long time and she's got strong woman credentials, but your mom displays a weird vibe sometimes."

I look up from my clay. "What's that supposed to mean?"

"She is controlling and creepy."

"Whoa." I work my fingers into the clay and try to find my way to a response.

"I'm sorry. That's your mom, I get it. But you've been sick for a long time, right, Cara? She should have figured some of this out by now. Brinks just does his job. Her job is supposed to be teaching you how to advocate for yourself. Lifting you up, not convincing you exams are too tough or classes are too exhausting. Your mom says she's protecting you. I don't see that. I see her holding you back."

It's strange to hear someone else criticize Mama, especially after last night, when I felt so angry and let down. But it's one thing for me to think those things. Hearing Xavier Barnes say them out loud, in the middle of the pottery studio, doesn't sit right at all.

"You don't understand—"

"I come pretty close to understanding, Cara."

"You want to call my mom overprotective and your mom wouldn't let you be alone with me."

"You're acting defensive."

"That happened *this morning*."

"It did." Xavier nods. "Sometimes, my mom does not fully grasp the magnitude of my nerdiness. But she has also made certain, from the moment of my diagnosis, that she understands sickle cell, that I understand sickle cell. And even more than that, she has guaranteed that I can explain it to other people so that I don't have to move through my days apologizing for my health."

I don't think I operate that way. I don't walk around apologizing for myself. But Mama's taught me to feel grateful for the days that I can enjoy. Maybe Xavier doesn't grasp how rare a trip to town is for me. I don't want to spend this whole afternoon of freedom talking about the limits of illness. I try to put the brakes on this whole conversation. "You know what?" I say. "Think what you want. I appreciate all your help, but really, let's just try having fun."

158

But Xavier keeps going. "Tell me about your illness, Cara. I want to understand what you're going through. I want to help."

Sometimes I feel like a stone caught up in a riverbed. Everyone runs over me like churning water. They don't mean to silence me or hold me down; they just keep rushing by, the way they are meant to. But all the same, they wear me out.

"I have an autoimmune disease." My voice sounds small and feeble. "That means that my body sometimes attacks itself, thinking it is fighting infection. That causes pain and weakness. It's tricky to find a combination of medicines that help address all of those problems."

"Right. And I get that it's just been you and your mom trying to get to the bottom of what's going on with your health—"

"Not anymore." I don't even know why I say it, why I feel the need to claim him. Maybe I'm just arguing with Xavier for the sake of arguing when I say, "We have Dr. Eric now."

"I know. I don't understand that either. Do you know how many doctors I've seen in my lifetime? How many of them do you think provide checkups in my living room?"

I parrot the lines I've heard from Mama these past weeks. "We're very lucky in that way—to have such a preeminent physician take an interest in my case. We never imagined a blessing like that."

"Yeah. But what about *your* interest in your case? Do you understand why I'm pursuing research science? Listen, there are mornings when I hurt so badly, I throw up oatmeal. When I'm in the middle of a pain crisis, my wrists feel like they're splintering. My hands don't work; they look crippled. But even if I just sit in the back and listen, I get myself to class. I want to learn. I don't just accept what doctors tell me. I keep asking questions. Because someday I'm going to find a cure for sickle cell. I have set that goal. It drives me. Then I met you and I admire you. I see how tough you are. But what I don't get is this: Why aren't you more curious, Cara? Why aren't you more driven?"

I remind myself that I am just a stone and that I can't control the current running over me. Xavier doesn't mean to wear me down. The clay in my hands right now is so soft. We'll paint it and glaze it, and after we leave, Manuela will bake it in a wood-fired kiln. She will stoke the fire and the fire will transform it from soft clay to solid ceramic. Maybe I'm less like a stone and more like a piece of wood-fired clay. I feel hardened like that—brittle.

I select my words very carefully, but they still emerge angrier than I mean them to. "I'm sorry you are better at being sick than I am."

Xavier reels back. "I didn't mean it like that." But of course he did.

Maybe Mrs. Barnes has taught her son to advocate for himself and search for cures that don't yet exist. Good on her. Mama has schooled me on plenty of other valuable life lessons. For instance, we Wakely women consider ourselves experts in almost destroying each other and then acting like nothing at all has happened. I employ that tactic at the pottery studio, next to the birthday party, under the watchful eye of my friend Manuela, immediately after Xavier Barnes has accused me of choosing to stay sick, of deciding to be complacent.

"Here, let me show you how to make a cylinder," I say, in the steadiest cadence possible. "You have to work the clay a bit with your hands. Once it warms up, it becomes more pliable." I direct him to the mason jar full of tools. "You can use one of those rollers too, especially for the bottom." Science Kid keeps looking searchingly at me, as if I should have more to say to him.

But I've already moved on. Xavier Barnes is not the first person to underestimate me. Or my coping mechanisms. Sometimes you need to fix a smile on your face and just muscle through. That's another way to deal with the sinking sensation that you cannot trust another person on the planet. That is another kind of remedy.

CHAPTER SEVENTEEN

If Xavier Barnes thinks genetics only applies to biological makeup, that hypothesis is disproven during the drive home from Mud Matters. I'm sure Mama knows something has gone wrong between us but she never lets on to Xavier or me that she's picked up on that. Instead she keeps up a constant stream of chatter as she drives us home.

I stare out the window and try to tune out their small talk. Mama chirps on so friendly, asking Xavier about his classes and his hobbies. "Well, today we discovered that pottery might not be my calling." He laughs ruefully.

"I don't believe that. I'm sure it just takes practice and studying."

"I don't know about that. Cara really has a knack for it." Xavier lays it on thick. "She has this complete command over the material."

"You've seen the vase she made for me, right? We could see it in a museum."

I shift my gaze back to the window. I don't want to hear him saying kind things to me. The two of them discuss Xavier's lifetime goals and Mama rapturously informs him that she believes he could become surgeon general someday. When she pauses, I get the urge to chime in and mention how he has already diagnosed her as creepy and overbearing. Eventually though, Xavier Barnes will step out of the car. He'll return to his home with his parents, who have probably installed a high-tech laboratory in his refurbished basement so that they can work together as a family to find a cure for his blood disorder. I will still be stuck drinking kale smoothies with Mama.

He rattles off directions and Mama takes several turns into the kind of posh neighborhood I didn't know existed in Middlefield. When we do pull into Xavier's driveway, his home stands as exactly the type of real estate in which I imagined he lived: stately and well-maintained, with columns in the front and those shrubs that someone actually takes the time to shape.

He twists toward me. "We should meet up again soon to make sure that you're all set with the math material. Even tomorrow, if you're up for it. The rest of break will fly by really quickly. Mrs. Wakely, if you could schedule that exam first, it would help us a lot. Cara really knows the material."

"Yes. That's the exam she was taking when she collapsed."

"I remember. Mr. Brinks has always met my mom halfway when working through my makeup assignments. Maybe he can count the first few sections Cara completed so that her first exam won't be so long. Right, Cara? That way you could ease into midterms?" I nod before remembering to be angry. Encouraged, Xavier presses on. "Feel free to call my mom, Mrs. Wakely. She might have some tips on dealing with Brinks."

Mama keeps her smile set, but her eyes are granite. "We appreciate your help tutoring Cara Jean. But let me stick to handling the school administration for my daughter."

"Of course, of course. Thanks so much for the ride. I'll text you later, Cara."

Xavier goes around back to grab his enormous bag of books from the back of the van. Mama and I hear a loud thud when he hauls the bag out of the car. "Oof," he mumbles. I can't just sit there and watch him struggle to drag all those books up his long front walk.

"Hold on a second, Mama." My voice surprises me. I hop out of the van to help Xavier. We each take a tote handle and split the weight between us.

Xavier stops halfway up the path. He waits to speak until I meet his eyes. "I shouldn't have said those things about your mom. I'm sorry. Sometimes I forget I don't actually know everything."

"Xavier the expert."

"Only about some things." He holds out his hand. It feels strange to shake a boy's hand. Mama's taught me to be vigilant about germs. I don't go around touching people without a reason. I can't recall the last time there was a reason. Xavier's hand radiates heat, probably from carrying the heavy bag. His palm feels smooth and his fingers squeeze mine and let go. I don't imagine lingering like that—what it would feel like to sit next to Xavier and keep our fingers tangled, the way some people who look forward to seeing each other do. I leave Xavier on his front steps and seal myself back up in my mom's minivan so that she can explain that no one understands us.

She starts in as soon as the door closes. "Sweet kid." That's her initial verdict, and then: "But a little bit clueless. It always amazes me how kids today feel empowered to speak up on subject matter they know absolutely nothing about. I know I raised you as more respectful than that."

"He has a chronic illness too," I explain with as little inflection as possible. I don't feel like defending Xavier right now, but he's not completely unqualified to exchange ideas about makeup work with my mother.

"Well, we certainly sympathize." Mama keeps her eyes on the road and I return to staring out the window. Maybe both of us want to be somewhere else. "He does have a way about him, though," she says. "I didn't want to say anything because you were so excited to have a new friend, maybe particularly a new handsome friend."

"I wouldn't call Xavier Barnes handsome." *Not out loud anyway.*

"Well, regardless, I almost spoke up. I just didn't appreciate how I heard him talk to you. You're a very smart young lady, Cara Jean. I hope you know that about yourself. And, while it was never my intention to eavesdrop on your conversations," my mother lies, "I couldn't help but overhear moments now and then. I noticed his patronizing tone. What do they call it now? Mansplaining. It seems to me that Xavier has been doing a lot of mansplaining."

"He's tutoring me. That means we've asked him to explain things to me."

"Okay. If you didn't feel disrespected, then I don't want to overstep. But I see patterns. You don't always give yourself enough credit. I'm not sure you need his help."

"Thanks for looking out for me. The sessions are really helping, though. I even feel ready to go back to school."

"Let's just take it slow, Cara Jean." I knew she would say that. Her cell phone buzzes then, right as we pull into the driveway. "Probably Dr. Eric," she mentions breezily.

"Speaking of mansplainers . . ." My voice sounds sour, even to me.

"He hoped to stop by and check your vitals. Which I certainly appreciate. You need a quiet night, especially after all of today's activity."

I can't argue with this. My shoulders ache from the day's trials and burdens: hunkering over schoolbooks and then strolling around town, perching on the stools at Manuela's studio and leaning over the craft table. And then holding in all the tension. My muscles throb from so much anger and forgiveness. From trying to figure what to say, and also what to stop myself from saying. When I step out of the car, my eyes travel up to my bedroom window, where my bed waits. I can almost imagine what it will feel like to sink under the covers and hide away in the muffled softness.

Right at the moment the idea becomes so vivid for me, Mama screeches in a way that is the opposite of quiet. "Cara Jean. My goodness. This is really happening."

I don't even have enough energy to ask. I head toward the door and she follows, shouting after me, "It's happening already. They plan to air our segment tomorrow morning—the feature about the fundraiser."

Mama practically hovers up the stairs, she is so propelled by excitement. "We have to make some phone calls, tell people to watch. I can't believe this. They must have loved the segment. I had no idea they would air it so soon. You know, I sensed this strong connection with the two news anchors but I just dismissed that. *Shaylene*, I told myself, *these people converse with strangers for a living. Of course the dialogue will run smoothly.* But we didn't feel like strangers; we had this immediate bond. Our story seemed to just land in their hearts. I swore I felt that this morning. And there you go. We are going to go to sleep tonight and wake up tomorrow morning and watch ourselves on television. How many people can say that?"

She finally seems to notice me again. "You are just stunned silent. Are you just so elated?"

"Yeah." I nod vigorously. "It's the best news. But you're right. All this activity today really drained me. I'm going to turn in early so that I can wake up with you tomorrow."

"Cara Jean." Mama's mouth opens and closes, searching for words. "Now? You haven't eaten supper."

"I know. But I'm way too excited to eat anyway. This way the morning will only come faster." Sometimes I think to myself, *Cara Wakely, how do you come up with this crap?*

Mama laps it up. "Well, I get that. That's not the healthiest choice, but I understand it." She leans forward to kiss me. "Are you going to call Xavier up and tell him?" Mama asks breezily, as if it's the most casual question. But she's measuring how much he matters to me.

"It's really not any of his business, right?"

She grins. "I think you're underestimating how interested he is. But you know what, sweetheart? You're allowed to set boundaries. You don't owe anybody anything. That's not a lesson I was taught as a young girl and I hope you'll take note of it."

I imagine Mama as a girl, in one of her glittery skating leotards. She cuts wide rings in the ice with the blades of her skates. These are boundaries and no one may cross them.

Tonight she's spinning in different kinds of circles. "I don't know how you'll manage to fall asleep. You need to take your evening meds," she reminds me. "And you shouldn't take the blue pill on an empty stomach."

I fix myself a bowl of granola with almond milk and eat it standing at the kitchen sink. Usually, Mama hates when I eat standing up, but she is preoccupied with the computer anyway, checking the daily tally on the Caring for Cara fundraiser. Lately, she opens and closes the page quickly, like she doesn't want me looking over her shoulder. She even has the app on her phone and I see her tapping away at it when we're out and about.

When she sees me notice, she slips her phone back in her pocket like it's confidential business. Her secrecy seems crazy to me because I couldn't care less. If I wanted to, I could just log on to the website—the site publishes fundraising progress as public knowledge, after all. I'd rather not know. It's not meant for me to decide about anyway—I understand that much.

When I'm done, Mama says, "Remember—no studying in bed. Make sure to wear your breathing machine."

My heart lurches. "But, Mama—"

"Don't fuss." The warning tone rings in her voice. "I've cleaned the device thoroughly; there's no risk to using it."

Just the memory of that pain sears the crescents of flesh below my eyes. I'll have to lie on my back like a mummy in a sarcophagus and try not to feel smothered by my mom and her miraculous inventions.

It occurs to me that Mama doesn't have anyone besides Dr. Eric to tell about tomorrow's news story. She could call up people from her support group, but maybe that's considered impolite, since everyone in that circle could benefit from media exposure. We don't talk to her family, on account of how they treated her when she had to give up skating. She doesn't have brothers or sisters and we've never done a good job of keeping up with old friends once we've moved. On the eve of Mama's big moment, she sits alone in the kitchen.

But not for long. I hear the sound of a kitchen stool scraping along the tiles as soon as I hit the first step upstairs. I linger just enough to hear the angle Mama takes in tonight's episode. "Hey there, wellness warriors." Her voice bounces through the house like an overinflated ball. "You will not believe why I am already parked in front of our humble little television set . . ."

CHAPTER EIGHTEEN

The next morning Mama tells me that my cancer is out of remission. Sort of. She sits on a blue leather armchair in a local television studio and casually mentions this fact to Stuart Porterfield and Stella Repollet, the cheerful hosts of *Channel 7 Sunshine*.

Stuart and Stella do not react as cheerfully to this news as they did to the collection of my baby pictures that Mama displayed or her funny anecdotes about learning how to work the camera for her YouTube channel.

"I'm so sorry, did you just say that Cara Jean's cancer

has returned?" Stella leans forward in her chair to ask.

I watch the TV version of my mother nod and lower her eyes as if to give over a moment of silence to my future. Next to me, my real-life mother keeps her eyes fixed on the television screen. She does not move to comfort me or offer any kind of explanation. I look to Dr. Eric, who my mom surprised with this viewing party. He arrived at 7:00 a.m. to take my blood pressure and some blood samples and then Mama sat him down in the living room and handed him the remote control. Currently, he sits on the opposite end of the sofa, rubbing his temples as if it physically pains him to be present. The remote control rests on the table in front of him. I'm tempted to reach for it to shut the TV off so that I can demand some answers.

TV Mama smiles bravely. "Mildly. We are very lucky that Cara Jean is now under the personal care of an extremely talented physician. He feels strongly that her disease is not only treatable but curable. That is the best news we've heard for quite some time."

"But the cancer represents a different issue than her auto-immune disorder, isn't that right?" Stuart asks as Stella looks on in her worried way.

"They are related. These kinds of complications occur when a patient suffers from certain forms of childhood cancer. And it's possible there's a genetic component at play; I am a survivor. My own cancer derailed my skating career." A picture flashes of Mama in her tiny, shimmering dress. "Oh my word—you have a picture ready to go!" Mama exclaims about the photograph she must have recently provided to the production team. "My greatest hope for Cara Jean is that she can pursue all of her dreams, that nothing has to take a back seat to these terrible diagnoses."

There is a lengthy pause, during which it's clear that no one knows what to say. Stella Repollet clears her throat and then regroups. "Shaylene, I'm sure that all of our viewers at home wonder one thing—how can we help?"

Yep, Stella. That's all I'm wondering. TV Mama launches into an explanation of the Caring for Cara website. Actual Mama sits beside me and nods along.

On-screen, Stuart reaches over to pat Mama's shoulder in a mechanically comforting way. "We understand now why Cara Jean couldn't join us today."

"Oh, she wanted to. Believe me. But it's crucial for us to be mindful of her immune system. Her doctor limits her exposure to any possible contaminants as much as possible."

I calculate the number of doorways I passed through yesterday, the people I grazed in my small adventures. I visualize my hands reaching for my cup of cocoa at the coffee shop, then buried in the clay at Mud Matters, then my fingers closing over Xavier's. As if she knows what I'm thinking, Mama reaches over to hold my hand. My palms go hot and sweaty.

Stella Repollet's hands flutter like swallows at her chest. She gestures in elegant arcs. "Of course. We absolutely understand. We hope you'll pass along our well wishes to her. Cara, honey, if you're watching this at home, your mom loves you so much." Stella beams into the camera. Next to me, Mama tips her head to rest on my shoulder. "We are all behind you a hundred percent. Stay determined, keep fighting, and may this coming new year bring you strength and healing. If Cara Jean was able to join us in the studio today, Shaylene, what would she say to us all?"

TV Mama grips the arm of her chair and tilts forward. She

speaks very carefully, as if she's worked hard to memorize these particular lines. "Stella and Stuart, how about we roll the tape and give Cara Jean the chance to speak for herself?"

I know what's coming.

The familiar website posts up on the screen along with the clip of me bellowing "I feel determined!" at the camera. I wince and Mama squeezes my hand.

"Well, that's just wonderful to hear." Stuart Porterfield's voice booms with approval.

"Isn't it?" Stella says. "Hey, Stuart, after this commercial break, let's talk about what we are determined to accomplish in the upcoming year. And all you viewers at home—what are your New Year's goals? We'll be right back after this word from our sponsors."

Dr. Eric flicks off the TV before the sponsors can get a word in. All our eyes move from the television to the coffee table. No one appears eager for eye contact.

I take the opportunity to issue the ultimate icebreaker: "So I have cancer?"

Dr. Eric tries to look comforting. "Cara, the complexities of your diagnosis may be difficult for someone of your limited experience and education to fully grasp."

"But Mama just said I have cancer. On TV."

My mother has rushed to the kitchen and come back with her clipboard. She flips through the piles of papers. "There's a set of test results here that I think will illustrate the numbers Dr. Eric's referring to."

"She's not going to understand those numbers." He turns to me. "Your mother needed clear terms to describe the health

173

challenges you're facing. We chose simple language that would garner a strong reaction. And it did. Your mother did a fantastic job, didn't she? She spoke graciously and articulately." He turns back to her. "I should never have doubted your ability to speak on behalf of Cara Jean."

Mama preens in the corner. I still don't understand. I don't feel anywhere close to understanding. "Do I have cancer or not?" I search my mother's face for answers but it's Dr. Eric who speaks.

"Let's try to stay calm. Hysterics won't help anything. Cara, you are no sicker than you were yesterday or the weeks and months before that. It's a matter of vocabulary. Your white blood cell count is elevated, indicating a high level of systemic infection. Paired with your medical history, that gives us a strong indication that you are out of remission, yes."

I turn to my mother. "This is how you decided to tell me?" Mama stares up at the gray screen of the television as if she wishes she could still find her face there. "You knew you said it like that. When you came home from the interview, you had to have remembered what they asked you and how you answered. You didn't think you should sit me down and maybe talk me through it? You expected me to look forward to hearing about it like this?"

"Let's not attack your mother for working so tirelessly to provide you with the best possible—"

But I am not hearing it. "Why aren't I in the hospital? Shouldn't I be in the hospital? I want to go to the hospital."

Mama reacts with a grimace and finally tears her gaze from the blank TV. "No, you don't, Cara. We've talked about why the hospital carries such dangers for a patient in your condition. You want answers and we are trying our best."

"This is your best?"

Dr. Eric leans toward me. "Hey, now. Watch your tone with your mother."

I swivel my head so fast to face Dr. Eric that immediately my temples begin to throb. "Why don't you mind your own business? Instead of trying to take on the role of my—"

"You're right. I should have done better," Mama interjects. I have her full attention now. "You're absolutely right about that. First, we said we couldn't be sure. So I made the choice to shield you from Dr. Eric's findings. I didn't want to scare you. And then you seemed so motivated with your schoolwork, with your new friendships. I don't want this illness to take anything else from you, Cara Jean. I can't explain why I just blurted it out during the interview. It must have been bothering me to keep such a secret. That's just not my way. Then afterward I put all those details to the back of my mind. That's when I really failed you because I should have prepared you. I didn't consider how you would feel listening to that conversation play out. I'm so very sorry."

Sometimes I wish people would just hold off on their apologies. Mama's saying the right lines, and they feel genuine. But I just want a little more time to be angry. My hands still feel jittery from fear and fury but now I'm supposed to manage forgiveness. Or else I'm the monster.

"Cara Jean should be able to understand that," Dr. Eric says. Both my mother and I turn to glare at him simultaneously. "Okay." He holds his hands up in surrender. "I see I'm intruding here. Why don't I take off for a bit and manage some of my other patients? Later on, when we've all regulated our emotions, we can answer any questions Cara Jean might have and discuss treatment options in a much more open way. Won't that feel like progress?"

I hear him call loudly after me, but I am already floating up the stairs. Let my mother fret over Dr. Eric and persuade him of his own importance. I retreat to my bedroom and slide back beneath the covers and try to fit together the factual fragments I've managed to collect. I start listing pieces of evidence that I want to get a hold of: Mama's clipboard with the last few weeks of my test results, the chart she insisted on bringing home with us from the hospital, even Dr. Abidi's business card. I have this idea that if I gather it all together and bring it to someone else, they might help me make sense of it. Maybe Xavier Barnes could treat my case as research. Or at least help me schedule an appointment with Dr. Abidi's office, since Mama canceled the one I was supposed to have, saying that Dr. Eric was the only doctor I needed.

But the word *cancer* chokes me. I think of the curves of its letters as snakes winding around my neck and waist. Constrictive and poisonous. I lie there, hiding under the layers of blankets, and trace my hands along my body, feeling for the source of sickness, for the rotten spot. Nothing feels that wrong, just the weariness that's always there, and now a rising panic for what's to come.

As soon as I hear my phone chime, I know it's Xavier. He must have switched on the TV this morning. Maybe his mom was making an omelet and she enjoys cooking with her morning shows on in the background. They were probably talking about whatever program for gifted students he'll apply to this summer. And then maybe Xavier Barnes looked up. Maybe he recognized my mother on the TV screen and his voice rose, just a little bit.

"Hold on a second, Mom. That's Mrs. Wakely."

He'll have questions and demand answers. And after that performance, he will have all sorts of something to say about my mother. I tunnel out to grab my phone from my dresser and glance through the yawning doorway to make sure that Mama's still downstairs. I bring the phone back under the covers to read in private. But the message is barely two sentences: *I need to skip tutoring today. Very sorry.* No jokes, no emojis. Just careful language canceling plans.

It doesn't mean Xavier didn't watch the *Channel 7 Sunshine* news story. I know that. It just might mean that he didn't believe it. Or maybe now he thinks I've been hiding this all along. I exhale under my blanket and try to breathe the stale air. It's not even nine o'clock. Life-threatening illness? Confirmed. Tutoring session with burgeoning romance? Abruptly canceled.

The last day of the year already stands as one for the ages.

I'm not the only one who gets stood up on New Year's Eve. Dr. Eric doesn't come back later on. I know it bothers Mama because she keeps checking her phone and sliding her eyes to the clock. But she doesn't mention missing him. When she asks when Xavier plans to come by, I just tell her I'm not up for studying.

I study on the sly, while she keeps track of the inevitable boost on the Caring for Cara website. "I want you to try to let go of the fear, Cara Jean," she tells me over dinner. She made grilled chicken with mango salsa and I appreciate the way she thinks she can ease the worst day of my life with homemade Mexican flavors. "Everything we've learned about healing tells us that staying positive is an enormous component."

"Then I'd like to move forward with my exams." I take a deep breath and launch into my pitch, knowing it's my best possible shot. "It would give me a piece of my future to focus on. Something to generate that sense of optimism that you say I need. Maybe you don't realize it but running the fundraising campaign has been really good for you." I see her startled look and quickly add, "Obviously, the campaign directly benefits me and I appreciate that. But you're learning as you're building it. You're pushing yourself to create a website and go on television. That inspires me."

Mama cuts her meat with enough pent-up frustration that her knife screams on the plate. But she hears me out. "I feel like it's the wrong time, Cara Jean. We need to reserve your energy and our resources."

"I think it's a better use of my nervous energy right now. And Xavier doesn't charge us for his tutoring. But when he goes back to school, his time will be more in demand."

"Well, I very much doubt he'll let that interfere with your study sessions."

I ignore that comment and plow forward. "I feel ready for this and would really appreciate your belief in me." And then because really, why stop now? I offer up my last enticement. "And we could do an amazing episode about makeup tests. I think our viewers would connect to that."

"A lot of our viewers are homeschooled," Mama counters. If I don't tread carefully, I might just join them.

"But they still sit for standardized testing, so they can relate to that aspect."

Mama nods thoughtfully. She even sets her knife down. "It could be an incredible episode. It targets a lot of our recurring themes of school support and accommodations. But it can't just be me yapping about you sitting for tests. You'd have to take a more active role."

I try not to look too eager. "I know."

When Mama takes out her spiral notebook and starts jotting down ideas for the makeup exam episode, I know it's a done deal.

After dinner, we indulge our longtime New Year's Eve tradition, watching the ball drop in London, five hours ahead of schedule. We bang on some pots and toast with organic apple cider and watch the fireworks explode over the Thames on BBC America. "Happy New Year, Cara Jean!" Mama says, and it's not an entirely terrible moment.

I make a big show of recording my vitals and then taking my meds in front of her, even though I still want to do a little studying in bed. I begin by reviewing biology and then switch to making history flash cards when my brain starts to get groggy.

Science Kid texts at nine o'clock: *Hey. All good there? Sorry to skip our study session.*

I wait a couple of minutes before sending my carefully worded casual reaction: *No worries. I am brilliant after all.*

Had a pain crisis this morning. All ok now.

I hold my phone in my hand like a fragile creature and try to measure out the correct response.

Glad you're ok. And then, because I want to understand more: *What does it feel like?*

The blue lights blink for a long time.

Living with pain is lonely. You feel so contained by the aching contraption of your body. You don't believe anyone could possibly relate. And sympathy just scrapes at the tender places. At the beginning, you feel noticed and seen. Maybe you lean into that understanding and really try to describe it. Maybe you let the carefully constructed mask slip and show the lines etched on your face, the sheer suffering there. But then you see the eyes glaze over and focus on a spot right past you. You have to add the worry about burdening other people to the already unrelenting burden of your own pain.

I decide to listen to Xavier better than that. I wait through the silence until he's ready to continue.

Like my bones are being pulverized inside my skin. Mostly it affects my arms and legs. If it gravitates to my lower back, then we usually have to go to the hospital.

What helps? I ask.

Hot compresses, breathing exercises. I try not to take pain medication.

I read this and my shoulders tense and hunch over. My defense mechanisms kick in. Xavier isn't talking about me, though. He is answering a question I asked. The three dots blink again and then he asks, *How is the studying going?*

Great! I now know everything. And then, because I want him to know that I listened to him yesterday, I say: *Good news. My mom agreed to schedule makeup exams.*

How did you manage that?

I don't say my mom feels guilty for how she told me I have cancer. Instead: *I told you. I'm brilliant.*

We don't tell each other happy new year or anything sappy like that. We talk about my history flash cards. We make plans to meet up the next day. Every once in a while, I listen out for Mama, who will wonder if I'm not knocked out by the time she turns in for the night. When the effects of my sleep medication overpower the thrill of incoming texts, I switch my phone to silent. I stash my flash cards under my pillow in case it's possible for historical facts to seep into my brain while I sleep.

If I were studying the record of my own life, I might make a flash card about texting with Xavier. I would label it *the night I was a good friend* or *accomplished a connection*. It definitely counts as a milestone. For the first time in a while, I breathe freely, even with the mask strapped across my face.

CHAPTER NINETEEN

My mother has apparently forgiven Dr. Eric for standing her up on New Year's Eve because the next day, the two of them seem resolved to put on a united front.

After he weighs me, takes my pulse, temperature, and blood pressure, the doctor with the man bun that my mom seems to listen to without question takes six syringes of my blood. Mama sets a spinach protein shake down next to me and Dr. Eric reminds me that it's important to replace my iron, like it's the first time I've ever had blood drawn. Then we all sit around the kitchen table, as if at a board meeting for a company going bankrupt.

It turns out that I'm the floundering company. Dr. Eric is apparently the drastic measure we have hired to turn my sinking ship around.

"We've all practiced a great deal of patience lately," he starts off. Because he's opening with optimism, I know we're headed nowhere happy. "Cara, I know it takes a great deal of patience to be a teenager, eager for independence and new experiences, and facing limits to your physical being. You're supposed to be a little rebellious right now. That's developmentally appropriate, after all. But in your case, rebellion could be deadly."

Mama looks stricken and I say, "Well, that took a turn." And then, because part of my resolutions has to do with leaning less on sarcasm and attempting to be more cooperative, I try to do better. "My mother and I had a long talk last night—you must have been attending to your other patients. Anyway, we came up with a plan about a new episode and my makeup tests." Mama chews her lip and refuses to meet my eyes. Now I feel like the CEO who understands she's about to take her spot on the unemployment line.

But Dr. Eric says, "That's fine, Cara. The wellness warriors channel and your school are areas of your mother's and your concern. I wouldn't dream of infringing on those decisions." Apparently, Dr. Eric has made some resolutions of his own. "Of course, I will continue to warn you against fatigue, which can be an enemy of good health."

"Dr. Eric believes we're not taking your test results seriously enough," Mama interjects. "We just want you to understand why you might feel a bit more ill in the next few weeks." She looks to Dr. Eric for confirmation.

He nods. "Weeks, possibly months."

"Because of what you told me yesterday? The new diagnosis?"

"Partly," Mama answers. "But the medication we've decided on works to eradicate diseased cells. It can also mistakenly attack healthy cells."

Dr. Eric wrinkles his brow. "*Inadvertently* more so than *mistakenly*. It's not an error—it's more like a calculated risk."

I know that my mother was sick, really sick at one time. She speaks about surviving reverently, like her relatively good health is a dispensation she can hardly believe she's been given. I've seen pictures of her looking almost skeletal with dark circles ringing her eyes. I've seen photos of her swollen face and learned that too was a result of medical treatment. I remind myself that Mama was once so sick because otherwise I would doubt that she could ever possibly absorb how tired I am of dealing with illness, and how I can't believe she wants me to take on more of it.

But I also think of Xavier Barnes. He places warm compresses on his limbs and does his visualization and waits for the pain to pass. On his good days, he tries to find a way to stop the bad days from finding him. It's not a terrible plan, considering.

"Well, I don't have a choice, right?" I say. Mama looks oddly relieved. "Will I go back to the hospital?" I ask, knowing that she'll shake her head no. "You know Xavier also deals with a major health issue—his parents might have a recommended doctor. Not to replace you, Dr. Eric. I know you're working so hard on my case, but maybe it would help to have a team."

I am not looking at Dr. Eric, whose last name I've never even known. Instead I search my mother's eyes for some reassurance that she has thought carefully about placing her full trust and my physical health and well-being in this man's hands.

Dr. Eric smiles benevolently. "I believe in teamwork, Cara. You and your mother are sensational teammates. And rest assured, I don't operate in a vacuum. My practice has a reputation built on collaboration with other medical professionals and I have reviewed your case with several colleagues whose input I respect. That is great self-advocacy, though. I applaud you. And I'm glad that you and Xavier have been able to share your experience in dealing with health challenges. But you need to be careful—what is his specific diagnosis? May I ask that?"

I consider whether giving Dr. Eric details betrays Xavier's confidence. But Xavier isn't like me—he doesn't seem ashamed of being sick. "He has sickle cell anemia."

"Oh, I see." Dr. Eric chuckles in this awkward sort of way. "It's wonderful that you two can commiserate. But try not to compare your experiences. Xavier's medical team is focused on gene therapy. That's the direction of treatment in which he needs to advance. You have very different challenges ahead of you. Cara, have you heard of chemotherapy?"

He still doesn't say the other C-word. "Yes." I swallow. "It's medicine you take intravenously, right, in the hospital?"

"Used to be. But pharmaceuticals keep evolving. We are so blessed that way. We can administer chemotherapy with a pill, taken right here at home."

"Lots of strides since I was sick, Cara Jean," Mama mentions, as if I have lucked out in some way.

Dr. Eric nods. "That's true, but it is a difficult medical protocol to follow. It's accompanied by serious side effects: nausea, lethargy, joint pain."

Mama tags into the conversation. "Cara Jean, do you remember the last time you were treated with chemotherapy?"

My mouth feels dry. I shake my head. "You've always said it was so damaging to me. You've partially blamed that for my symptoms now."

"Well, it's complicated. These are chemicals and sometimes we just don't know how our bodies, which are complex organisms, will process them. But I wouldn't have chosen to forgo treatment. That wasn't an option." She looks to Dr. Eric for help.

"Certainly any residual effects that we've seen play out in more recent years might be traced to earlier treatment choices, but we just don't know. Your immune system is so compromised. We need to do this. It's our only shot to stop the disease from progressing. Do you understand?"

"Yes."

Dr. Eric goes on. "There are other side effects to chemotherapy that I understand might be difficult for an adolescent girl. It's likely you'll lose your hair."

My eyes snap open, like a doll that's been dropped and then sat up. "I'm sorry. What do you mean?"

My mom leans forward over the table. "Do you remember when you were little?" She sniffles a little and reaches for a Kleenex from the box on the counter. "Your hair thinned out until you had these patchy wisps." Mama dabs at her eyes. "You always looked cute, but you were so sad, pulling out tufts of your hair."

I think back. "My head always itched." That's the only thread of memory I can grab at. "It grew back though, right?" I reach to slip a strand behind my ear and catch myself feeling to measure its length.

"Of course it grew back, sweetheart. That's what hair does. Hair always grows back."

Dr. Eric stands and looks down at both of us. "Thank you for hearing us out, Cara. We're all in agreement. I'm going to write a scrip for this medication and get started on placing an order."

Mama meets my eyes as if there's a possibility I might refuse. I search for the possibility of an opening.

"I mean, we have to, right?" I say.

"Right," she says.

"Then okay."

"Okay. It's just that it's very expensive, and completely ineffective if taken irregularly or incompletely—"

"I'll be compliant."

"That's great to hear." Dr. Eric heads to the door and reaches for his coat. He is so comfortable in our home, coming and going and hanging his clothes on the hook we leave open for him at the door.

"Why is it so expensive?" I ask just as Dr. Eric shakes a knit scarf out from his sleeve.

"What's that, Cara?"

"If it's treatment I need, why wouldn't our insurance cover it? Chemotherapy is pretty traditional medication, right? No one considers it experimental or alternative."

Dr. Eric sort of snickers while he wraps the scarf around his neck. "Shaylene, you're going to have to step in and field this question. None of us have the time for me to explain how broken the health insurance system is in this country. I'm sorry, Cara, I just wouldn't even know where to begin."

He makes a big show of snapping his heels together and saluting my mother and me. As if all this time he's just been following our orders. "All right, ladies. I'll leave you to it." He heads out the door.

I look over at my mom, expecting her to take me through the issues with our insurance coverage. But instead she raises her chin and sets back her shoulders and says, "I think we should cut your hair."

"Why?"

"Because it will be too painful to watch it fall out. I don't want you to have to suffer through that. Not all over again. Not as a young woman. You'll see strands of it hanging along the tiles in the shower, in the tub's drain. You'll find clumps on your pillow each morning. It's horrifying. Plenty of girls absolutely rock a short haircut, sweetheart. And you certainly have the cheekbones for a pixie cut." All of a sudden Mama sounds like a columnist for *Seventeen* magazine.

She leaves the room briefly while I sit frozen at the table, trying to make sense of her reasoning. I hear her babbling about standards of beauty and faces with dramatic impact. Then my mother swoops back into the kitchen with a bath towel draped over her arm and a pair of scissors in one hand.

"Can't we at least go to a salon? If we have to do this?"

"I've always cut your hair." She has the nerve to stand there, looking flabbergasted.

"You've always *trimmed* my hair. It's not that I don't trust you, Mama, but maybe a professional could give me a style that's flattering to my face shape? Maybe that will help it look a little . . . more normal." I can hear the tears in my voice and I try to quiet my own surface. My chest tightens and my lungs constrict. My head starts to pound and I feel woozy.

"Your face has a beautiful shape. Do you really want to go to a professional and explain to a total stranger why we have to cut your hair? You want to say those words out loud? Not to mention how it will make everyone at the hair salon feel. I know how you loathe strangers fawning all over you."

"I don't mind seeing my hair fall out a little. Really. Let's just wait. I promise not to argue about it later."

"Believe me, this won't get easier." She's using her soothing voice, her nurse voice. "It's not like you to shy away from a challenge. Let's be brave. Let's just get it done."

I think of that stone at the bottom of the riverbed again, how it doesn't fight the powerful current running over it. That stone just withstands all that pressure and somehow stays itself. Maybe Mama doesn't believe she means this as a consequence. But I know differently. Dr. Eric takes my blood and my mother takes my hair.

At first when I stand up, I consider running. I imagine my legs pumping, my feet pounding on the sidewalk. I could reach Main Street. Then I imagine Mama driving slowly beside me, ordering me into the car. Where would I go? What choice do I have? She drags one of the kitchen stools into the center of the room.

When I sit down, I forfeit any fight.

She lets me braid it so that she can cut it more quickly. "I think I could shape it better if you just let it hang down," she tells me.

"I don't need you to shape it if it's just going to fall out anyway." My hands tremble as I divide the strands into three sections and start carefully overlapping them. It makes me think of Manuela's braids and how they glint in the warm light of the pottery studio—so black and shiny they look almost blue.

It's been a while since I wore a single braid down my back. I've had this feeling that tying back my hair pulled at my scalp and worsened my headaches. My fingers start out clumsy but then they work through my hair expertly. They fall into the motion of braiding like they have it memorized.

I try to weave all my emotions into my hair. I tell myself to hand over my fear and worry and resentment and rage. I tuck every bit of tenderness I feel for my mother into the strands. All my helplessness. That way, when my mom cuts off my hair, she will sever every weakness from my body. That's what I concentrate on.

The braid is longer than I expected. It feels heavy between my shoulder blades. I feel that weight lift a little and realize that Mama has picked up my hair with her hand.

She doesn't just snip off the braid. My hair is thick enough that she struggles to close the scissors. I feel her breath at my neck and feel the blades hacking through, like she is pulling the teeth of a saw across my braid over and over. She cuts as closely to the back of my head as she can and the cold, flat metal of the scissors presses against my skin.

I feel a painful yank and then a lightness. I look down and to my right and see the braid in my mother's hand. She holds it uneasily, like a gun she has wrestled away from me. I feel her exhale behind me and realize that she is experiencing relief. "Okay," she says. "Okay, sweetheart." I hop down from the stool and reach toward her, and at first, she steps back as if she is afraid.

"Please may I have the braid." My voice sounds robotic, though. I don't pronounce it as a question.

"Okay, but why don't you let me clean it up a little, in the back? That cut didn't go as smoothly as I expected. It's just a little uneven." I shake my head no, only once, and she does not press again.

She hands over most of my hair. The top of the braid has already unwound a little, from where she hacked it. I can see a few stray locks of my hair on the floor. "Where are you going?" Mama asks. She sounds shaky and a little afraid.

I turn away and trudge upstairs. I stand up straight, with my arms at my sides. I do not give her the satisfaction of seeing me feel the back of my head. She does not get to see my hand raised, searching for the bald spot.

There's not a door to slam once I get to my room. Instead I go directly to my dresser and pull open the top drawer. Bury the braid beneath some old T-shirts and then close it as quietly as possible. I don't want my mother to know where it is hidden. I tug the top sheet off my bed and use it to cover the mirror. Then I sit on my bed and start working methodically through my study materials.

I have work to do.

CHAPTER TWENTY

Still on for tutoring? I text Xavier after lunch.

Yes. At 2? 2toring? I groan in spite of myself. Somewhere on the other side of town, in his fancy house, with his full head of hair, Xavier Barnes is doing finger guns. I'm sure of it.

I need you to promise me something.

The three dots blink but not for very long. *Sure.*

You can't ask about my hair.

Ok?

Promise.

I promise.

Xavier Barnes remains true to his word. When the doorbell rings, I skip down the stairs and answer with as much energy as I can muster. "Happy New Year!" I call out, the way people in movies do at midnight. I wave to Mrs. Barnes in her car and usher Xavier into our house and wait for the horrified expression to wash over his face.

"Happy New Year, Cara Wakely!" Xavier's eyes widen and his mouth drops open slightly but he recovers quickly and he does not ask.

My mom comes out of the kitchen with a tray of snacks and two bottles of water. "Thanks, Mom!" I say with canned enthusiasm. She looks from me to Xavier and I can tell she is measuring whether she should offer up some explanation for the state of my appearance. I still haven't actually seen my reflection.

Mama tells him about the wellness warriors video we're drafting about how I'm going to take my exams, before I interrupt and tell her we need to get to work.

She nods. "I'll bring in your meds in half an hour. I know that might affect your ability to concentrate but we discussed the importance of staying on schedule."

"I understand. I can handle it."

Xavier doesn't look up at me for the longest time. I figure he can't deal with my hair. It stings but it's not like I think of him like that anyway. I don't need to look pretty. But then Xavier Barnes says, "Man, I'd forgotten about *wellness warriors*," and he's permitted to mock that. I might even encourage him to mock the vlog.

But I say, "Stop it." Just like he wants me to. We don't laugh out loud in case my mother is listening.

At 2:59, Xavier's phone lights up and I point to my flash cards to show him I can keep going if he needs to take a call. But he taps at the time and nods to the door, and sure enough, my mother strides through a minute later.

"How's it going with the young scholars?" She's even got the pills in a little Dixie cup and brings along a smoothie. "Xavier, can I interest you in an apple-spinach protein shake?"

"Oh, thank you, that sounds like brain food right there, but I'm good."

"Too many veggies for you?"

"No, I love my veggies, Mrs. Wakely."

"Cara Jean had blood drawn this morning, so I have my eye on her iron levels."

"Makes sense." Xavier keeps his answers polite and short.

I suck down the last of the juice and take Xavier through a few proofs so that he sees I'm ready to sit for the Algebra II exam without belting out a single lyric of Celine Dion. "Those look good. Let me show you another way to get to the same answer." Then he flips over the graph paper and writes, in the tiniest of letters, *Are you okay?* When I don't answer, he underlines the words adamantly. I stare at him. He stares back. I nod. He points to the question again. I nod again.

He reaches over and erases it. I don't know what kind of strict mother Mrs. Barnes is, but Xavier sure knows how to sneak around.

What happened to your hair? He writes these words even smaller. My fingers spring back to the top of my head and the corners of my eyes immediately seep tears. We sit there in silence. He moves to draw a single line under the question. "You promised you wouldn't ask about it," I remind him, without even trying to be quiet. He nods quickly and then reaches to rub that off the page too.

"Right. If that way works better for you, then you should choose the method that you're most comfortable with. Let me show you one last version of this proof in case. During the exam, if you get stressed out and panic or forget what you've learned, this could also work to solve the problem." Xavier's explanation matches up with Algebra II, but his eyes describe a different scenario. This time he barely presses his pencil to the page; his handwriting is silver and feathery.

If you ever need help, text or call. My mom and I will come get you. Dad is a lawyer. He'll know what to do.

I read Xavier's message but when I nod it's just to make him feel better. The way when I ask him about a pain crisis, he tells me he can handle it. He meticulously erases the last message and we move to biology. We review the short stories that will be on my English exam and he makes me compare each one to *Antigone*.

"Is that the essay question?" I ask.

"I can't tell you that. That would be an insane advantage."

"It's totally the essay. I'm going to write an outline."

"Don't. Durand might like you, but he'll still give you a different essay question."

We work for forty-five more minutes and I stay focused and sharp, pummeling through my notebooks like a boxer training for a fight. Xavier runs me through my historical timelines and quizzes me on biology terms. We talk through three different English essays and he asks, "How do you feel about your Japanese class?"

"Completely ready."

"You sure?"

"You don't take Japanese. You can't help me with that class."

He smiles. "For you, Cara Wakely, I would try to learn."

Once the break is over, my mom and I work out my makeup exam schedule with Mr. Brinks and my teachers. They let me choose the dates and even the order of the tests.

Mama has already carefully lettered JANUARY at the top of the dry erase chart on the wall. I've never noticed that our days consist almost entirely of medicinal doses. I'm sure other families list picnics and soccer practices, violin lessons and sleepovers. But Mama's and my days are composed only of numbers.

I figure if everyone goes back to classes Tuesday, I should plan to start exams by Wednesday morning at least. That way, I can sit for two sessions, morning and afternoon, and still finish up by the end of the first week.

In addition, Mama and I craft a more unusual request to Mr. Brinks that reads in part:

From the recent coverage of our family by local news outlets, you may have learned more about Cara's health struggles. In order to showcase the generous support that you, her teachers, and her classmates have given her, we respectfully request permission for a cameraman to rec-

ord footage of Cara returning to school and taking her exams.

To my surprise, he doesn't say no.

My morning routine alters, to some degree. I pad into the kitchen and face down the wall calendar that Mama keeps so carefully. She still itemizes my medications there, but since the talk about chemo, the list has grown longer. Names I don't recognize and pills that it takes even more effort to work down my throat. My whole body feels like it's marooned at sea. Sometimes I can stand still—staring into the refrigerator or fixing a cup of tea at the counter. I stand there and notice myself tilting to the side. I drink a lot of tea and as much water as possible and tell myself it's possible to flush all the medicine through my system before the side effects can latch on. There's nothing that tastes good to me anymore. The inside of my mouth smells sour. My heart races like I'm frightened all the time.

The squares on the calendar don't feature only my mother's fastidious lettering. They also wear sashes emblazoned with the subjects of my exams. I will not provide my mother or doctor a reason to interfere with this week's plans.

Wednesday I will sit for history in the morning, break for lunch, and then meet to take the last part of my Algebra II exam. Mrs. Fontana has agreed to count the sections I completed last time, before I hit the gym floor. My first day back in the squat brick building won't require me to sit for four whole hours of testing. Instead it will add up to just a little more than two and a half. Hopefully, that will give me a chance to get used to the crushes of classmates in the hall, the smell of canned peaches that permeates the cafeteria, those rigid half-desk, half-chair monsters that you have to sit in.

Then there's my hair. Currently a wool cap covers the hack job of the century, but I've been instructed to report to Mr. Brinks first thing upon arrival. I know that as soon as I cross the threshold, one of the secretaries in the office will order me to take off my hat and then they'll gasp and cluck with sympathy and that will feel even worse.

I put gel in this morning, which just brings the look to a whole new ridiculous level.

Mama asks, "Cara Jean, do you have your water bottle and your travel thermometer? You probably won't be able to have your cell phone on your person, and that worries me. You should let me ask Mr. Brinks to make an exception."

"No way. I'm going to get As on these tests. I don't want Brinks to be able to claim that I cheated. Besides, my own doctor will be there, filming me."

We had agreed that having my mother record me wouldn't have the same prestige as a man who looks like he could be from a news channel, so Dr. Eric's been drafted to get the footage Mama wants. Now he tilts his head and frowns, saying, "I thought I'd just record for a few minutes and then we would splice several scenes together for the episode. I'm not monitoring her through the whole test, correct?"

"Correct," I say. When what I really mean is *I really hope not.*

I'm surprised by the way my heart leaps when we turn the corner and see the high school appear in the distance. It doesn't make sense to feel the joy of homecoming while we approach a place in which I have never felt at home. It's not that Xavier's there or because I am just so thrilled to spend a couple of hours writing about history. The sprawling cement fortress now guards my goals. I'm not a soldier, giddy to return home. I'm just feeling ready and eager to return to battle.

In contrast, my honorary fellow wellness warrior, Dr. Eric, climbs out of the car reluctantly.

He clearly feels uncomfortable with his new role as part of my entourage, but I appreciate him being here. Hopefully, his man bun will distract my classmates from my new haircut.

Mama drops us off in front of the main entrance and Dr. Eric sort of stumbles around. If I were a news network producer, I probably wouldn't hire him. He opens the back door of the minivan for me and helps me out to the curb as if he's accompanying me to a daddy-daughter dance. Then he lunges past me to grab the camera. I am so wobbly on my feet though that I topple a little. A gentleman, for sure. But we are an utter mess.

In the main office, Dr. Eric causes a little stir. The secretaries flutter and fawn. They are so busy trying to figure out what news station he's from that my hat goes unnoticed.

"We're supposed to report right to Mr. Brinks," I volunteer. "We've made previous arrangements."

"Cara Wakely. It's so great to see you. I almost didn't recognize you. How have you been? You know, you gave us all quite a scare. Theresa, do you remember? During midterms, Cara left in an ambulance. Honey, we were all so worried. But you're back—look at you. You look . . . great."

I know exactly what I look like. I look like the kind of homeless person who sits on a street corner with a dog and makes you want to rescue the dog. I use my meek and quiet voice to say thank you.

For one thing, that voice comes in handy with ladies like these. And also: I need to conserve my energy.

Mr. Brinks comes in the office behind us. His enthusiasm is only a little less unbridled than that of the office ladies. "You must be the newsman." He reaches out to pump Dr. Eric's hand and Dr. Eric tries to shake with the same hand that's holding the camera. I cannot make sense of how clumsy Dr. Eric is, how nervously he acts this morning. All this time, maybe I have underestimated his pure heart. I feel awful that Mama and I have asked him to lie; he obviously can't handle the pressure.

"Thank you, thank you." He sounds as if he's about to launch into an Oscars speech. I stare at him and silently urge him to stop talking. "Totally appreciate the access today, man. I just need to grab a little footage and then I'll get out of your way." Dr. Eric now speaks with a surfer dude accent. I guess maybe that's how cameramen might sound in LA?

"Of course. We always want to accommodate the media. And support Cara. She is a remarkable girl." Mr. Brinks smiles benevolently at me. "How are you feeling?"

My stomach has settled a little bit since we stepped out of the car. My legs still seem unsteady and my mouth has that metal taste from the new medicine. I would describe myself as sleepy rather than groggy.

"Ready to take my history exam," I answer Mr. Brinks, with as much excitement as I can muster.

"Okay. We're going to set you up in the conference room. Please leave your backpack and your phone with Mrs. Arsenault in the office. We walk through every now and then and I've arranged for

Mr. Cohen to stop by periodically to check on you and answer any questions you might have. Sound good?"

"May I keep my water bottle?"

"It's important that Cara stays hydrated," Dr. Eric says. Then he remembers he's not supposed to sound so competent and adds, "Her mom says that."

"Of course. Why don't you follow me?"

I remember the conference room from the teacher meeting with Mama. I haven't prepared myself to return to that scene.

Dr. Eric balks at entering. "I thought we'd be in the gym? Cara described taking exams in the gymnasium?"

"Oh, we only set up in the gym when we need to accommodate the entire student body. Hard to fit six hundred kids in one place. But it's just Cara testing today. The conference room will serve our purpose well."

Dr. Eric grimaces and shifts his camera. I'm not quite sure when he developed an allergy to conference rooms. Until he says, "Makes sense, makes sense. It's just not gonna have the same visual impact of the gym, you know what I mean?" Then I know he's only trying to follow my mother's orders.

I step ahead of them both and sit down at the table. I look up at Mr. Brinks, waiting for him to hand down my exam. He seems baffled to be having the debate with Dr. Eric. He obviously hasn't grown up on a YouTube channel. He's not sure what to make of all this. "I hear what you're saying, but surely you understand we have a school to run. And I do want to make certain that Cara has the chance to focus on the task at hand. Listen. I'll tell you what. I'll have a desk set up there for a few shots this afternoon. That's the best I can do."

"Sure, sure." Dr. Eric holds his hands up and almost bangs himself in the face with the camera. "I fully got you, man."

Mr. Brinks passes a manila envelope to me. "You've got two hours, Cara. There's a blue book in there for your essay, and remember to simply note your questions for Mr. Cohen to answer when he swings by." Then Mr. Brinks crouches down next to my seat, the way adults lower themselves to eye level with you when they want to believe they're making a connection. "Please, Cara, if you start to feel ill, simply walk out that door and tell one of the ladies in the office. We'll have a nurse here, pronto." Mr. Brinks looks up and sees Dr. Eric filming and flashes a wide smile.

"Thank you." I slide the exam out of the manila envelope and get to work. I skim through the questions as quickly as possible, the way Xavier taught me, so that I can fill in all the answers that are just straight recollection before tackling the questions that call for more interpretation.

I don't even hear Dr. Eric leave. After that, it's just me and all I've learned in the conference room. Mr. Cohen stops by but I just smile and shake my head when he offers to answer questions. "It's good to see you," he tells me, which seems to stand as the common refrain from the adults I see at school. Which is kind.

Once I'm out of the conference room, kindness isn't exactly the rule. My classmates react. Later, when I sit at a lunch table with Xavier, they actually stop and turn to stare, full-on craning their necks to see us. But Xavier doesn't seem fazed by that. Neither do the two other kids at the table, who say very little to us, but dice their food into tiny cubes and talk to each other about Pokémon cards.

"Alistair and Vishnu," Xavier says by way of introduction.

"Oh. Hi." Neither answers. Fair enough. "Where's the rest of the library crowd?" I ask.

"Probably at the library."

I eat my turkey roll-ups and watch him devour the cafeteria tacos. I wonder if maybe Xavier is embarrassed by me, with my knit cap and my too-loose clothes. He says, "Sometimes I sneak a sandwich in the stacks or eat during a break during lab. But I wanted to make sure you had someone to sit with. You need to eat more, keep up your strength."

"Thanks. My appetite is sort of in flux." By that, I mean it doesn't exist. All the new medicine makes me feel like my internal organs are somehow rotting.

I watch Xavier guzzle almost a full water bottle. I've never seen anyone drink as much water as he does. He says it's good for his body to flush out toxins and stay hydrated. But I don't understand how Xavier has time to discover new species of amoeba or whatever he does in his free time when he must spend so much of his day standing at the water fountain, refilling his water bottle at the cup holder station. Or peeing.

"Hey," I say, "how do you cut your hair?" I lean over the cafeteria table to peer more closely at Xavier's style.

"You're going to start asking me about my hair now?"

"What do you use? Clippers?"

His hand reaches up and runs along his even fade. "I do use clippers. Usually by myself, with minimal assistance from my mom." He brushes taco crumbs onto his tray.

"Can I borrow them?"

"Why do you need clippers?"

I look over to see if Alistair and Vishnu are eavesdropping

but they are too busy arguing about the rarity of a first-edition holographic Shadowless Charizard. I tap briefly on my wool cap.

"I have kind of a situation going on."

"Umm-hmm."

"What does that mean?"

"I have been instructed to refrain from asking questions about that situation."

"Yes. That still stands. But may I borrow your clippers?"

"Cara. What are you planning?" Xavier shakes his head. "I don't know what happened with your hair. You'll tell me eventually. But why do you want to make high school even harder on yourself? It will grow in soon enough."

"It won't though. It's just going to fall out anyway."

"What am I missing? Why do you think that?" Xavier looks at me as if he wishes he could put me on a microscope's slide. Anything to be able to study and make sense of me. But then he snaps out of it. "Good luck, Cara Wakely. You know this stuff and it's just a couple of sections. This should be a walk in the park."

"Thanks. Clippers," I remind him, and then hurry back to the main office.

It takes me forty-five minutes to finish up the math exam. Right after I complete the last problem and start checking my work, the bell to switch classes rings and I hear the commotion of everyone moving from period six to period seven. It sounds louder than usual, the second day back from winter break, everyone reconnecting and reporting back on vacation adventures.

Whatever news about my health that Mama unveiled last

week, I feel pretty hopeful. Two exams done—already that's the most I've accomplished in a long time.

I bring my exam out to the secretaries in the office and text Mama to let her know I'm finished for the day. We figured I wouldn't stay until 3:00 and didn't pack my afternoon meds, so we need to make quick work of it. When Dr. Eric arrives to pick me up, he says, "I thought we could still hit the gym real quick, but I'll follow your lead. How are you feeling, Cara?"

"Not too shabby." I do not add *for a kid who just took midterms with cancer.* Instead I embody positivity. "Not as much fatigue as we expected. And I knew all the material. I can humor my cameraman. Hey, where'd you learn to do that, anyway? This morning, you became a whole other person."

"Not really. I just adjusted the way I talk. I didn't dress differently or radically change my appearance."

"It was pretty cool," I admit.

"I've noticed that you can get away with more if others underestimate you. I have a feeling that a lot of people underestimate you, Cara. You've really impressed me with how you've dealt with this latest round of treatment. I know you're hurting, but you just keep pressing forward."

When we close in on the school gym, we find that Mr. Brinks has set out the single desk as promised. The lights are on, but the empty gym looks vast and a little bit spooky. Dr. Eric has me lean forward and wrap my arm around the desk, like I'm guarding my test answers. "Maybe take the hat off? It might read better?" For a second, I sit perfectly still. "Cara? It's just us."

It's just us and Mama's two hundred thousand viewers, but okay. I grab the hat from my head and stash it under my thigh.

Rake my hands through my hair to fluff it out a little and then bend my neck forward. "That's great, Cara. Beautiful." And then just as I steal another look up at the clock, he says, "All set."

We walk quickly. Dr. Eric hurries for Mama's sake and I rush to avoid running into the entire Middlefield High student body while accompanied by my own personal cameraman. The large glass panes of the lobby gleam in front of us by the time I work up the courage to ask, "Dr. Eric—do you really think I'll get better?"

When he turns to face me, the sun lights him up from behind. The light surrounding his man bun glimmers like a halo. I get why Mama floated home that first time after she met him, how she could have seen him as a savior, sent to rescue us from our desperate lack of answers. He looks like that. Like he could save us.

He winks at me and nods toward Mr. Brinks's office. "Totally. Like for sure." Then as we head to Mama's minivan, Dr. Eric clamps a hand around my shoulder and tells me: "Absolutely, Cara. Just keep staying the course. We'll get you there." When Mama arrives, I climb into the van's back seat and all my effort gives way. I try not to vomit out the window on the way home. My afternoon collapse may be the price I have to pay, but for once I don't mind paying it.

CHAPTER TWENTY-ONE

Three major victories occur the next day. I basically channel the spirit of *Antigone* for my English essay; I survive my biology exam even though Dr. Presley included two diagrams that I have never before seen in my life. And Xavier Barnes brings his clippers to school.

He spends lunch period in the nurse's office and I sit with Alistair and Vishnu by myself. They tolerate my presence fine.

I throw a few Pokémon names into the conversational mix and they murmur appreciatively and then go back to dicing their sandwiches. It's comfortable. No one stares at me, and if they do, I just decide it's because I'm the only badass bold enough to wear a hat in front of Mr. Brinks.

I text Xavier back after he tells me where he is. *Why are you at the nurse?*

Just dealing with some pain. Everything's under control. Sorry to leave you hanging for lunch.

Nope. Lunching with the boyz.

Xavier's three dots blink a while. I like making him wonder. Finally: *???*

"Hey, Vish, Alistair—okay if I snap a picture?" I hold up my phone and they both shrug. Vishnu smiles; Alistair keeps eating. I snap the photo to Xavier and he writes back.

This sincerely makes me happy.

Can you drop the clippers off at the office?

That sincerely makes me worry, he fires back quickly.

Still, when I drop by the nurse's office on the way to my bio exam, he's left them with the nurse to hand over.

I use every minute available for the bio exam. I mine every question, looking for clues to use in the short answers, and I check the details of each set of directions just like Xavier instructed. He describes science as a process and says there is a step for everything. He has this theory that science teachers make up their tests that way either on purpose or because it's so inherent to their nature.

Mrs. Arsenault comes into the conference room to collect the exam promptly at 3:05. "Honey, I'm so sorry, but you know the faculty are very strict about timed exams. I'm afraid you need to turn it in now."

"That's okay. I understand. It has to be fair." We both stare at each other then, and maybe we're both thinking it. Nothing is ever fair.

I feel the weight of the clippers in my backpack as I make to leave. I text my mom: *Ok to stay for xtra help?*

She writes back immediately. *Meds??*

I sigh. Always, always the meds. *Just need half hour.*

See you at 3:30.

The bathroom in the back corridor is empty except for one closed stall in the back. I see feet: black Converse, but they face sideways. Black Converse isn't peeing. She's full-on crying in the bathroom stall. I turn on the faucet so she knows someone's come in and to give her a little privacy while she calms herself down. The sinks turn off automatically so we don't flood the school, I guess. When the stream of water shuts down, Black Converse's cries have quieted to little gasping breaths. I hit the water again and check my time to make sure that I still have minutes to spare before Mama's minivan pulls into the lot.

When the door to the last stall swings open, I remind myself not to look up. I concentrate really hard on washing my hands so that my eyes don't meet those of Black Converse in the mirror. But she just stands there for a second. It feels like she's waiting. I keep my hands under the faucet. She stays there next to me. We both remain there, frozen. Then the water shuts off.

There's nothing else to do but look up. When I do, I work hard not to let my shock and recognition play out on my face. My eyes travel up and see Libby Gilfeather staring back at me.

"Hey," I say before I realize I should think of something better.

"Hey," she replies. Her voice sounds raspy. "You're back."

"Yeah. Making up exams now."

She nods. Maybe she's picturing me falling facedown in the gym, smacking my head on the shiny wood floor. But it's possible she's not thinking about me at all. Libby Gilfeather has her own concerns.

"Well, good luck."

"Thanks."

She nods and heads out. I should follow her. I should chase her down and offer to listen and make sure she has my number in case she wants to text later. I should tell her that it means a lot to me that she always makes a point to greet me, after I've missed weeks, even months of school. But I don't have time to intrude on the life of Libby Gilfeather. There's something else I have to take care of first.

The clippers sound really loud in the Middlefield High girls' bathroom. The sound shocks me into acting faster than I mean to. When the blade cuts its first path through my cropped hair, I figure out quickly that the setting is correct. A stripe of white scalp materializes across my head. A fringe of chestnut hair floats into the sink's basin.

I turn my head to see it from all angles. It feels powerful, like I just took back all the control my mom wielded with her dull pair of scissors, sawing at my braid in the center of our kitchen. Once the initial shock wears off, I get into it. Each strip shaved signifies an accomplishment, another boundary highlighted, another railing of my emotional fence hammered into place. A couple of times, I nick myself and see bright specks of blood flecking my skin. But even those marks satisfy me.

Libby Gilfeather has left the building. It's just me now. I meet my own eyes in the mirror and take a long look at my own shaved head. I look stronger this way. Like an army recruit or a girl who goes to punk rock shows and throws herself into the pit in front of the stage.

Then of course I do the least punk rock thing ever. I wet a paper towel and dab up all the stray hairs that don't travel down the drain of the school sink. I fit my wool cap over my head again. It hangs more loosely now and itches a little bit, but I can tough that out.

"Good news or bad news?" Mama asks in the car. It's pouring out and she leans forward as she drives.

"Maybe a little of both. English seemed easy. I don't think he changed the essay question at all. But there were a couple of sections on the bio that I hadn't prepared for."

"Tomorrow's Japanese?"

"I'm not worried about that one. I'll run through vocabulary and charactery tonight."

"And rest a little."

"Yes. Also rest."

"Actually, if you're feeling up to it, I thought we might put together the episode, maybe record your voiceover? Dr. Eric stopped by and the cinematography looks fantastic. We just need your vocals." My mother just used the word *cinematography* in conversation about the wellness warriors channel. She has officially achieved extra status. "I understand if you're too tired. You just seem so chipper, so I thought—"

"I can do it."

"Really? That's wonderful. It makes me happy to see you with all this energy. You're like a different person today." I smile to myself and resist the urge to take off my cap. Mama continues, "Maybe before afternoon meds?" Apparently, she doesn't want me to slur through my words this time.

"Sure, Mama. That sounds good. Xavier and I had this plan to celebrate getting through my exams by going to Mud Matters this weekend. That's great I can get the video done before."

"That sounds like fun. But I worry about you spending so much time with Xavier. You don't need to lean on a boy."

"I think Libby Gilfeather's going too." I make that up on the spot. "You know—Libby? From my English class. I saw her in the bathroom after school. She was crying. I couldn't get her to tell me what was wrong, but I thought maybe if we planned something fun, it might give her space to open up." I've realized this about telling a lie: It helps to start with a kernel of the truth. Then maybe you just get the details wrong. After all, I'm on so many meds now, maybe I just imagined inviting Libby to the pottery studio. Mama can't prove otherwise.

"Isn't that wonderful? We never know whose path we might cross, who we have the chance to inspire."

Poor Libby might find herself guest-starring in a wellness warriors video if I don't handle this deftly. "Exactly. I hope she'll come. I didn't want to put too much pressure on her since she

seemed so upset."

"You can only open the door," Mama offers sagely. We sit in the driveway, watching the sheets of rain come down. "Ready to make a run for it?"

"I can manage a jog," I joke. We hurry into the house with our jackets pulled over our heads.

"My goodness!" Mama unwinds her scarf and shakes out her hair once we're inside. "Make sure to get out any wet clothes, Cara Jean. We can't have you catching a cold on top of everything else. Your immune system—"

"I know." I take off my jacket and hang it on the hook. I wait until she sorts through the mail and faces away from me before I lift off my cap and hang it there too.

The envelopes and advertisements make a slapping sound when they drop to the counter.

"Cara Jean." What is there to say? I just gaze right back at her. "What have you done?"

"It was going to fall out anyway." I say it lightly, like it's no big deal. And it shouldn't be. I've seen plenty of photos of me as a baby and then as a toddler with no hair. Mama's only shocked because I chose it for myself.

"But what you put me through the other day—" It takes a lot of strength for me to stop myself from smirking when she says that. I remember that fierce girl in the mirror and try to live up to her nerve. "When? At school?"

"This morning."

"With what?" I picture Xavier's clippers stashed in my locker at school and know that I can't let Mama link him in any way to my newly bald head.

"Just a razor."

"You did this with a disposable razor?" She steps forward to inspect it and I step back.

"Should I have used something else? There's a training salon in the vo-tech wing at the high school, but I figured you wouldn't want me to make a scene at school. I'm sorry, Mama. I just figured I should embrace what's happening with my body. You noticed yourself—my energy's up. Dr. Eric's medicine must be working. Why should I care about losing my hair? I can grow it back when I beat this disease."

"You impress me so much." Mama wrestles with her feelings in front of me. It's strange to observe. She knows I'm right and she has no call to be angry. But it makes her so uncomfortable to loosen her grip on the territory of my body. "What did your friends say?" She means Xavier. She's testing still.

"He hasn't seen it. I kept my hat on all day. It seems like Mr. Brinks will allow that."

"Well, he absolutely ought to. I'm glad I don't have to fight that battle. *Channel Seven Sunshine* would have been only too happy to feature an update about the heartless bureaucrats running our education system." Mama has moved on. She's settled on a new target for her outrage. She moves to the computer to check in on Caring for Cara and to prep for my voiceover.

We do about a dozen takes before she's happy with my narration. "Hey there, wellness warriors, it's Cara Jean here. Your positive energy has already powered me through four exams this week. I'm well on my way to catching up after a long absence from school."

Mama has me add in *necessary*.

"I'm happy to say I'm almost caught up after a long and

necessary absence from school. Don't let deadlines turn deadly."
Mama insists on that line. "No matter what your teachers or
school administrators say, your health comes first. I was lucky
enough to find a peer tutor to help me study. Consider reaching
out to the local honor society for classmates who might be willing
to assist you. It's also a great way to build friendships." Those
lines are my contributions, and Mama urges me on. She wants
the focus back on me. "Even without the tutor, all the donations
to the Caring for Cara website have taught Mama and me that we
are not alone in this battle. This new treatment regime is tough
in terms of side effects but tough on my disease. We thank you
for all your donations, thoughts, and prayers. Sayonara for now.
I have only one last exam tomorrow—Japanese language. I'm
signing off to study and rest."

"I'm not sure about the *sayonara*. If they don't speak Japanese,
they might not get it. I hate when you ad-lib on the last take."

"It's just hard to say the same thing over and over again."

"When I record the vast majority of wellness warrior videos, I
manage it just fine." Mama is still feeling salty over my bald head.
I don't let her bait me into an argument.

"People will know the word *sayonara*."

"It's a foreign word. And we've branded you as more of an all-
American girl."

You mean an all-American sick girl. But that's one of those
things I cannot say. I busy myself at the counter instead, flipping
through the mail that Mama left scattered. I find two letters.
Mama has gotten some mail since appearing on *Channel 7
Sunshine.* I've seen her slice open the envelopes. But if they don't
have checks enclosed, she tosses them on the pile in the dining

room. These are addressed to me, though, so I slip them into the front pocket of my backpack. I can read them later, alone in my room.

Mama leaves me to go to her parent group at the hospital. She warns me to keep the TV off and not to cram for tomorrow's last midterm. "We know this about language acquisition," she reminds me. "It's a process of gradual repetition." Somewhere, a wellness warrior's eyes glaze over, bored by another video about gratitude and generosity. Mama knows all about repetition. By the time I eat lentil stew and roasted squash and take all the meds brimming in the tiny cup, the energy that had buzzed through my body has fizzled.

I manage to text Xavier, but he says, *Don't check on me.* I understand the sentiment. When he asks, *Did you use the clippers? How does it look?* I answer *Yes.* And then I add, *Like I've become my own person.*

Here if you need me, he writes, and it occurs to me that phrase sort of captures our entire non-relationship. *Here if you need me.* We'll write it back and forth until something major changes. Or one of us dies.

CHAPTER TWENTY-TWO

The house feels different when I wake up. Sometimes in January, you step outside and sniff the air and think to yourself, *It smells like snow.* Almost always it snows that afternoon. This morning the house feels chilly in a different way. I'm certain that Mama is so angry but can't figure out why. I can sense an incoming storm.

She slams my bowl of overnight oats in front of me. I jolt, then recover. "Is Dr. Eric coming by?"

"Not this morning."

I change directions and try to remind her how cooperative I am. "Did you finish up the video?"

"Yes."

"Did you keep the *sayonara*? It's okay if you didn't keep that part."

"I didn't. I cut it off right after you thanked the viewers for their thoughts and prayers. That was a better way to end." I nod vigorously. My enthusiastic agreement does not appease her. "I know it's okay if I don't keep that part."

I nod again. "Mama, are you angry that I shaved my head? It's just that I took to heart—"

"If I am angry, Cara, and I think that the better word would actually be *disappointed* or maybe even *bewildered*, it is not because you chose to shave your head. Although I had to suffer through your histrionics when I took the far less dramatic and attention-seeking route of simply cutting it. While your choice was shocking and unnecessary, I understood it, considering the side effects of your chemotherapy. But do you know what isn't a side effect of chemo?"

She waits for me to shake my head, to make sure I am paying close attention.

"Lying." Mama sounds triumphant. "Lying is not a side effect of chemotherapy. You didn't shave your head with a disposable razor in our bathroom and I am embarrassed that I spent any amount of time last night believing that. But I generally don't expect my daughter, for whom I have sacrificed everything, to lie to my face."

"I don't understand, Mama, I—"

"Did you think Xavier would be intrigued? He was only too happy to help, he's *there if you need him.*"

There's a certain ugliness in hearing Xavier's words in Mama's mouth.

"You read my texts?"

"I have the appropriate parental access to your cell phone, yes. Part of my duty as your mother is to make sure you are making safe choices. Ethical choices."

"But that's spying."

"It is protective. You have no idea what's out there in the world, Cara Jean. You are so naive."

"I don't need protecting from Xavier Barnes."

"No, you need protection from yourself and the choices you make to impress Xavier Barnes."

"You read all my texts."

"I pay for the phone."

No. Generous donors pay for the phone. My illness pays for the phone.

I don't say these things aloud, though.

Mama goes on. "This is not a conversation about whatever privacy you believe you deserve. I asked you a direct question. You lied to me. I send you to school to take these exams that you claim are so important and you use that time away from me to lash out. What's the point, Cara Jean? What did you want to prove?"

I remember the satisfaction of running the clippers over my head, watching the little tufts of hair float down, erasing the way Mama had turned me into a freak the week earlier. I can't say that aloud either.

"It's not much different," I say. "I don't see what the big deal is."

"If it wasn't a big deal, you wouldn't have done it in secret. You wouldn't have plotted it. Take off your hat."

In this moment, I actually might hate my mother. She issues commands. I follow directions. Slowly, I pull off the wool cap.

Her reaction? "It doesn't look terrible. I understand your feelings of loss and confusion. My issue is with the lying." I detect the slightest spot of softness in my mother's voice—a tiny bruise blooming on a piece of fruit.

"I don't know why I lied to you, Mama. Something just came over me. I apologize."

Mama crumples into the kitchen chair next to me. We have moved into the part in which I am supposed to feel bad for her because she struggles to parent a sick kid. "I expect you to take more accountability than that, Cara Jean," she tells me. "But an apology is a good place to start." I nod as meekly as possible and fix my hat back onto my head. "Last exam today?" I nod again.

"I'll pick you up at eleven." I blink.

"I'd like to stay for the whole day."

"Not a good idea."

"I planned to meet with Mr. Brinks and my teachers. Figure out the work I missed this week." I blink again. She asked for honesty. "I'd like to eat lunch with my friends." It stretches but reaches the truth. I picture the table in the cafeteria: Xavier, Alistair, Vishnu, and me. We could start our own really bizarre band.

"Okay. Three o'clock."

"Thanks, Mama."

Her turn to nod curtly. I clear the dishes and take the pills she has set out for me, in the unquestioning way that she prefers.

Later on, I work at the conference table in the room outside the main office. I write out my short answers carefully and speak the oral portion into the tiny microphone on the computer. More than any other test this week, I relish filling in the answers, carefully composing the characters. My mom would not be able to spy on me in Japanese. She would not understand the language.

"I don't speak Japanese either, though," Xavier says in his cheerful, pragmatic way, after I catch him up at lunch.

"Well, right. We wouldn't actually need to text in Japanese. You could run it through Google Translate."

He shrugs and moves his spaghetti around his plate. "So could she." He glances at Vish and Alistair but they are focused on other things. "Cara, you shouldn't have to write in code. It's not cool that your mom has been reading your texts. It's developmentally appropriate to give teenagers a measure of privacy. That's just basic psychology."

Xavier has never gone upstairs in my house. He doesn't know about my unhinged door. He obviously has opinions about my unhinged mom, though.

"Do you want me to ask my mom to talk to her?" he offers.

"No way. That would not go well."

"You met my mom. She can be convincing."

"How do you know your mom's not reading your texts?"

"If she were, she'd tell me."

I say, "You're totally right. I'll talk to her tonight. If I explain how much it bothers me, I bet she'll stop." I force myself to make eye contact so that Xavier believes me. He looks suspicious and I slide my eyes away.

I can't appease everyone at once.

He reaches out his hand and for a split second I think he means to touch my face. But it's not that kind of moment. Xavier reaches out to tug on my wool cap.

"Can I see?" I give him a look I hope counts as withering. "Come on. I bet it looks fresh." And then, when I still don't take off my cap: "Why go through all the trouble of shaving it just to keep it hidden like that?"

When he sees it, he lets loose a low whistle. Not the way skeevy men do on women's razor commercials but the way someone might whistle at a spectacular natural disaster. "You really went for it."

Vish and Alistair just keep on gaping. It's more eye contact than we've shared all week. "Your head resembles a frozen turkey," Alistair announces.

I nod to him. "Thank you. I appreciate that."

But Xavier corrects him. "Not at all. It is fresh in a savage way."

The reaction around the rest of the cafeteria lands somewhere between Alistair and Xavier. We hear some buzz on our way out. On my way to the office to meet with Mr. Brinks, a few heads spin around to get a better view. Most of these kids have barely registered my existence, let alone my extended absence. Now they've cataloged me as "the bald girl" in the directory inside their heads.

When it's time for me to meet with him, Mr. Brinks wins the vice principal award for professionalism. He barely reacts. "Cara. A new look. Okay. How did exams go, from your perspective? Did you feel prepared?"

"Yes. Thanks for letting me use the conference room. And I studied so much over break; that time helped a lot."

"Good, good." He nods past the time that seems natural or warranted. "How about treatment? You've continued with treatment? Under a doctor's care?"

I wonder how Mr. Brinks would react if I told him my doctor was the surftastic cameraman he fist-bumped earlier in the week. No need to get into it. If Mama were here, she would squeeze my hand. "Thank you. Yes. To both. Treatment and a doctor."

"That's great to know. Well, listen, we want your focus to stay on your health. If you need to take a day for treatment, or maybe afterward, just have your mom or the doctor call in to one of the secretaries."

"I thought I'd stop by my classes and get this week's assignments. I'm glad to finish up midterms but it means I missed the first few days of the spring semester."

"That's all right," Mr. Brinks rushes to reassure me. "I'll reach out to your teachers. Expect detailed emails this evening and make sure to check the portal for updates. That will allow you to get a start this weekend." He immediately puts one finger up. "But I do mean a start—don't go overboard. We have plenty of time to catch up."

"Thank you, Mr. Brinks. I appreciate it."

"Of course. Now go get some rest."

I want to reach across his desk and pinch the skin on his arm, just to make sure this version of Mr. Brinks is real and not a cyborg engineered by Xavier's friends on the robotics team. Maybe Mama sent him a link to her *Channel 7 Sunshine* episode or Dr. Eric sent a report of all those test results.

I don't text Mama for an early pickup. I'm simply sticking to the original plan. In the library, everyone whispers, so I can't tell if people whisper about my lack of hair. I choose a carrel and settle in, logging on to the portal at a school computer. Click through and piece together enough material to start.

While digging through the front pocket of my backpack, my fingers close around the two letters. They're not official-looking like bills. One looks like a card and the other is a small rectangle inked with meticulous script: *Miss Cara Wakely.*

I open the card first. There's a yellow Labrador on front, wearing a white jacket like Dr. Eric's. In a speech bubble aimed out of its mouth, the dog says, "Lab results are in: You need to get well soon." The yellow lab clutches a bouquet of test tubes in his paw and looks attentive. Inside, the card reads:

> Dear Cara Jean Wakely, I hope this doggie brings you a bit of good cheer. I saw your story on the news this morning and wanted you and your dear mother to know you were not alone in your journey. I wish you a new year full of many blessings and moments of comfort. May the good Lord bless and keep you both in the palm of his hand. Most sincerely, Patrick Neary

What a kind and random note. It amazes me that some sweet little old man watched *Channel 7 Sunshine* in the morning, saw my story, and went to all the trouble of picking out a funny card.

I read the letter again. I'm moved when I realize: Patrick Neary doesn't expect anything in return. He just reached out to show a little kindness to a kid he thought needed it.

When I think about the palm of God's hand, I have to believe it feels that compassionate and loving. I know that on the Caring for Cara website, Mama's barometer of donations keeps rising. Of course, I'm grateful for those people too. But the people sending money are sending it to Mama. It means a lot to me that Mr. Patrick Neary went to all that trouble of picking out a card just for me.

The other envelope is thin and slightly glossy, like the skin of an onion. I open it with great care, fearful that one quick movement could tear the delicate paper. I skim it and notice that it concludes with a mention of prayer. Lots of God in this week's mail delivery. Then I read more closely and then I force myself to slow down and read the words another time.

Dear Cara,

We saw your mother speak on the news this morning and felt shock and sadness for many reasons. We had no idea the two of you still lived so close. She had indicated a move to the Boston area and we took her at her word. Our mistake, I suppose. While we are overjoyed to discover your proximity, we remain concerned about your health. Cara, please reach out to us. Please know that whatever mistakes your father has made, they were born from an excess of trust. While we will not make excuses for him, we ask for our family bonds to be honored on their own accord. Cara, please consider getting in touch. It would answer our prayers.

Love, Grandma and Gramps Wakely

Below the signature, they've written a telephone number with a Cleveland area code. The numbers lilt right and slightly up, as if buoyed a little by hope.

I don't have a grandma and I certainly don't have a gramps, the kind of jovial fellow who pretends to steal your nose and pull quarters from your ears. I have never known either set of grandparents on account of Mama's estrangement from her family and the fact of my father's absence. Mama has told me how she tried, how they would hang up on her when she called, how the Christmas cards she sent would arrive back in our mailbox, stamped *Return to Sender*.

This letter tells a very different story. I touch the thin paper between my fingers as if knowing where my mystery grandma bought her stationery would solve the mystery of her long absence. My father's mistakes and our family bonds? The words sound like the title of the debut album of an alternative country rock band in which one sister plays the mandolin and another plays the fiddle. I don't know that song. I know a family of two people—quiet holidays and tight budgets and no place to turn if you argue or get sick of each other. Or, you know, just sick.

Everyone else in the library goes about their business. Studying chemistry or economics as if more pressing issues don't exist. I clutch at the letter and follow the sentences with one finger, trying to feel for the truth. My phone slips easily out of my pocket and I start to dial the number Grandma Wakely has listed.

Just in time, I drop my cell phone. If Mama can keep up with my texts, then she can certainly log my calls. I delete the digits entered and set out in search of an untraceable phone.

At the circulation desk, the school librarian seems surprised by my request.

"My battery died." I hold the phone up. "I need to call my mom for a ride home."

"I'm sorry, dear. You can't talk in the library."

But we are *talking in the library*, I want to say. Instead I take my cap off. "I really need to call home."

The sweet librarian is absorbed with my bald head and my tearful voice. She nods to the glass-enclosed space behind her. "Okay, just do me a favor and close the door. We wouldn't want to disturb your fellow library patrons, right?" Most of my classmates are recording TikTok videos in the stacks but why should I draw attention to that?

I nod solemnly and say "Thank you very much" the way I am supposed to. I sit at her desk and shield the envelope from her sight. I use the landline to dial the telephone number that apparently belongs to my paternal grandparents.

It rings four times and I almost hang up. I imagine an old lady, swinging a walker, trying to catapult herself in the direction of her phone. I let it ring a bit longer. When she finally picks up, the little old lady sounds as wheezy as I expected. "Hello there?"

I panic and find myself unable to pronounce even a standard greeting. She repeats, "Hello?" with an even higher-pitched squawk. And she says to someone else near her, "Burt, I hear breathing." Immediately, I stop breathing. "Burt, the caller ID says Middlefield High School—do you think . . . ?" Then the little old lady says my name, as if it is a familiar name, as if she says it often. "Cara? Honey, is that you?" I gasp, and that must sound like a sizzle through the wire, a jolt of electricity.

I recognize her voice. I can't recall a specific sentence or a song sung, but that voice pronouncing my name rings a bell at the iron door that stands guard over my earliest childhood memories.

The old woman's voice trembles like she's trying not to weep. "Well, Cara, if this is you, let me just say that Gramps and I love you very much. We worry for you, honey. We were sad to learn you were unwell again and hope to help if we can. We want to be involved and I know that your dad—" I can't help but gasp again and it short-circuits her voice or reminds her of the secrets she's required to keep. "Well," she says. "We have so much to tell you. If this is Cara."

Her expectation fills the silence. The librarian turns from her desk to make sure I'm okay in the little glass room. After all, I'm just supposed to be calling for a ride. I move to hang up the phone and it's like the little old woman can sense that.

"Gramps and I can pick you up from that school," she rushes to say, but I am already in motion; her voice keens and fades in the air. The receiver clatters into place. My eyes dart around, half anticipating my long-lost grandparents to arrive at the library any minute. *Now they know where I go to school*, I think to myself, even though I'm sure that *Channel 7 Sunshine* already included that little tidbit of personal trivia. I remind myself: Mama and I are not in hiding. Mama and I are not on the run.

Except I definitely don't mention the letter later, on the way home from school. Both pieces of mail rest folded between pages in my Japanese notebook.

"You're all done with those wretched exams!" Mama exclaims. She mimes shoving a microphone in my face. "Tell the studio audience, Cara Jean—how does it feel?"

"Really terrific," I answer, trying to take the temperature of her feelings. We seem to have ventured back into the realm of friendly chitchat and manic us-against-the-world machinations. "Tons of energy," I lie. "I have a clear head and plans for a relaxing weekend."

"Well, let me tell you about this weekend," Mama says, and I do my best not to cringe. Usually that means she has planned activities for us to do together and of course record for our viewers: clay masks or manicures. One time we knit an enormous blanket together and she made me list things that provided security. Now she asks, "Wait—you're sure? You're really feeling great?" and I worry that she wants to do something more active like an at-home yoga retreat, which usually only entails a new instruction video and slices of cucumbers floating in a jug of water.

"I really feel fine, Mama," I say, but a little more subdued now, in case I need to make an excuse to miss tai chi on the front lawn or something.

"Well, okay. I'm really glad to hear that because I've decided to take a little trip away—a three-day weekend, including Monday."

This is, perhaps, the worst-case scenario. How do I tell her I don't feel at all fine? The idea of a road trip summons my weak stomach to pitch and heave. My head hammers with the idea of sharing a hotel room with Mama, with the sleep machine strapped over my face, her five feet away with her teeth grinding like forks banging around in a slammed drawer.

"Oh, Mama, I don't think I can. I just finished exams, but there's all this makeup work now. Mr. Brinks says to take my time—and I will—but still I have to make a start."

"Cara Jean, I don't mean . . ." Mama trails off. "This is hard to say." She sounds genuinely regretful. I grip the armrest beside and closely watch her lips move, trying to predict what she is about to plunk down. "I planned a weekend away for myself. By myself. Maybe that sounds strange to you. It seemed like an ideal time. You've completed midterms. Your numbers have consistently hit high on the health chart's target areas. I've packed the fridge with meal prep—veggie lasagna and lentil soup. Turkey meatballs too. But you're fourteen, you know, Cara Jean. You have studying, friends to text—you'll have your own weekend."

I'm fourteen and unsure that I've ever had my own anything. It doesn't even feel like my illness is my own. And that last bit that Mama mentions about friends I can text—she's just pretending those messages with Xavier don't matter. They matter. That last bit shows me they do. "I don't understand. You're leaving me alone?" It sounds pathetic voiced like that, like a little kid demanding a night-light.

At home, her suitcase already waits by the door. She can't wait to leave.

"How long have you planned this?" I ask, and once again the forlorn chord in my voice surprises me.

"Oh, sweetheart—I've been thinking about it for a while. But I decided this week. I got a great deal for a resort retreat and just leapt at the chance. You inspire me, Cara Jean—seeing you take on such responsibility for yourself. I'll worry less, and that's a testament to your newfound independence. Maybe I need to be a little more independent too."

She sounds like a sitcom mom, with her answers underlined in positivity. But there's another thread running through her words—a sharp and silver anger that needles beneath her sentences. When I was little and the local church group took us to Disney World, Mama made sure to show me how we demonstrate thankfulness. It didn't matter that the church elders traveling with us smelled like butterscotch candy and Vicks VapoRub, that I hardly knew them, and they shouted deafly about the Lord every time I sat on a ride. Mama taught me that you had to display gratitude. The giver was owed a certain performance.

The flip side of that? You do not get to exhibit impatience. You sit on the kind man's lap and smile for the camera when instructed. You keep quiet about sunburn or blisters from your secondhand sandals. My mother and I are experts in swallowing our anger. But sometimes it coats our throats and seeps into our voices.

"What if I get sick?" I ask. But of course what I mean is: *What if I get more sick?*

"You've been doing such a good job taking care of yourself. And Dr. Eric will be over in a few minutes for a quick checkup. I'm sure he'll reassure us both. But, Cara Jean, really, I hope you don't intend to make me feel guilty for this. I realize it's extravagant, but can you remember a time I've taken a weekend to myself? In your entire life?"

"No, Mama."

"That's right. When I shared that at the parents' group the other night, people registered genuine shock. Caretaker burnout is a reality and I simply have to put myself first once in a while, especially since you're growing up and can obviously do the same."

There it is. The silver thread of my mother's anger gleams. "Of course, you're right. I wouldn't dream of guilting you. You work so hard. I just got scared for a second—that's all." I don't know if I've ever spent a full night home alone. In the hospital, sure—but hooked up to machines monitoring me, with nurses rotating through every hour.

"Hopefully, Dr. Eric can put both our minds at ease." Mama starts flipping through one of her notebooks. She's listed all the info I'll need, she tells me. "I've arranged for Mrs. Barnes to pick you up on Monday morning and bring you to school."

"Xavier's mom?" I can't imagine my mother actually calling up Mrs. Barnes. To tell her she needed help during her vacation.

But she says, "Of course. She offered that one time, right before Christmas, don't you remember? She could not have been kinder on the phone. She encouraged me to spend the whole week away, but I could never do that. Who knows? Maybe I won't be able to do it. I'll have to come home early just to take your temperature." Mama chuckles like this is a ridiculous scenario and not an actual possibility.

A little while later, I sit with my arm in the blood pressure cuff and Dr. Eric reviews all my vitals.

Mama lurks close by, ducking in to read every number and record them on the wall chart behind her. "So how are her vitals? Cara Jean has been telling me how she feels the healthiest she has in years." I don't remember saying exactly that. But Mama steamrolls on. "What do you think, Doctor? Is she as stable as she says she feels?"

Dr. Eric nods. "Her numbers look great. I'd like to take some blood to get a sense of your response to this most recent round of treatment. That'll make you a bit weak and woozy tonight—any wild plans?"

"Nope." I smile wryly. "Had I known Mama was going away, I would have thrown a rager."

We all laugh like this is the most typical conversation.

Dr. Eric sticks my arms with the needle and grins at me. He gives me the raised chin of the Cool Guy. "Hey. I'm digging the new haircut."

"Yeah?" I look to my mom, but she busies herself making lists.

"Yeah. Very high impact. Hollywood ready." He means for me to remember Wednesday's caper, his Californian cool, his crazy accent.

"Thanks." The vial fills with my blood and I feel my heart quicken as it tries to replace the lost platelets. All our conversation acts like that—attempting to replenish the sense of normalcy. We try. "Where did you say you were going, Mama?"

She looks up from her latest list. "I'm sorry—what? Where? I've written everything you need down—a phone number for the hotel, Mrs. Barnes's number—although you could just text Xavier." Dr. Eric doesn't blink. I'm the only one who hears the bite in that side note.

"What hotel?"

Mama sighs like she's losing her patience with my pesky questions. "I'm staying at the Ravenwood."

"At Ravenwood Castle?" I'm sure my nose wrinkles. I'm certain my eyes blink too much, trying to compute. Ravenwood Castle is actually a medieval castle. In Ohio. You see commercials for Ravenwood Castle during episodes of *The Bachelor* and *Judge Judy*. Apparently, it's the place for romantic reckoning. People get engaged there, and married, and maybe embark on illicit relationships that end up triggering divorces. It's not really a casual, me-and-my-mom-jeans-deserve-a-spa-day kind of place.

I'm pretty sure they have a Princess Suite with a Jacuzzi

233

that's shaped like a giant glass slipper. And Ravenwood Castle is expensive. On account of it being a castle. But I don't have to ask how Mama can afford a weekend retreat at Ravenwood. After all, she's been "Caring for Cara." It turns out that's fairly lucrative.

"They offer discounts through the hospital," Mama explains.

"That's just what every parent of a sick kid needs—a weekend of role-playing romance novels in a cheesy medieval castle."

"Cara! That's enough." The blush that creeps up Mama's neck surprises me. Dr. Eric keeps his head down as he packs up the vials of my blood and his various instruments of torture. Mama sighs. "You promised not to make me feel guilty."

"I'm sorry—I didn't mean that. You should not feel at all guilty." She should feel a little ridiculous, though.

"Thank you for saying that. Now come over here so I can take you through all the steps and resources I've set up." My mother has listed my meds in her notebook—both dosages and times.

"Isn't this already written up on the chart?" I motion to our wall of pharmaceutical agenda.

"The notebook has more precise times and instructions. See? This supplement requires a sixteen-ounce glass of water. You should always take this one on a full stomach."

"I know all this, Mama."

"I just thought it might reassure you to see it recorded in one place. And it's portable if you decide to go to the library or to the studio."

"What?" Dr. Eric glances up, the concern obvious on his face. "Shaylene, we talked about this. Cara had a full week and she should rest."

234   "Well, yes."

"Wait—I can't go anywhere? At all? We had planned to go to the studio this weekend; I told you about that." For all Mama knows, Libby Gilfeather's mental health relies on our planned pottery outing.

"Cara Jean, let's just look at plans realistically. You don't have transportation and I don't want you taking Uber alone. If Xavier wants to come over—"

"His mom won't let him if you're not home." My voice barks before I pull back on the leash of my own anger.

"Well, then good on Mrs. Barnes for enforcing rules and boundaries." Mama slowly claps her hands. "I am thrilled to have the backup of another parent setting healthy parameters." She glances at Dr. Eric, who is preoccupied with packing up my lab samples. She lowers her voice into a hush. "Honestly, I don't see the harm in a short pottery session as long as a parent picks you up and brings you back home. But make sure to lock up. I left the spare key in the drawer with the chargers."

Her voice raises its volume: "But you know, Cara, you might find that both you and Xavier could stand a little space. You'll see all your friends on Monday." Mama gives me an exaggerated wink and then directs me to the pill caddy. "I've sorted out every dose, organized by day of week and time of day. You should take your afternoon meds now and before I go, I'll set a timer for tonight's scheduled supplements."

Dr. Eric speaks up then. "Cara, remember, we don't want you to miss your dosage, but overmedicating can be even more dangerous. Your mom and I don't want a repeat of the Christmas Eve incident."

It bothers me to hear the phrase "your mom and I" emerge

from Dr. Eric's mouth. Mama must see me tense up because she reaches over to rub my shoulders in gentle circles. Then she grabs my hand and gives it a quick squeeze. "Cara knows. That was scary for her too. Sweetheart, if you need anything at all, I've written out a list of emergency contacts on the inside cover of the notebook: my cell, the hotel, Mrs. Barnes . . ."

"Not Dr. Eric?"

His man bun slides a bit as Dr. Eric shakes his head. "Yeah, I'm sorry about that. I've scheduled a trip into Cleveland this weekend. Driving the harm reduction van. You know how I roll."

"Hard to be a saint in the city," I mutter, and he misses the sarcasm completely.

"We all do what we can."

My mom reviews her notes one last time. "There's an envelope of cash on my dresser beneath the stack of books, but I prefer that you don't order meals delivered. Food industry people rarely take allergies seriously. I also listed Stella's number under emergency contacts. But that's really only if it's an absolute emergency or you need the media's presence."

Dr. Eric and I both go completely still. My eyes skid to the right and find he looks as horrified as I feel.

"Why would I need the media?" I ask.

Mama breezes past the question. "Stella's just another resource. It can't hurt to have her as a contact. Anyway, did you look in the fridge? Am I forgetting something?" Dr. Eric stands at the door, shrugging on his coat.

"You've taken care of everything," I tell her. That's not untrue. Even still, I try not to let my rising panic show on my face. I reach up in the new way I do and rub the back of my freshly shaven head. That calms me now. Remembering how strong I felt with the clippers in my hand—that settles me.

"Well, okay. You'll take your afternoon meds right now." I nod obligingly. Mama looks from Dr. Eric to me and then back again. "If I leave right this minute, I can still avoid rush hour traffic. I love you, Cara Jean. Rest a whole lot and absolutely call me if you need anything. Lock the door behind us and turn off the oven or stovetop as soon as you're done using it. Don't take baths at night, after your medication. And don't tell everyone you're home alone—people just don't need to know that." She fusses with the flowers in the vase I made, rearranging the stems.

Dr. Eric says, "Let me get your bags, Shaylene." Mama and I stand in the kitchen, facing each other. I think she won't actually be able to leave. She's planned this whole trip, fueled by her fury. I insisted on taking my five exams. I shaved my head and lied. I spoke out of turn. But maybe she's stuck now, unable to back down in front of Dr. Eric. She's already called Mrs. Barnes.

I could cry and beg my mom to stay home, explain how my head aches, my joints creak, and my thoughts seem muddled. But she would never let me forget that. Asking would add another strand to the rope that already tethers me to my mother. Then she says it. She starts out kindly, her tone encouraging: "You're going to be just fine, Cara Jean," she tells me. "You've grown so much in the past few months." And that's when her voice steels and I realize that Mama means to scare me a bit. She believes I've taken her for granted. I have disobeyed. Her chin lifts and the lines around her mouth deepen like parentheses. The words from my text to Xavier echo when she tells me, "I suppose I need to become my own person too."

CHAPTER TWENTY-THREE

Mama's parting shot sets my stomach churning. The panic rises in my chest and my knees quake and quiver. But honestly, I have felt queasy and feeble for ages. I can handle these feelings.

I watch Dr. Eric load her suitcase in her trunk and hug her lightly before climbing into his jeep. His face pauses at her ear and I'm sure he's reinforcing her decision. I bet he tells her, "Cara will be fine. She needs to learn a little gratitude. You deserve some time away." Whatever Dr. Eric is saying, I know he's taking her side.

The car doors slam; the keys turn in the ignitions; the cars back out of the driveway.

I sit on the couch and stare out the window to the street outside. I exhale and try to release the worry and fear. And then I let myself enjoy the quiet of the empty house.

I stand up and lean on the sill of the front window, peer up the street, half expecting to see Mama's car circle back. But it doesn't. I don't believe she's tricking me. She wouldn't have gone to the trouble of packing the suitcase just to make a point.

The ocean on the computer's screen saver looks tropical and inviting but I power it down. I don't want to spend a minute of my freedom thinking about the website. I don't want to feel beholden to anyone.

Besides, there might be a way for Mama to check in on me through the camera.

I dash up to the linen closet and grab a bunch of sheets. Drape one over the computer center and then take two thumbtacks from the junk drawer in the kitchen. It takes work and a queen sheet to cover up the giant wall chart. But afterward, I stand back and look up with satisfaction. No more calendar dictating my hours. Not for three days at least.

For three days, my time is my own.

"My time!" I shout it and the house reverberates its understanding. It's probably the loudest I've ever spoken in its walls. Mama meant for me to warm up the vegetable lasagna, but I go straight for the turkey meatballs instead. Such a rebel. I eat on the sofa, in front of the television, like a heathen. I watch

Divorce Court even though Mama considers that smut. She has been gone for half an hour and I have broken about six rules.

I am just getting started.

I take out my phone to text Xavier, considering my words carefully. She'll be following every keystroke from her castle tower at Ravenwood. I stick to basics, facts that Xavier must already know.

Japanese exam went well. Thank you for all of your study help. Must celebrate soon.

He writes back, *Tonight? Pottery party?*

No ride. Stuck home. But better for resting.

You feeling okay?

I don't know how to tell him to meet me in town without typing *meet me in town*.

Yes. Working on bio project now. Sketching out antlers. It's all I've got and not particularly clever. I hope Xavier figures it out. Though if I have to sit and sip cocoa by myself and sculpt a herd of deer all on my own, it will still count as amazing.

I shake myself awake and propel myself forward. I move my dirty plate to the sink and promise to rinse off my dish later. Drink some carrot juice and run upstairs to get a hoodie from my closet. I take two twenty-dollar bills from the bank envelope beneath my mom's book and don't even feel greedy. She's not exactly pinching pennies with her escape to spa castle. I smear on lip gloss and tell myself it's to soothe my chapped lips. I tuck the spare key into my pocket and bundle up. And then at the last minute, almost as an afterthought, I dig out the slim envelope from Grandma Wakely and fold that into my pocket too.

240   Outside, the air stings in my lungs and tears spring to the

corners of my eyes. My body is fueled by turkey meatballs, adrenaline, and the alien experience of independence. I catch myself checking for Mama's minivan, until the cold distracts me.

There's a line at the coffee shop but I force myself to stand there anyway, try to eavesdrop without being obvious. I'm not the only person there by myself, but maybe the youngest. I keep my wool hat on; I am aiming to blend in, to be forgettable. I keep my phone in my hand so that it seems like people need to reach me urgently. Once I have my mug of cocoa, I make my way to the small sofas next to the potbellied stove in the corner and sit for a moment, drinking it all in—the chocolate, the warmth from the stove, the night stretched out in front of me. I relish the musical rumble of other people's conversations.

I expect Mama to text any minute. I have an alibi ready to go—I even selected a movie on Netflix before I left in case she reviews my queue.

When I bring my mug up to the plastic bin, the woman behind the counter smiles and thanks me. She has lavender streaks in her hair and my mom might cluck about that and call them a cry for attention. I think they are beautiful. When my hair grows back, I'd like to try that too.

"You okay?" she asks me, and I worry for a second that it's radiating off me—illness or worry or just a general wistfulness for my own brunette waves. My hand rushes to my head, to make sure my hat sits securely there. She tells me, "You just looked so sad for a second."

"I'm okay," I answer. I hear how strong my voice sounds. It doesn't quiver or catch at all. "But thanks for asking." She nods and turns back to take more orders.

241

Mud Matters is just as lively as the coffee shop. Maybe the citizens of Middlefield have resolved to try more handicrafts in the new year. Manuela rushes around, the long layers of her skirt swishing behind her.

"Little fawn, where is the young buck?" she asks. Then she places her hands on my shoulders and steers me to a spot at a table toward the back.

"I knew you would ask about him."

"He is worth asking about, correct?"

I feel my cheeks redden but still nod, knowing that too is the truth. "He might meet me here."

"Splendid!" Manuela claps her hands together. "I will be happy to see Mr. Sensitive but we will both play it cool, correct? What are you making tonight? Another present for your mom?"

"No." It comes out sounding rigid, so I try to temper it. "I think I want to make something for myself." As soon as I pronounce the words, I hear Mama's voice in my head, hissing, *Selfish*.

But Manuela only celebrates more. "Wonderful. I believe that, you know. Sometimes the very best presents are the ones we give ourselves."

I throw the clay on the table until it feels soft and pliable and then shape it with my hands. No deer tonight. I set about pulling the clay like taffy with my fingers, trying to make the mane of a lion. With one of the sharp tools from the canister in the center of the workspace, I score the strands carefully and then attempt to capture the heavy muscles of his body. The tail throws me off and I work to make it look like it hangs against the big cat's back legs.

"That is one messed-up deer."

When I hear Xavier's voice behind me, my hand slips and I almost slice myself with the X-ACTO.

"You. How did you know I was here?" It's not that I'm shocked he understood. But even though I expected Xavier to figure out my cryptic message, it surprises me a little that he dropped everything to come.

He says, "I only canceled plans with the Nobel committee." And I want to hug him. Because that's the most exciting night Science Kid can think of. "Which is too bad, because I might get a Nobel next year for solving your coded texts, Wakely."

I look around for Manuela, thinking that Xavier needs his own portion of clay. I study his face to try to judge how he's feeling. I take stock of his clothes to see if he put in any extra effort into his appearance. But really I am stalling. There is so much to explain to Xavier and I don't know how to begin. "Hold on one second." I dart to the back of the studio and find the portions of clay wrapped in cheesecloth, soaking in shallow pools of water. I grab one, shake it out, and put it on one of the ceramic plates stacked on the shelf.

I catch Manuela's eye and show her. She gives me the thumbs-up, saying, "Don't make me give you a job, little fawn."

Xavier looks flummoxed when I set the plate in front of him as if it's a home-cooked meal. "I really need clay?"

"Well, that's the whole point of this place." Then I try to explain the past few hours.

"What do you mean, your mom just took off? To a spa? Are you sure it wasn't planned?"

"I really think it just occurred to her. Maybe Thursday at the earliest. She's mad about my hair and the texts with you. She goes

243

to this group, for parents of sick kids. She says they talked about burnout. But it was weird—the whole thing. Like there was a threat implied?"

"What kind of threat?"

"I can't explain it." I watch Xavier roll a small piece of clay between his fingers.

"Like a physical threat?"

"No!" My voice shrinks. "Like she'll stop loving me. That kind of threat."

"Well, you know that won't happen, Cara Jean. You have to stop thinking of yourself as a troublemaker. You worry so much. But look at you. Your mom's away for the weekend. You're sculpting ceramic animals."

"This one's a lion. He's fierce."

Xavier smiles but shakes his head. "Do you think she's with a man?"

"What are you talking about?"

"Maybe she's a little less patient lately because she met someone. Maybe this has nothing to do with you at all—your mom's just dating and moody about it."

"She's more than moody." I can't say to Xavier that it *always* has to do with me. I know how that would sound but I also know what is true.

Xavier reaches into his backpack for his water bottle. He drinks in long gulps. I know he goes through a bottle every three hours like clockwork. Keeping hydrated keeps his blood circulating and helps stave off pain crises. I can't imagine that Mrs. Barnes ever needs to post a giant chart in her kitchen. Xavier probably takes care of all that on his own, without any reminder, every day.

"Oh crap." I shut my eyes when the realization hits me. "I forgot my meds. Mama told me to take them as soon as she left, and I had dinner and watched terrible TV. I just completely blanked."

"Do you want to go back and get them? I could call my mom for a ride."

"But I've already messed it up, and if I take too much, I'll feel all doped up. But I have to keep up with . . ." Xavier sits very still and I know he notes every word. I choose the next ones carefully and tell him, "I have to keep up with the treatment plan."

"I see." He studies me. "So how do you feel?"

"What do you mean?"

"How do you feel, physically, right now? You've missed a dose, right? Do you feel sick? Do you notice pain creeping in? Maybe you notice a little confusion?"

"I'm actually more clearheaded than usual." I stop and turn the clay lion in my hands.

Xavier shifts in his seat. He looks reluctant to share his observations. "And clear-eyed. Your pupils aren't dilated, for one thing. You just seem more alert in general. When did you last take your medication?"

"This morning, before school."

"Any withdrawal symptoms? Skin crawling? Headaches?"

"I get that every day, just from fatigue."

Xavier wrinkles his nose. He drums his fingers on the table, thinking, thinking.

Right then Manuela sails by. "Mr. Sensitive! You have arrived after all. I knew you would." Manuela winks and clasps her hand to her heart. "The intensity. I can sense it just standing near the two of you. Put all of those unspoken emotions into your art." And then she glides away, leaving us to find a way to speak through our embarrassment.

Once she's gone, Xavier straight-up asks, "Why did you shave your head, Cara?"

I focus on the lion's mane, how I have painstakingly outlined every filament. "First my mom cut it all off, but that looked awful and just left me waiting. It would have just fallen out anyway."

"Why would you think that?"

Maybe I decide that pronouncing the word will make it become real. Or maybe I avoid saying it because I don't believe it's true. But I can't force the words out, even for Xavier, who stares at me so intently. His fingers drum on the table. I am waiting, waiting.

Then he tells me, "Cara, you thought your hair would fall out because you thought you were on chemotherapy. You thought you needed chemo because you believe you have cancer."

Behind Xavier, I see Manuela floating from table to table. She stops to chat at each station, her hands waving expressively. Each time she moves on, her black braids whip to the side. Most of the eyes in the room follow her movements.

Not Xavier's eyes. Xavier stares steadily at me. He asks me, "Cara, did your mom tell you that you have cancer?" I nod, slowly enough that my chin moves by fractions of inches. "Was that diagnosis confirmed by a doctor?"

After I nod again, he asks, "At a hospital?"

"No, my doctor comes to my house."

"Were there ever any CAT scans? MRIs? Even X-rays done, to lead to this diagnosis?"

"No."

"No biopsies? Lab work?"

"I've had blood taken."

"By the doctor at home."

"Yes."

"Not anyone else."

"Nobody else."

"You haven't talked to any specialists? It's that same doctor who was treating you for your autoimmune disorder who diagnosed your cancer?"

"Yes."

"Because your mom won't let you see anyone else?"

I don't even answer that one.

Science Kid leans forward and drops his voice. If Manuela were to turn back and look at us, she might think he was confessing deep feelings for me. The older couple at the table nearby probably see us and think: *How sweet*. Xavier speaks slowly and clearly. He grabs a pen out of the jar in the center of the table and even carefully prints out notes for me. As if maybe this is a topic we're investigating for biology class and I might be quizzed later on. He tells me, "I don't believe you have cancer. I've been doing a lot of research and I think it's something called Munchausen syndrome, actually Munchausen syndrome by proxy. Do you know what that is?"

This time, my chin moves from side to side. I hear the rush of cold air across my ears when I shake my head.

Xavier says, "Sometimes Munchausen is also called factitious disorder. Patients with Munchausen, or factitious disorder, deceive others by appearing sick or intentionally sickening themselves. Sometimes Munchausen, or factitious disorder, occurs when a parent falsely presents her child as ill or impaired somehow."

247

The rush across my ears builds into a roar. "Falsely presents?" I repeat. "You think we're making it up?"

"No. I do not think that. I think you are very sick. I think your mother is actually sickening you. The medications, the supplements—I think she has been creating symptoms."

"She would never do that. Why would she do that?"

"Mostly for attention—from what I understand. She wants devotion from you. Pity from other people. Media interest. Sometimes, according to what I've read, there can be financial incentives, either from insurance payouts or fundraising campaigns."

He waits for me to say something. I wait for him to tell me he's kidding.

"Look," I say, "I understand my mom creeps you out. I get it. She hasn't been acting like herself lately. But I've been sick my whole life."

"Says who?"

"What do you mean? Says me, says my own body. I've gone to doctors since I was a baby, stayed in hospitals, switched schools, anything to manage my health."

"Exactly. Who has been there with you through all that?"

"My mom." Xavier sits back as if I've proven his point, but the fact that my mother was with me doesn't prove *anything* sinister. I ask him, "Who has taken you to all your doctor's appointments, Xavier? Who has decided how much pain warrants an emergency room visit? Who has met with your doctors?"

"It's different."

"Why is it different? What makes your disease valid and mine factitious?"

"That's not what I mean."

"That's *exactly* what you mean. I thought you understood me. I thought you saw me fighting, just like you. I've never questioned anything about your illness, Xavier. Imagine if I interrogated you about sickle cell? Asked you if it really hurt that badly or suggested it was just something your mom made up for attention? How would you react? Are you that egotistical that you cannot allow for the idea that someone else might experience suffering? What's the problem? I wasn't threatening as long I was too dumb and tired to attend class? But now that I'm catching up, you might have to share the tragic limelight with another sick nerd?"

"That's not fair."

"No, it's not." I stand up then and half expect to feel unsteady on my feet but actually I feel quite strong. I stride up to the counter where Manuela keeps the register and leave a twenty-dollar bill near the machine.

"Little fawn, what's the rush?"

"I'm not a fawn, Manuela. I'm a lion."

The other patrons at the pottery studio murmur behind me. I've made a scene. I know I should turn back to fix it but instead I head out the door, whipping off my wool cap with one hand as I push open the front door with the other. The bells hanging on the door jangle and draw even more eyes to me. Let them look.

I reach up to rub my bald head, to warm it up in the cold night. It occurs to me that I keep sculpting boy animals. Deer with antlers. A lion with a majestic mane. In the wilderness, it's the females who have the strength to remain unadorned.

I remember how I placed all my hurt in that braid, twisted all my resentment into its strands. Pictured how my braid looked on the floor, like a girl in a long gown who had collapsed from too much dancing. My face is wet with tears. My phone is silent. No one texts me to say *Wait, are you okay?* No one calls to make sure I'm home safe and resting.

Walking up our driveway, I consider how few times I've approached our house on my own. If *Channel 7 Sunshine* canvassed the street, what would our neighbors offer about Mama and me? They might say, *The two of them mostly kept to themselves.* Maybe someone would mention: *We wondered if she really had a daughter— we never saw a young girl in the yard or walking with friends from town.* Wish I had remembered to leave the porch light on. I spook myself, trying to fit the key in the door. I worry Mama has come home and I worry Mama will never come home.

She has wheeled her little travel suitcase into the great hall of Ravenwood Castle and Xavier would have me believe she is stocking up on poison apples. Inside the house, I stop at the kitchen first. The plastic box labeled with the days of the week stares up at me. The capsules from Monday through Thursday yawn open. Pills still pack the compartments for Friday, Saturday, and Sunday.

I open up Friday's container and line up the pills end to end. The row stretches out the length of my hand. I could swallow them all. They have been assigned to me. I could curl up in my bed beneath the white cotton blankets and try to forget the doubt shadowing Xavier's face. I will just wake tomorrow though, woozy and worn before the day even gets going. That doubt will be a soft spot I drift back to—the same way I can't stop my hand from brushing against my shaved head.

I toss the pills into the basket of the sink's disposal and imagine a crowd going wild, points racking up on a scoreboard.

Turn on the water and then the disposal. No going back now. The machines churns and rumbles. Consider sending Saturday and Sunday down the drain too, then decide to wait and evaluate my symptoms each morning and night. I won't trade blindly following my mom and Dr. Eric for blindly following Xavier Barnes.

My phone sits still in my pocket, a dead weight of uncaring. I take it out, craft my text to Mama carefully. *Hope you are settling in. Feeling worn out, going to sleep soon. Love you.* Then I wait.

It takes her longer than I would expect to respond to me. *Miss you, sweetheart! FaceTime?*

That stops me. I set the phone down on the counter, like it's a grenade, and consider how Manuela and Xavier both noticed a difference in me. Mama always observes me so closely. *Too tired,* I write, and wait.

Rest up. Call if you need me. Love you.

I turn the ringer off then. No sense waiting for the chime to signify someone else reaching out. I don't need that.

For once, I have energy to spare and find myself pacing around the kitchen. The computer center beckons me, a ghost cloaked with the white sheet. But I know not to leave clues in the browser's search history. And if Mama monitors my phone, she might have spyware installed on the computer. That research will have to wait. For now, I start in the room where it's all written down, where piles of bills spill out of folders and envelopes. On wellness warriors episodes, sometimes Mama refers to our dining room as our own hall of medical records.

For a Friday night, it's still pretty early. I sit down and begin reading. I start sorting the pages and try to organize the documents into a timeline that makes sense.

CHAPTER TWENTY-FOUR

It turns out that it's impossible to categorize my medical files into any kind of logical account. I order bills by dates and discover that at certain times, Mama has had me seeing three or four doctors at once. Maybe I should look at Dr. Eric as an upgrade?

None of my previous other doctors refer to each other's findings ever. Most of them keep offices in locations at least forty-five minutes from towns where we've lived. I find a lot of bills past due or marked SENT TO COLLECTIONS and a few official-looking letters referring to inaccurate insurance information provided, requesting updated policy information.

I find one folder packed with several different versions of the same letter, addressed to a variety of children's charitable trusts. In those, Mama appeals to whatever charity and claims several different diagnoses: pediatric cancer, autoimmune disorders, diabetes, Crohn's disease, Lyme.

I also find letters in which she claims to be a widow, a military widow, and also raising a child on her own while her ex-husband serves time related to a domestic violence conviction. I don't find any other reference to my father.

I read until my head spins. I jot down notes and keep one folder for pages I find particularly mysterious. Maybe I mean incriminating. At first, I try to leave everything as I find it, to set pages down carefully in the exact places where I pick them up, but I don't stick to that. It's too easy to get caught up reading one page after another. It feels like falling down a hole, and as I fall, I catch glimpses, but it's confusing to try to arrange those fragments into any kind of coherent story.

All the fragments follow one pattern: Mama claims I am sick. Mama requests money. I don't find a lot of actual diagnostic information. I find prescriptions scrawled on green, pink, and light blue memos and signed with different initials. I find physical forms, like the one the school nurse demanded, complete with different allergies and medical histories listed. One form says my appendix came out five years ago. Then I find a form dated two years ago. On that form, under previous surgeries, I recognize the flourishes of Mama's handwriting: *None.*

I can't believe what I'm reading. I keep reaching for the last page read, trying to cross-reference, trying to fit all fragments together. It only works as the medical history of a dozen different people. Not one person. Not just me.

Otherwise none of it makes sense. And then that begins to make a different kind of sense.

The lies.

So many lies.

To doctors. About doctors.

To other people. To me.

I don't allow myself to fully absorb it. I need to keep reading. I have to find everything I can. Later, I'll let myself actually think about it.

The night ticks on and my eyelids weigh heavy. I worry about missing some small detail—a note that would explain away everything, a key that could decode aspects I don't yet understand. It's strange to not know what to root for. She hasn't been gone a full night and Mama has become less a person in my head and more a trail that I am following. It's a thrill to catch her in a lie. But when I see where we are headed, all I feel is dread.

Eventually, the folder of saved documents grows crammed and heavy. I have enough to show someone if I can think of someone to show. Xavier would make quick work of interpreting all the data. But he has already decided on his conclusion. I bring the one folder to the kitchen counter and pile it with the notebook of instructions Mama left me, and the letters at the bottom of my backpack. I empty the pills from the Saturday, Sunday, and Monday compartments into a Ziploc bag.

Then I transfer everything into my backpack—all the evidence I have gathered so far. I push the kitchen cart in front of the back door and throw the dead bolt across the front. Mama might come home early, but at least I will have bought myself some time. *I got nervous sleeping in the house on my own*, I will tell her. I practice saying out loud in the empty kitchen—"I'm sorry you cut your trip short, Mama. But I'm so glad you've come home."

When I let myself sleep, I tuck myself in under a blanket on the living room sofa, with one of the throw pillows propped under my head. The television glows and drones softly from the wall. I let the ridiculous desserts of a baking show distract me. Mama always says that watching TV interferes with your body's ability to actually rest and recharge. I don't find that to be the case. I dream of sweet pies piled around the kitchen, cakes emerging from the oven in droves.

In the morning, Netflix scrolls suggestions across the screen for me. If I enjoy baking shows so much, then perhaps I want to explore tree house living? Perhaps I want to learn how to design fashion for dogs? Their version of my life is so much more interesting and prone to self-improvement. Mama has left a Tupperware carafe of kale smoothie and I drink it suspiciously. It's a little strange to drink a beverage without using it to wash down a pill.

I try to take inventory of how I'm feeling. I stretch and notice that even though I slept on the sofa, my muscles don't ache. My head feels okay. My appetite roars to life and I polish off the turkey meatballs. I shower with the phone nearby, get dressed and ready with it right within reach. Mama calls at nine thirty.

"I wanted to make sure you woke up okay. You were so worn out last night—did you sleep well?"

"Sort of. I kept waking up, thinking I heard noises."

"You woke up? Even after taking your meds?"

"Well, I still felt a little dazed, but it was hard to feel settled in the house all by myself."

"Cara Jean, you know—"

"I wasn't implying anything, Mama—just explaining. That's all. How is the castle?"

"It's very grand but a bit drafty. I have a massage scheduled. I'm hoping the therapist might be able to work on that knot in my back. Mobility is of course such a crucial component of self-care. Are you seeing Xavier today?" Mama asks in her carefully casual voice, but I can feel her waiting over the phone line.

"No. I don't think so."

"Is everything okay between you two? Should I have tried to arrange a different carpool?"

"No. Xavier just sees himself as an expert in everything, you know?"

"Well, he has certainly helped with your academics. But don't let anyone else dictate your own self-worth."

"Of course not, Mama. You taught me better than that. I'll call at some point and check in about homework, just to reinforce his major ego."

"People enjoy feeling needed." I'm not used to talking to my mother like this. We don't normally spend enough time away from each other to require catching up and she sounds distracted; she's answering questions I'm not necessarily asking. "See if his mom will take you to make your pottery. Or reach out to your friend Libby."

"Maybe. I have a lot of studying."

"That's right. But if you go, bring along some organic turkey. Don't go crazy with junk food just because I'm not home to monitor. We don't want another allergic reaction."

"Right, Mama. I'll probably just stay home."

"Well, have fun. I'll call you later, sweetheart. To check up on you. In the meantime, make sure to take your meds on time and with meals according to my directions."

"Right. Enjoy the massage."

"Well, it's therapeutic, but sure." And then the phone clicks and somewhere, maybe in the tallest turret of Ravenwood Castle, my mother returns to her royal obligations.

I force myself to call Xavier next. He answers during the first ring.

"You okay?"

I keep it short and factual. "Yes. But I need you to do me a favor."

"Well, hold on, before we talk about favors. Cara, I'm really sorry if it felt like—"

"I don't really have time. Even to apologize. I said terrible things. But I might have meant them." I practically shout that last bit at him and wonder if a complete lack of social graces counts as a symptom, or maybe it's who I am when all the pharmaceutical enhancements have been stripped away from my basic personality. I try again, telling him, "I would have texted but—"

"Your mom."

"Right. And I don't know about phone calls."

"She might be listen—"

"That's not important." I leap to speak over him. Xavier may be a brilliant scientist but his spy skills seem rusty today.

"I need you to order me an Uber."

"What?"

"I don't have my own credit card. If I use the app on my phone, then—"

"She can trac—"

"Thank you," I interrupt again.

"You have to give me the address. Where you're going." I hadn't considered that. I don't want anyone tracing my steps, not even Science Kid. "It's just so I can order the car. You know what? It can't hurt either. For safety." Xavier's speech lands just as unevenly as my own. We don't know how to navigate this kind of conversation. Our anger makes us clumsy, like Vish and Alistair arguing about their favorite Pokémon cards. "Listen, I could just ride along with you. Moral support. We don't have to talk or anything. I don't have pressing plans."

"I don't need anyone's help," I snap at him. To Xavier's credit, he does not immediately point out that I, in fact, telephoned him for help, that we are currently negotiating the terms of that help. I take a deep, cleansing breath. When I speak, I select each word with great care and patience. "It's important that I go on my own. I know it costs money. Of course I'll pay you back."

Xavier sighs sadly before he answers, "It has nothing to do with money, Cara." I know that but I don't want to say I know that. After last night, I don't want to give Xavier any credit for our friendship. I hate that even now it's required that I feel grateful to someone. Even now I have to grovel to move forward in the smallest possible way.

So my speech is still gruff when I add, "There are other stops. Other places I need to go. I might as well tell you now." Silence fills the space between us and maybe I've finally pushed him too far.

"Just get me the first address. We'll go from there." I give it to him, and he calls back in four minutes. "Reuben will pick you up in twelve minutes. He's driving a blue Honda Accord. If you feel weird at all, just get out of the car at a red light. Preferably in a populated area. No matter where you are, we'll come get you."

"Do you really think Reuben the Uber driver plans to kidnap me?"

Xavier clears his throat. "I would like to talk about some of the things that were said last night."

"Sorry. Can't right now. I'm busy writing a letter. Thank you for arranging the ride. I really appreciate it."

Maybe Xavier Barnes believes that I'm writing to him and that brings him some comfort after I cut short our phone call. But I've decided to write Mr. Patrick Neary, the kindly man who doesn't claim grandparent status, who just took the time to send me a card with a cute dog illustration and let me know he had prayed for me. I use a sheet of heavy stationery from Mama's dining room files and stick a stamp I found there on a matching envelope.

I keep it short and direct.

Dear Mr. Neary,

Thank you so much for your kind card. It made me smile and feel cared for. Please don't spend a lot of time worrying about me. Lots of other people deserve your prayers. I'm not sure if I'm really sick or if my mom has been pretending. Maybe that sounds crazy and more complicated than you bargained for. Just please know your card mattered to me and helped me through a hard time.

Your friend,
Cara Wakely

I copy the address from the lime-green envelope and seal it up. Then I grab my backpack and a bottle of water, zip up my jacket, and tug my wool cap over my ears. I lock up the house and walk the stamped envelope down to the blue mailbox on the corner, dropping it in the slot before I have the chance to change my mind.

Then I stand in the cold until Reuben arrives in his blue Honda Accord. He pulls up right in front of the house and nods when I open the door and ask, "Reuben?" He's all business. Xavier might be worried about safety, but Reuben waits until I've buckled up before he hits the gas.

"So what's waiting for you in Aurora?"

I pronounce words I've never spoken aloud before. "I'm on my way to see my grandparents."

"I bet they'll be glad to see you." Reuben has no idea.

"It's a surprise, actually."

"Even better. Hey, you warm enough back there?"

Reuben meets my eyes in the rearview mirror. My hands flutter up to check on my hat before I can stop them. "Yes," I tell him. "Thank you." With that, I focus my gaze out the window and watch as the houses start spacing farther out from each other and the fields on the side of the highway look wilder, less carefully groomed.

I don't try to act unfriendly but the more I chat, the more chances exist to screw something up. Ever since I could talk, I've been told not to say too much. To let Mama describe my symptoms and explain my absences. She has schooled me in the rules of family privacy, of HIPAA laws. She has taught me what counts as private, what counts as privileged. When she's needed to, she has corrected me just by reaching over and squeezing my hand.

Now outside my window, the houses stand few and far between. I see them and understand how keeping me distant has also kept me quiet. We never trick-or-treated at neighbors' houses or opened the door to carolers at Christmas. When we moved, we packed quickly, without goodbyes to teachers or classmates. In all the paperwork I found last night, I didn't see a single envelope with a forwarding address.

I reread my grandmother's letter, noting the formal language, the looping letters: *We had no idea the two of you still lived so close.*

I start rehearsing my response: *Well, Grandma Wakely, maybe you could have investigated a little.* And it's not like Boston counts as some unmapped territory. How could they not have looked for me? Maybe Mama never allowed me to speak up, but it doesn't seem like my grandparents ever asked many questions.

The spaces between houses shrink when we reach the village of Aurora.

Mr. and Mrs. Burton Wakefield live in a neighborhood people would call charming—with big porches and mailboxes carved into the shape of animals. We pass a little general store and a diner that has a vintage car embedded in its roof.

When Reuben slows the car, I keep my eyes peeled for house

numbers and try not to visibly panic at the sight of 122 Prospect Street. I'm not feeling so distant now.

I step out of the car and stand at the curb as Reuben drives away. Somewhere forty-five minutes south of here, I'm sure Xavier is tracking his departure time.

I ring the doorbell, and it's the kind of chime I would expect from someone with my grandmother's vocabulary. It plays a little scale, and as each note lowers, I brace myself for the door to open.

No one answers. I cross the lawn and then the gravel driveway to reach the garage. It is organized, sheltering a great deal of wicker furniture, but no car. Around back, I find a little deck. I count four different bird feeders, so I seize on that newly discovered fact: My grandparents are generous to birds.

There's a mat near the sliding glass door but no key under it. I find the key in a fake potted plant right near the covered grill. I don't spend a lot of time debating it. I have their letter clutched in my hand so that if they come home and find that some crazy bald girl has broken into their quaint little Aurora house, at least I can prove they invited me.

I don't know why it surprises me so much to see the key turn in the lock. I push open the door, lean most of my body in, and call out, "Hello? Grandma Wakely? Gramps? I hope it's okay that I stopped by." Let me introduce myself—I am the most courteous prowler Aurora has ever seen. I take off my hat because older people find that respectful and my bald head makes me look frail and nonthreatening.

"It's Cara," I announce, hoping no one smacks me with a cane. "I just came by after receiving your letter. Hope that's okay—I have some questions for you." The house remains still and quiet.

For one panicked second, I worry that I've mixed up the addresses and have broken into another home, the residence of another couple who are complete strangers to me. But in their living room, a little desk sits beside a grandfather clock. There, I find a pile of mail on top, a neat arrangement of envelopes that makes Mama's dining room look like the aftermath of a tornado. Two piles, one featuring the precise handwriting that matches the envelope clenched in my fist. The other a set of bills and correspondence addressed to Mr. and Mrs. Burton Wakely. Burton. Burt. Grandpa Burt, but he prefers Gramps.

My heart ticks in my chest louder than the incessant progress of the clock's minute hand. I feel for my phone and debate calling Xavier. But what would I say? *I broke into a house. Now I'm snooping through their mail and talking to myself. I am handling my first weekend home alone like a professional delinquent.*

Then I see the photos. They are matted and framed, artfully arranged on the wall beside the staircase. I imagine that Grandma and Gramps Wakely move down the steps slowly on some mornings. Maybe once in a while, they pause for a rest, with a mottled hand resting on the banister. They look at the photographs while they catch their breath. There is a large wedding picture in black and white. My grandmother's veil resembles a sheet of froth. My grandfather's chin rests on her head and their fingers are intertwined in front of them. They're posed to look like they've just paused their dancing. I see a color photo, in sun-washed shades—a small blond boy, wearing denim overalls and presenting a toy train to the camera.

Framed at the top of the arrangement is another picture. The boy's hair is darker and his chin more chiseled. But it's him; I can tell it is him, wearing a graduation robe and slightly off-kilter hat. He keeps a leather-bound diploma tucked in his arm and seems like he finds all the formality a little silly. It looks like he might have burst out laughing right after the photographer snapped the photos. It's just the three of them—at the beach, in front of a watercolor sunset. Arms around each other, skis stuck in the snow like fence posts beside them. The Wakelys have lived a good life together, it seems.

In the center of the arrangement, there is another small photograph. A toddler with chestnut-colored pigtails, poised at the top of a slide in a cheerful-looking playground. Her little hands grip the slide's side rails. She's cheesing for the camera. I can almost feel the thick plastic of the slide's edges, how they warmed in the sun. What it felt like to let go and rush down, to bounce back after hitting the rubber at the bottom. I remember.

I remember ice cream pops bought at a truck and riding on someone's shoulders, my fingers tufting his hair, his arm crossed over my leg to keep me balanced and secured in my perch. I remember the burnt-match smell of blown birthday candles. I remember a lot of shouting. High fevers in footie pajamas. The metal rails of a hospital crib. I remember my father standing, framed in doorway after doorway, watching over me.

The little girl in the photo looks clear-eyed and happy. Her cheeks are pink and chubbier than I ever remember my cheeks being. Every day Mr. and Mrs. Burton Wakely must walk up and down these stairs, at least twice. How many times do they stop at that particular photograph? I wonder what they wonder about me.

I hear the crunch of the gravel under tires and it takes me a second to place the sound. The car's motor thrums loudly.

Evidently, Gramps Wakely believes in horsepower. My first rattled steps take me up the stairs. I dash up there madly, as if I can just crouch behind a shower curtain or up in an attic crawl space. Makes no sense, so I backtrack, taking the stairs two at a time. Then I can't stop myself. I snatch first one framed photo off the wall and then another. My father's graduation portrait and then me on the slide. Taking both feels greedy, so I leave the picture of me on the little desk by the clock. The gaps in the staircase display will tell the story of my visit.

The car doors shut with muffled thumps and the slow footsteps shuffle across the pebbled walk. The front door creaks open while I try to slide the kitchen door closed. It sticks. I stand there for a second, framed by the glass door, the portrait of my father tucked beneath my jacket. I see her. Her silver bob wisps around her face and she wears a silk scarf knotted at her throat. "Who's there?" she shouts loudly as the screen door screams in its track. "Burton!" she yells in warning, and for a sick second I worry that she will fall backward or collapse, clutching her chest. But then she sees me and shouts "Hello?" with less anger in her voice and more curiosity.

I stare back and face her fully. I want her to see who I am now. "Cara." She says my name like she is certain. I take off running, holding my father's picture to my chest. I don't turn around to look back.

CHAPTER TWENTY-FIVE

The Comet Diner in Aurora, Ohio, serves breakfast all day, even to teenage troublemakers who arrive winded from breaking into the homes of their estranged grandparents. I only have twenty dollars in my pocket, so I peruse the menu carefully. I catch my breath and keep an eye out the window for Mr. and Mrs. Burton Wakely.

The diner is shaped like a train car. I cower in the red vinyl booth and wish it sat on tracks attached to a steam engine, something that could transport me away pronto.

Almost noon and I have not accomplished nearly enough for the price I'll ultimately have to pay for these adventures. I know I have grandparents and that they appreciate hummingbirds. I now have a photo of my father, but I'm scared to take it out and examine it because it's technically stolen property. Instead I unzip my backpack and sneak it in there beneath the table in the diner's booth. I wait for a squad car to careen into the tiny parking lot in front of the building.

The waitress snaps her gum when she takes my order. My hand rests in my bag and feels for the Ziploc bag of pills in case they're needed. I don't think they're necessary, just reassuring. I just ran farther and faster than I can ever remember actually moving my body. A stitch in my side hurts and my chest hurts from sucking in the cold air, my ears ache from the extreme temperature changes, but I feel otherwise invigorated. I feel otherwise healthy.

I order pancakes. I stutter while pronouncing them because Mama and I rarely go out to eat and, if we do, we certainly don't order gluten. I order buckwheat pancakes, but even still. Pancakes.

"Something to drink?" The waitress has her pen ready to jot down my order. She has no idea how new this is to me.

"Juice. Please."

This earns a subtle eye roll. "What kind of juice, honey?"

"Orange. Thank you." After she saunters off, I take three cleansing breaths and really spend a moment appreciating my surroundings. I am alone in a diner, taking myself out for a meal. There is a tiny jukebox on each table and I flip through the selections. Mostly Motown. I try to look without staring. It's a small town, this quaint village, and I am a bald girl on my own, out to breakfast. I expect to attract attention.

No one else speaks on a cell phone. Some couples are bent toward each other in conversation. A few older men read the newspaper, unfolded enormously in front of them. Some people just sip their coffee and look bleakly out the window. I'm sure it qualifies as rude but I call Xavier anyway. When the waitress drops off the juice, she frowns in disappointment.

Xavier tells me I should have called earlier. "I've been worried. Where are you?" He sounds angry and then I remember he *is* angry. I remember our argument, and the smallness I accused him of.

"I'm sorry. It doesn't matter."

"You're in some place called Aurora." He can track me with Uber. If Reuben had turned out to be sketchy, Xavier would have had me covered. I sit back in the booth and drink my orange juice, feeling well cared for.

"Yes, at the moment, but I think I should head back. There's nothing here for me." That's not entirely true. I remember the look on Mrs. Burton Wakely's face. She seemed hopeful. I could walk back, calmly this time, and knock on their front door. Wait for them to let me in this time. I would sit in their freshly vacuumed living room and she would bring out a plate of little sandwiches. We would talk about the letter and I would ask about the affable graduate in the photo. I would show them my mother's letters, the charitable appeals in which she claims my father has died in the Middle East. Maybe Grandma Wakely would fill in the earliest part of my timeline. Maybe she could tell me about my first symptoms.

But I would be working at a disadvantage, trying to build that relationship only hours after I broke into their house. Better that she thinks on it all for a while. I remember my own rosy cheeks in the playground photo. She's had a decade or so to get in touch.

Xavier is talking about my return. "Maybe you should just come straight to my house. We can talk to my parents. I've been thinking, what if we brought you to a clinic or something? We could get an independent physical exam?"

The waitress sets down the plate of pancakes and clears her throat. I cover the phone with my hand and say, "Thank you."

"Great." Xavier misunderstands. "I'll look up places with walk-in appointments."

"No." I lean forward and speak urgently into the phone. "No, Xavier. Don't do that." How can he think that I'll go so readily to another doctor? The whole point is all the time I've spent seeing doctors. "Listen, I appreciate your efforts, but I don't need you to fix this."

"Cara, I'm not try—"

"I just need your Uber account." I cut myself a bite of pancakes and chew, waiting for him to argue. I recognize that I am being obnoxious, but somehow can't stop myself. After all, acting grateful never really got me anywhere. Right now, I can't find words for how angry I am. I keep picturing me as a toddler in that photo—the perky little pigtails, the carefree smile. Sunlight streaming into the strands of my hair. Fearless at the top of the slide. No one stopped me from falling. No one protected me afterward.

It's been a while since Xavier has tried to speak. I try to gentle my voice. "Listen, I still have some things that I want to investigate. That's my priority right now. If we still think it's a good idea for me to have tests done or something, then fine, we can go tomorrow. But I don't even know where my insurance card is."

Xavier exhales mightily. "Will you please stop worrying about money? We'll figure that part out." He talks exactly like a person who has never had to worry about money, who has never washed his hair with food-pantry shampoo or received the free cartons of milk at school. Then he says, "Please let me tell my parents. They'll want to help."

"No. Don't tell them. I'm serious. You have to promise."

"Yeah. I promise." There's a chance Xavier has already told his parents. I know that. There's just nothing I can do about it.

"I'm eating pancakes."

"Oh yeah?" I hear the laugh in his voice. "And what do you think of pancakes?"

"From now on, I'm only eating pancakes."

"Just wait until you try cookie dough."

I laugh like this is all there is to talk about: various desserts and the order in which I should explore them. But then the waitress swishes by and my voice drops to a whisper on the phone. "Do you really believe everything you said last night? Do you think my mom is making it all up?"

"That's not exactly what I said." Science Kid chooses his words very carefully. "I don't think your symptoms fit with the typical manifestations of pediatric cancer. I believe your mom is making you sick. I think she is suffering from a psychiatric disorder that causes that behavior. Our goal should be to get you safe and get your mom some help."

"I need for you to allow for the fact that I could still be actually sick. My mom might act weird. She might be defrauding all these people. But the fatigue and chronic pain that I experience is real. There have to be valid reasons for the way my body feels like this."

"How do you feel today? Are you still abstaining from medication?"

I know that Xavier Barnes is smart. I register and file away every point he makes. But Xavier loves research and experiments. Some kids play video games and some watch horror movies. Some play hockey and some collect expensive sneakers. Xavier enjoys formulating scientific hypotheses and then proving them. Or disproving. I am more than a theory that needs disproving.

"If you could order the Uber, I'm just about done with these pancakes," I announce. "I'm at the Comet Diner in Aurora. I'd like a ride to Tri-Point Medical Center, please."

The next driver who picks me up is named Grant. He's older and Middle Eastern and he rushes to open the car door for me when he sees me emerge from the Comet Diner. "Hello, hello."

"Thank you, Grant?" I say politely. The question in my voice confirms he's actually my Uber driver and not just a random man picking up a girl at the diner.

"You're going to the hospital—you okay?" His voice is kind and concerned.

"Just fine, thank you." He looks back at me, still waiting for an explanation. "I just have to look into a few things there."

Grant gestures to my hat, my bare ears. He seems to know about the hairless mess I have going on up there. "Listen, I am very sorry for your hard time." I nod. The tears spring to the corners of my eyes before I have prepared to intercept them. If I speak, I will weep. But the driver says, "You just sit back, okay? Grant will take you where you need to go."

I try to soak in the scenery as we leave Aurora. I search my memory for any familiar remnant—a family picnic, a Christmas morning. For some reason, I remember a parade with a marching band and a brigade of girls twirling ribbons. I picture them trooping past the general store and down the tiny Main Street. But I don't know if it's an actual memory or just a story I have begun to tell myself. The way on exams, you sometimes have to guess. I resent the need to fill in the blanks.

I text Mama, *Miss you. Hope the castle is a fairy tale!* in case that she has worried over hearing so little from me. It's sort of true. I hope for a dungeon or a drafty tower. Something with shackles bolted into the stone walls.

But she sends back a string of happy face emoji. *All ok?* And I answer, *Of course! Maybe watching too much reality TV,* just to keep her off my trail.

I slide the photograph out of my bag. It must be a high school graduation portrait because my father doesn't look much older than me. I knew his face as soon as I saw it: the long, straight nose, the square jaw. How could I recognize the width of my father's shoulders but not remember the sound of his voice? I doze a little in the car and wake to hear Grant up in the front seat, softly calling, "Miss, miss. Which entrance do you think? The visitors' reception area or maybe emergency?" He seems genuinely fearful—humanely concerned but also eager to get me out of his car's pristine interior.

"Visitors' reception would be just fine, thanks. My friend booked the car for me. I'm sure he's paid already."

"Oh yes. Please don't worry." Grant looks sadly after me as I

hurriedly pack up my knapsack and practically dive out of the back seat. Somewhere, there has to be a support group for Uber drivers who have seen some drama.

At the hospital, I operate with neither accomplice nor getaway driver. It's just me looking around, not even sure exactly what I'm searching for. I have this sense that someone here should have answers. I bypass the reception area completely. At first the little old lady working there calls insistently after me, "Excuse me, miss. Miss?" A security guard steps forward and that's when I strategically remove my hat and enjoy the spectacle of everyone around me backing off. No one questions the bald kid in the hospital. Maybe that's how Mama has felt pushing my wheelchair ahead of her through the lobby: the power of the powerless. I don't enjoy it more than my own hair but it's a satisfying consolation prize.

I take the elevator up to the fifth floor: pediatrics. I catch myself looking for Omar. At the nurses' station, my shaved head doesn't achieve the same reverence. "Hey there." The nurse wears scrubs with otters printed all over them. When I lean in slightly, I can read the phrase *otterly awesome* screen-printed between the animals.

"I like your scrubs."

"Thanks. How can I help you?"

"I'm just visiting. I was a patient here last month. I thought that maybe I could see my chart?"

"Yeah? That's not something we typically make available." I think of the fuss Mama kicked up just so she could bring a copy of my medical records home.

"I thought the law required it. I'm sorry—maybe I misunderstood."

"How old are you? If you're a minor, a parent or guardian needs to request it."

I want to ask if there's any oversight on parents and guardians. I feel that surge of rage again and I want to inform the smug nurse that it's otterly outrageous I need my mom to request my records in order to figure out how my mom has been manipulating my medical records. I want to tell her and any other medical professionals who treated me over and over when my symptoms were suspicious or remain unresolved that I consider them complicit in stealing my childhood.

Instead I ask, "Is Dr. Abidi on the floor today? She was my attending physician."

"She's not. She's on call, though. If you want to leave a message and a phone number, I'll try to pass it along."

I stand there chewing my lip, trying to pick the least dangerous option. Who can help me? And what I am willing to risk?

"It's confidential, to leave a note for my doctor, right?"

"Yeah. Pretty much. Unless someone was worried you might hurt yourself. Do you feel like you might hurt yourself?"

"No. Not at all." *The opposite*, I want to shout at her. But I try to see myself through her eyes: pale and skinny with a shaved head and a bulging backpack. Fangirling over a doctor. "She gave me her card, in case I had questions. I just realized I wasn't asking the right ones."

"Sure. She'd be happy to help." The nurse hands over a notepad. I try to think like a doctor and make my message straightforward and brief. *Cara Wakely, 14. Patient from December. Mother refused to schedule follow-up visit. Started treatment for cancer?* Then I spell it carefully, the way Xavier wrote it out for me. I don't want Dr. Abidi to think I'm some drama queen, making careless accusations. _Possible_ Munchausen's? I write, underlining forcefully. _Please don't text. Mom has access to phone. Student at Middlefield High._ It's another step I can't take back, another note I can't unsend.

"Do you have an envelope?" I ask, praying the nurse doesn't reach for the note to read right there in front of me.

"I can get you an envelope." She's studying me more carefully now. She watches while I fold the note into the envelope and seal it carefully closed. "Do you need anything else?"

Suddenly I feel so tired. I worry that I'm wrong after all, that Xavier is wrong and now something terrible is about to happen because I accused Mama of this kind of craziness. It's almost a relief to feel this tired. It's more familiar this way. I rally long enough to respond to the kind and vaguely suspicious nurse. "Thanks. I'm all right. I just got super tired all of a sudden."

"You look like you've had a long day. There's a cafeteria downstairs if you want to refuel and rest up."

The cafeteria looks inviting, but I left my last twenty dollars on the table for the waitress at the Comet Diner. On the first floor, I walk like I know where to go, my hat in my pocket with a handful of spare change. I find a corridor full of conference rooms and keep wandering in hopes of finding the snack machines. A sign posted on one of the doors stops me in my tracks: PARENTS OF CHRONICALLY ILL CHILDREN—A SUPPORT GROUP FOR PARENTS WITH PATIENTS. Just like Mama's group. This must be where she meets.

It hits me then how awful I am, how I've betrayed my mother over what exactly? Some bills that don't add up. The fact that she finally took a weekend to herself. In the meantime, how many years has she spent devoted to my care? Going to groups like these and comparing notes on her efforts to care for me. I reach out to trace the poster's letters and then, to my absolute horror and embarrassment, the door swings open.

About a dozen adults sit in a circle in the room, in chairs arranged in the center. Some of them sip from Styrofoam cups. I see more than one box of Kleenex. They all turn to stare at me in one motion. One of the women rushes to her feet and lumbers over. I notice she's wearing lavender toe socks with Birkenstock sandals. A long caftan with swirls of bright colors floats around her. I decide she's probably an art teacher, someone's very liberal aunt. "Hey there, butterfly, why have you landed here?" It's me she is speaking to. She's calling me *butterfly*.

"I'm so sorry," I say. "I accidentally pushed the door. I saw the sign and got curious. My mom goes to a group just like this. You know, for support."

"How wonderful." I see her taking in the vision of me then. She registers my lack of hair, probably even my weariness. "Well, we meet every Saturday afternoon at three p.m. You should tell her to drop by. We'd love to have another parent in the group."

"My mom comes to the group on Thursdays."

The art teacher lady blinks. She looks back at the rest of the parents behind her. "Oh, lovey, well then, never mind! This *is* the Thursday group. We switched our meeting time to Saturdays. Too many conflicts. Maybe your mom is here?" She opens the door wider.

"No, she just went to the group on Thursday. This past Thursday." We stare at each other, blank and friendly, the art teacher and me.

I don't know why I keep arguing with everyone. I'm just trying to keep everything straight and the rest of the world seems determined to confound me.

"Who's your mom, lovey?" she asks me in her sociable manner. It's all just a mix-up; we just have to figure it out.

"Shaylene Wakely." The low murmur of the group suddenly quiets. I see on the art teacher's face that she knows exactly who my mom is.

"I don't know her." She grits her teeth.

"She comes on Thursday."

One of the men comes over then and stands beside the art teacher. He's burly, a solid wall of muscle. If this were a bar rather than a hospital support group, I might think he was the bouncer.

"Your mom's not here," he says.

"I know that. But there's a Thursday group, isn't there?" My voice rises in panic at having uncovered another random lie. "What about Dr. Eric? Is Dr. Eric in this group too?"

The burly man shakes his head sadly and says, "I'm afraid we can't help you, and we really need to begin. I'm so sorry." Then he firmly shuts the conference room door. It's not soundproofed, though. I listen carefully.

"Do you think she meant Eric Andrianakis?" That's Art Teacher asking.

Another voice. "She called him Dr. Eric?"

"Well, that does make sense though, doesn't it?"

"I hope for her sake it's not."

They return to their seats, too far from the door for me to hear. That is my cue to leave, but not without first writing down the name Andrianakis before I forget it. I scrawl it across the

277

folder of unresolved paperwork questions, remembering how Mama explained why I could call Dr. Eric by his first name. His surname was Greek and hard to pronounce, she had said, even though the parents at the support group seemed to be saying his name just fine.

I stop at the front desk.

"May I help you, miss?" The kindly old woman behind the counter smiles at me.

"I'm not sure, but I'd appreciate it if you'd try. A friend of our family practices medicine near here. My mom asked me to please check in with him when I was in the area. Could you tell me if he works out of this hospital?"

"Sure. I can look that up. What would his name be?"

"Dr. Eric Andrianakis?" I sound it out, trying to get the spelling as close as possible.

"We don't have any doctor by that name."

"Maybe I'm misspelling it?"

But she tips the monitor up so that I can see it. She's got all the names that begin with *A* listed. "I'm sorry. No one even close."

I could call Xavier and ask for a ride. I know he'd ask his mom to pick me up or he'd order another Uber. Truthfully, I want a little space from Xavier's kindness. I open the maps app on my phone. I have had a long day—maybe my longest day ever. It's more than seven miles to get home. If I have cancer or some other serious disease, there's no way I can walk that distance. But if I don't, that's good exercise. It's wide-open time to clear my head and really think in the cold January air. Leaving now will time my arrival back to the house right before dark. I tighten my shoelaces, shift my backpack so it's centered on my shoulders, and start following the directions home.

CHAPTER TWENTY-SIX

Seven and a half miles is actually much farther to walk than it sounds. Particularly in January, particularly when you're used to moving only from bed to chair to couch for most of your days, particularly when the more you think about your life, the less you understand of it.

It is a long walk. It is hilly and cold. By the time I get within sight of home, the bottoms of my feet actually hurt from all the steps. My belly growls with voracious hunger.

But I don't feel sick. I feel satisfied to have completed the task. Just in time too—as I turn onto our street, dusk just about sweeps through, adding its gray strokes to the brisk blue sky. My body aches in a strange and good way. I reach the porch, unlock the door, and pretty much launch myself onto the sofa. I put on the British baking show in the background, but it just makes me feel hungrier and oddly English. I warm up vegetable lasagna and then watch all these people bake pheasant pie.

I text Xavier. *Thank you for your help with the bio project. Lots to learn. Still working on it.*

He replies, *Of course. Happy to help!* And then he immediately calls. "Where are you?"

"I'm home."

"How?"

My eyes dart around the room. But I suppose if Mama had cameras and microphones set up, she would have made a beeline home by now. "I walked." I have to move the phone away from my ear—Xavier squawks that loudly in response.

"What do you mean, you walked? From where?"

"From Tri-Point Medical Center."

"Girl, what? You don't see that as a self-destructive choice? I call that self-destructive. Are you all right? Why would you walk all the way home from the hospital?"

"To see if I could." He's silent then. "It's more than twenty-four hours now since I've taken anything—even ibuprofen. I'm keeping a log to try and track what are symptoms and what are side effects."

"Brilliant. That's super smart." I feel full of food and now warmth, basking in Xavier's praise. "But listen, Cara. You need to be careful. That's not actually a long time to be off any kind of medication. Most pharmaceuticals have a half-life—do you know what that means?" My turn now to stay silent. "That's how they work their way out of your body. Substances cut themselves in half, day by day or week by week and so on. But it takes a while to get them fully out of your system. That's why you can't take any other meds right now, because it could throw your body chemistry off at a critical time. Do you understand? I've been reading a lot about all this."

"I understand." I imagine Xavier all worried, designing different models to see how I could best get clean.

"What about headaches? Restlessness?"

"Nothing to worry about."

"Everything is something to worry about right now. Did you find out anything at the hospital?"

"More complications. Less sense. I think my mom has been lying about going to her support group. Or maybe she's been going to another support group. But the members of this one seemed to know her. The support group had serious beef with my mom."

"Well, okay. But that fits, right? If she's manufacturing some of these medical issues?"

It fits with his version. I wanted to remind Xavier that a scientist doesn't just gather evidence to support one theory. "I tried to check in with a couple of doctors."

"Good. That's a really good step."

"I didn't connect with anyone."

"But you reached out."

"Oh, I definitely reached out. All day long, I reached out." 281

"Even now." I can tell by how he says it; Xavier is smiling.

"Oh yeah? How is that?"

"You didn't make me text you. You contacted me, to let me know you were home safe and sound. You didn't need a ride or anything. I consider that progress. What's the plan for tomorrow?"

"What do you mean?"

"We are sans plans. You want to come to church with me?"

"Are you joking?"

"No. It's another way of reaching out." The only thing I know about church is the bags of donated groceries. I don't want to be surrounded by other people right now, a magnet for all their pitying looks. To be bald and sallow, the weird white girl trailing Xavier's family. I don't want to listen to a preacher lecture me about forgiveness or gratitude. "We could go to church and then swing by an urgent care clinic. Then we could sit down and explain possible scenarios to my parents and come up with a plan." Xavier has thought this through.

"That sounds like the worst Sunday ever." I mean, I've had worse Sundays. I think of all the Sundays I've spent at home, overmedicated and grappling to complete homework, only for Mama to keep me home from school the next week anyway. "I don't mean to dismiss all your suggestions," I tell Xavier as I dismiss all his suggestions. "Really I need to take some time, to figure things out on my own and to get some sleep."

"I get that. You don't have a lot of time though, Cara. We need to get you out of the house. My guess is that your mom will notice a difference in your presentation almost immediately. From what I've read, Munchausen's moms lash out when confronted. They don't ever admit their actions and can't seem to stop themselves from medically interfering with their children."

I stand up then and walk around the house, flipping on lights. With Xavier tethered on the phone line for reassurance, I make sure Mama's not waiting in the shadows, listening in on my conversation, planning more medical interference. "Okay, but slow down. We're not certain all that's happening." I feel myself fading. There are pieces I haven't made sense of yet, fragments that haven't fallen into place. "More than anything right now, I need some sleep."

Perhaps the most convincing evidence I have that Mama has stunted my adolescence is the fact that alone on a Saturday, I fall asleep before 8:00 p.m., on the sofa, while watching *The Great British Baking Show*. I wake up sore but alert and have enough expertise in body aches that I know to draw myself an Epsom salt bath and let the fizz soak into my resentful muscles. My phone pings at seven thirty.

Last chance to come to church?

Thank you. But I'll stick to godlessness.

When my phone buzzes on the bathroom tiles again, I figure it's him, texting back something cute about Jesus. But it's Mama. I almost drop the phone in the tub with me.

FaceTime?

It terrifies me to hear from her so early, but I can't think of another valid reason to put off the call.

I hold the phone up in front of my face and hit the button. Mama swims into place on the screen. "Cara Jean. Sweetheart! I know it's early but figured maybe you're up. How are you?" We dodge the fact that she's been tracking my texts. She probably just read my exchange with Xavier.

"I'm okay, Mama. Don't worry." I try to make my voice sound sleepy and end up overdoing it. I try again, using my tiny-kernel-of-truth lying technique. "I woke up with really sore joints and muscles, so I ran an Epsom bath."

"You're in the bath? My goodness! We could have talked later." My mom is so adorable, the way she pretends to have boundaries. "So you'd categorize your muscle pain as severe? Anything else? Fever? Should I come back early?"

I focus on speaking in my long-suffering and brave way. I try to channel Beth from *Little Women*. "No, Mama, you deserve this time away. No new symptoms. Just feeling really run-down and fatigued. Maybe those exams took too much out of me."

"Well, you know how much I hate seeing you worn down like this, Cara Jean. But I'm glad to hear you admit that those exams might have tipped you over the edge. Can you take a break today, practice some self-care?"

"Yeah." I let my head nod and am maybe too convincing. Mama gets all nervous about me soaking in the tub.

"Why don't you put the phone down for a second and get out of the bath? Put on some comfy pajamas and go back to bed for a little while. Are you keeping up with your meds? No skipping, right, Cara Jean?"

"Right. Except I didn't take anything yet this morning. You said not to take my meds before a bath," I call louder into the phone while I dry myself off, throw back on sweats. When I bring the phone back in front of my face, I'm sitting on the edge of my bed, hoping Mama doesn't notice how unslept in it looks. I see her mouth open to speak, but then the castle chimes ring and we laugh, having to wait through their melody so that I can hear her.

Finally she tells me, "Good girl. I wrote that down too. If you have any questions, I left clear instructions. And you can always call. Do you have big plans today?"

"No. Xavier invited me to church," I tell her.

"Did he, now?" I appreciate her feigned surprise. "Well, that's a kind gesture. I'm not sure that's what I intended when I asked Mrs. Barnes for help, though. You know, Cara Jean, people will always try to inflict their faith on you, especially under the guise of charity. But we are Wakely women. That gives us the strength to decide our own beliefs."

I spend the rest of the day deciding my beliefs—organizing paperwork, trying to build a timeline. After two days of vigilantly avoiding the computer, I finally whip off the sheet and fire it up. I go to our wellness warriors channel and rewatch as many of our videos as I can stand. I try to track side effects. I make a calendar of recorded videos and try to evaluate how heavily medicated I'd been on those particular days. Then I cross-reference those dates with activities I missed, chances I lost.

Up in Mama's bathroom, I move each item with great precision and care—noting distance and height so that I can place them back exactly where I found them. I search everywhere for her zippered bag of prescriptions. I take inventory of both medicine cabinets. I find antibiotics, old nasal spray—nothing that looks like the kind of pills I've been taking, the ones stashed in the Ziploc bag in my backpack. And none of the doctors' names on the bottles are the same. None of them identify Dr. Eric as the prescribing physician—not any spelled version of his name.

I take pictures of pills on my phone and list all the topics I'm too scared to type into our search engine at home, and then I head out to the library to look them up at one of the public terminals. I learn about Munchausen syndrome and Munchausen's by proxy. If I were faking my own illness or making myself sick, that would be Munchausen syndrome. I think about the little I know about Mama's life before me: the figure skating and injuries. The illnesses, the allergies. The cancer she still frequently mentions. Mama fits the profile.

Then there's me: the allergies and vague diagnoses, the frequent hospitalizations and visits to different doctors. The way we have packed up and moved so often and the picked carcasses of relationships that Mama has left behind us. I keep clicking and reading and start wondering why doctors never reported us. They sure followed up when Mama refused to pay their bills. I have the billing records to prove that. Our co-pays mattered to them. Our deductibles mattered. But no one stopped to investigate how I managed to develop so many different health complications so young. No one ever intervened.

I consider everything I've missed out on. The elements of a normal childhood. And all the procedures I've undergone. I try to calculate the IV sticks, the exploratory examinations, the medications and their cascade of side effects. Last night I found paperwork from the year I turned eight; two different doctors wrote prescriptions for spinal taps that winter. I remember lying on my side, with my knees drawn tightly up to my chest, feeling the needle pierce deeply. Twice my mother convinced a doctor I needed that.

My spine vibrates at the memory. The tiny dots of scars on my arms—marks where someone has punctured my skin—prickle with pain and rage.

On the way back from the library, my knees ache in a new and different way—they remember all the walking from yesterday. Xavier Barnes would be proud of me. I am proud of me. I have approached my research scientifically, gathering data and drawing conclusions. But I still don't know who to turn to for answers about what to do next.

At home in the kitchen, watching our most recent episode, I finally land on a viable option. I remember how easily we joked together, how without Mom to impress or a lecture to give, Dr. Eric almost seemed human.

I decide that it's worth just getting his perspective. He's the physician in charge of my most recent treatment, after all. I'll phrase my questions carefully, as if it's just me taking more ownership over my health—the way he's advised. Dr. Eric can tell me how my mom presented my case, how she described my symptoms. He'll probably be defensive. I know that. After all, he fell for her lies.

If my mom has been monitoring my cell phone, I don't want to set off alarms with a call to Dr. Eric. So I text her. I keep it brief. *Feeling a little short of breath. Don't worry. Calling Dr. Eric.*

No need to bother him. Try using the humidifier.

I leave her response on unread. Then I dial.

Dr. Eric's voice mail message is briefer than I expect, just "Hey, you've reached Eric, but I can't take your call right now. Please leave your message after the tone." Nothing about office hours or pager numbers or any of the other ways most doctors remind you that their time is billable in a way that yours aren't.

Alarm bells are going off in my mind.

He calls me right back. "Cara—are you okay?" And then: "Your mom texted me. She mentioned shortness of breath?" Wow. Mama is on it and Dr. Eric is responsive. It's too bad I'm not legitimately sick because they make a great team.

"Yeah." I make sure to pause to take deep and labored breaths. "That's part of it. And I'm trying to fill out this form for school—it's got me all stressed out."

"Well, don't worry about forms. I'll stop over on Tuesday. We'll look at it together."

"It's due tomorrow, though. I just wondered—well, do you have a minute?"

"I do. I do have a little bit of time. After that we're going to make a food run. Lots of hungry folks milling around who need our help."

"The form asks about medication I'm taking. They need a list?"

"What? Cara, we've sent over a treatment plan already. That's not a form you should have to fill out."

"I think it's a standard thing. In order to use the science labs." That is not a lie that makes any sense, but I come up with it quickly. Then I just go with it.

"No, that doesn't check out, Cara. I can't just rattle off prescription names. Physicians need to be really careful with information like that. I'll look at the form when I come by on Tuesday."

I feel myself getting desperate. By Tuesday, Mama might have traced some of my steps. By Tuesday, I might have run out of unmedicated time. "How about my initial symptoms?"

"Your what?"

"My initial symptoms? What did my mom report, when she first met you?"

"This is in order to use the science lab?"

"Well, this is for something different. But my initial symptoms? Do you remember?"

"Let's see. Your mom sought me out because she was so worried about your condition. Mostly the debilitating headaches and persistent fatigue. You're very lucky to have such an advocate in her. Most kids just hear that they're making it up. I don't know why people feel the need to do that."

I look across the living room at all the piles of evidence I've accumulated. "Do what, Dr. Eric?"

"Try to convince the chronically ill that they're actually well. You're not lazy, Cara. You tell that school you're working as hard as you can."

"Thanks. I appreciate that. And I will."

"Okay. Gotta get back to work. I'll see you Tuesday."

You can't stop knocking just because one door doesn't open. Mama used to say that about raising money, but those doors seem to be swinging on the regular now. It's not going to be Dr. Eric who ends up rescuing me; that's okay. I have built a whole network of options. I take my deep cleansing breaths, make time to drink water. I warm up some lentils. With each action of self-tending, I compose myself.

Then my phone bings. It's a text from Mama:

Worried about your breathing issues. Heading home early.

That's when I give myself permission to panic.

CHAPTER TWENTY-SEVEN

I program the address into the maps app first and it's a drive of about an hour and a half from Ravenwood Castle to our little house. I text Mama a quick response: *Please don't cut your trip short. All ok here.* But I know she's on the way back, in the same way the field mouse feels cold when the hawk's wings block the sun. I can sense her coming.

It's probably ridiculous that the first task I tackle is the pile of the dirty dishes in the sink. As if Mama might discover that I've been snooping in her financial records, covering her beloved wall chart with bed linens, and taking Ubers all over Northeast Ohio, but the thing that will really stick in her craw will be my lack of housekeeping. But the dishes give me a place to focus while I create a plan for what happens next.

The dining room stands as the most daunting program. How do you unsort something? I decide to simply start moving the piles of papers back onto the table and pray Mama doesn't have her own mysterious logic to all the paperwork. I aim for a kind of cultivated chaos so that at least she can't tell what exactly I have found at first. It hurts to scatter the pages all around—like shaking free all the pieces from a half-completed puzzle.

Then I find a safe place for the contents of my backpack—I slip the folder of odd bills and strange correspondence and the framed portrait of young Mr. Wakely under my mattress. It's when I grab the Ziploc bag of pills that I promptly panic. I don't remember which pill goes in which compartment and there should still be a few remaining in Sunday's part of the pill container. All of Monday's medication should still be in there. The bag dangles in my hand—a problem that even my cleared mind can't solve. I take my three cleansing breaths. Then I take three more. I check the time. It's running down quickly.

I fold up the sheets and slide them back into the linen closet. I even remember to drop the spare key back in the drawer. I move to shut down the computer but then, in a desperate burst of innovation, I access the school's learning portal. I search through the directory and pull up the profile of Mr. Brinks. Sometimes you have no other choice but to believe the best of people. I remember how patiently Brinks sat at my bedside in the hospital, how kindly and calmly he spoke when it counted.

Dear Mr. Brinks: If I am absent on Monday, January 13, please contact Xavier Barnes. He may have relevant information. You might also reach out to Dr. Abidi at Tri-Point Medical Center.

Then I clear the browser history in case it could possibly matter and shut down the computer. I send a carefully innocuous text to Xavier. *Good news!* I write. *Mom coming home early. Probably don't need ride tomorrow.* I watch the blue dots blink and understand that there is nothing that Xavier Barnes can write that could help me now. I had told myself that we had options. Mrs. Barnes would pick me up for school and Xavier and I could talk to her right then and there. She could drive me to a walk-in clinic or another hospital and then we might have test results to bring to the authorities. Or I could avoid involving the Barnes family completely and just ride along in their back seat, then report to the counseling center as soon as I arrived at school. I could call Mr. and Mr. Burton Wakely and demand that they step in, to make up for all those years of doing nothing.

Xavier writes, *It's such a sunny day. You should make sure and get out.* I appreciate that we are still the worst at speaking in code. It is a beautiful day. The sunlight streams through the trees. The air is crisp but not freezing. I sit on the porch and feel my ears turn pink. There's no place to run now. I breathe in and out. I breathe in, hold it, and then out. I breathe in. Then I exhale and try to let go of my worries and worst-case scenarios. I go back inside the house and wait for my mother to return home.

I only have to play dumb and keep quiet long enough to get myself to Middlefield High tomorrow. I just have to fake it for a little while and of course I can do that. After all, Mama has taught me well.

She comes into the house looking, her eyes scanning the way I bet Libby Gilfeather mom's might peer around to make sure she didn't throw a wild party or find her way into the liquor cabinet. Her glances skip over the dining room, but she checks the fridge and takes quick stock. "Well, good job on food intake. You seem to have your appetite back. How's your breathing? Does it feel like chest congestion? What about your vitals?" She studies the chart where I have plugged in estimated numbers.

"I'm really fine. Except for feeling lousy that you cut your trip short."

Mama sighs. "But you weren't fine. For goodness' sake, you telephoned Dr. Eric and caused him such concern. And what is this about medical history? Did Mr. Brinks reach out again? At this point, this man's behavior would absolutely constitute harassment, and we are well within our rights to contact his superintendent."

I am finally seeing how Mama operates, how she has been able to scare off anyone who has scrutinized us too closely. She is intimidating, the way she cries harassment or unprofessionalism every time someone questions her judgment. She has cultivated a far-reaching platform and a following who are virulently protective of us. And she doesn't hesitate to put someone on blast for simply causing us an inconvenience.

Mama abruptly halts at the counter and opens each of the pill compartments. "Cara Jean, what's going on with your medication?" She holds the case up, as if she needs to convince me it's empty. If I admit I stopped taking my meds, she will notice how focused I am. She'll start asking questions. All I can take is the opposite route and hope to confuse her enough to avoid providing answers.

"I don't know," I answer flippantly. "I took the pills that were in there, just like you said."

"Cara Jean! I left very clear instructions. The pills were separated by day of the week. Where are Monday's medications, Cara Jean? Come on." She snaps her fingers in front of me. "When did you take them, all of them like that?"

My mind scrambles. If the time is too recent, she might try to get me to vomit. I go with "This morning. I accidentally missed and so I tried to make up."

My mother throws up her hands. "That's specifically what I told you not to do. Cara Jean, what were you thinking?"

"Mama, I feel fine. Really. You have to stop worrying so much. I can't believe you came back from that castle . . ." I let my words trail off.

"Well, this little mishap sits squarely on Dr. Eric's shoulders. I hold him completely responsible. I said that an overnight trip was out of the question and he swore up and down that you could handle it, that it would be good for us. And now here you are, totally doped up. Placing odd phone calls. And he calls himself a doctor."

That it would be good for us.

There's something in her inflection. I realize: She's not talking about her and me.

She's talking about her and Dr. Eric. On my usual meds, I might not have picked up on it.

While Mama's back is turned, I reach for my phone in my

pocket. I scroll through recent calls until I find his number. There's only one way to find out if he's still in Cleveland . . . or a castle. I hit call. And then the strangest thing happens. In the distance of the front porch, we hear a phone ringing.

Dr. Eric's voice soon follows. Not on my phone. From the front porch.

"For Christ's sake, Shaylene, I will examine her in a second. I asked for ten minutes to catch up on emails." He opens the door and stands there, digging for his phone from a pocket inside his coat.

Mama's look of confusion mirrors my own. "I didn't call you. We said you'd come in a bit later."

"It's too cold to just sit out in my car." He walks into the kitchen, glancing at his phone and then at me. "Cara? What's up?" I slip my hand out of my pocket. He asks Mama, "Did you tell her I was here?"

"I did not." I think of all the ways that Mama has changed over the past few months, dressing a little younger, trying to reinvent herself. Her trip away. I remember Xavier saying *Maybe she's with a man?*

"It was voice-activated, I think. Because we were talking about you." I don't have to work to sound dumbfounded anymore.

"Well, then that's sweet. Why were you talking about me?" But it's Mama he turns to and asks.

"She's overmedicated again."

"What are you talking about?"

"Just look at her. She took all the pills at once. I told you. She's completely noncompliant with meds now. We have to switch to injections."

"Hold on for a second. We've discussed this. IV drugs are an entirely different animal. The trip was cut short and you're feeling frustrated. This isn't the right time to make any major decisions. Let me check her out." Dr. Eric whips out his penlight and shines it directly into my eyes. I don't know how to react. I giggle and cover my face with my hands. Peek through to see Dr. Eric looking thoughtful. "You said she took everything."

"She admitted it."

Dr. Eric keeps studying me. "You okay, Cara? Something you want to talk about with your mother and me? Do you still want more information about your initial symptoms?" I shake my head. "What's that, Cara?" Dr. Eric cups his hand over his ear. "I can't hear you."

"No, thank you."

He nods at me. He knows. Mama is too preoccupied with the Caring for Cara website to notice, but Dr. Eric understands that I'm pretending. He just doesn't understand why.

"Let's try it," he says.

"What? The intravenous? Now? Isn't it dangerous to administer that on top of what she's already taken?" Mama barely looks away from the computer screen.

"I think we'll be okay, actually. Just sit tight, Cara." When Dr. Eric comes back into the kitchen, he carries a zippered metal case. "Good news—we've got some different medicine. This will help with those symptoms you were experiencing earlier—the chest pains and shortness of breath." He unzips the case and I see a wide row of glass vials. I watch him load up a hypodermic. He screws the tube onto the needle and taps its side with his fingernail. "You don't want air bubbles. Okay, Cara, make a fist, and then when I tell you, relax your arm. Hold on, now. You have to wait for me to tell you. We don't want to have to do this twice. Tight fist, please."

I obey.

I sit there with my arm out because I don't know what else to do, where else to reach for help.

I don't feel anything at first. It stings and then aches, going first through my skin and then my muscle. The kitchen stays our kitchen and Mama remains sitting at the computer. She asks me, "Cara, did you clear the browsing history? Why would you do that?" When I move my lips to answer, they don't move quickly enough. Then it feels like my whole body is hit with a wall of warm water. "Cara, did you hear me? Oh Christ. Eric, she's drooling." I hear my mom but can't turn my head to speak to her. I try to lift my hand to wipe my mouth but the cables in my arms have loosened. My hands dangle heavily at my sides.

Dr. Eric points the penlight at me again. I can't even command my eyelids to blink. "It's fine. She's just fine," he says softly. "She's not going to mess around with medication again, I bet."

"Well, honestly, if that's how we have to handle it from now on, that's how we handle it," Mama rants on. She doesn't look at me, floating in the chair while she talks.

"That's a very simplified view of a complicated issue," Dr. Eric says. "When you give her the pills, she takes them herself. She's fourteen; she's not seven. If you need to, you can spin that. She has a history of raiding your medicine cabinet. Across the country, that's an epidemic. No one in their right mind would judge you for that."

He taps the metal case. It makes a chiming sound. "Harder to spin this. And I don't like carrying the risk of administering it.

An overzealous investigation can land on assault for dispensing medication intravenously."

"She has never been an uncooperative child."

"You know my opinion on this, Shaylene. Come on. Follow the model that has worked before. You've done a fantastic job taking care of your special-needs daughter all on your own. But this time around, you gave her a little too much freedom. Maybe, just maybe, because you wanted some time to yourself too. Okay. Lesson learned. We move on. We move away from some of these negative influences that put all kinds of ideas in her head. You stick to homeschooling and you slow down the internet self-promotion."

"So we just pack up and leave again?"

"Would you rather sit here and wait for the division of youth and family services to knock on the door? Because they're on the way. I'm telling you." Dr. Eric nods at the computer. "You have to shut the site down too." I sit there absolutely still in the chair, unable to move without pooling to liquid on the floor. Tears slide down my cheeks, but no one mentions them. I can't lift my arm to wipe them away. I want to go up to my room now. I don't want to sit here and watch them like a show I can't shut off.

Out of one wet corner of my eye, I see my mother pet the laptop, like it's an animal to be comforted. Dr. Eric reminds her, "Don't get greedy. Cash it in and pack it up. How long before the viewers tap out anyway? Everything has a shelf life, Shaylene."

"And what about us?" Again, I know my mom doesn't mean her and me.

"We've talked about this too," Dr. Eric reminds her. "You'll move on. I'll spend some time missing you. And then you'll send up a flare. I'll come running."

"Sure you will. And until then—all the money I gave you for Cara Jean's treatment . . ."

"Shaylene, that's my living, my ability to treat scores of other patients. Let's not confuse my calling as a doctor with my feelings as a man."

Mama looks so forlorn. I almost feel sorry for her. "We had a really lovely weekend."

Dr. Eric reaches for her hair, twists it at the back of her neck and then lets it go. "I promise, we'll have a lot of lovely weekends." Mama just nods sadly. I wonder how difficult it was to not touch each other in front of me, whether they texted back and forth late into the night.

Tomorrow I won't show up to school. At first no one will question that. It will just be another long stretch of absences. By the time Xavier Barnes can convince someone to look in on me, we'll be on our way to some other town, our cell numbers disconnected, our lease terminated.

"Can you help me get her up to her bed?"

"Sure." I don't think of Dr. Eric as particularly muscular, but he throws me over his shoulder like I am a sack of flour. My limbs all stiffen when he lifts me and then he scolds, "Relax, Cara," and I immediately go slack. *Look at me*, I want to tell them. *I am finally your cooperative patient.* "You'll need to call her out sick tomorrow. She won't remember going under. And then I'm serious. You need to consider your next move carefully."

"I got it."

I feel myself lifting up, the way your body slightly floats on an elevator. My head itches me. My head itches because my hair is growing in.

"Here's her phone."

My hand reaches into the pocket of my hooded sweatshirt but doesn't actually move.

"I still can't believe she called you."

"We're lucky she called me." They lower my body onto the soft white mattress. I feel myself sink right until my shoulder leans into something flat and hard. I think of the framed picture shoved under the mattress and my eyes leak more tears. People sometimes disappoint you. Sometimes people don't come through.

Dr. Eric instructs softly: "Make sure she's on her side." Then he says, "There you go, Cara. I'll see you soon." I clench my eyes shut— the only set of doors I can close between them and me. I remember imagining myself as that stone, resting in the silt at the bottom of the rushing river. It turns out that sometimes the current is too strong to withstand. Sometimes the water dislodges the stone and the stone loosens and travels downstream.

CHAPTER TWENTY-EIGHT

The first car to pull up in our driveway the next morning is Mrs. Barnes's white Mercedes. I barely register its engine's thrum. My eyelids still feel weighted with coins and my mouth is so dry my voice just scrapes out of my throat. The horn beeps and then, a short time later, the doorbell rings. I know Xavier is seriously concerned when I hear the voice of Mrs. Barnes herself at the door. He's sent his mom for me.

"Cara, honey, aren't you ready for school?" she calls out.

I hear Mama's low murmur and then Mrs. Barnes's insistence on volume. "Well, Xavier did *not* tell me that. He is a certifiable zombie in the mornings." I hear her heels clacking against the floor and understand that Mrs. Barnes is just filling silence, trying to buy some time so that she can snoop around. "I thought she was just running late. Well, goodness, that's too bad. Poor girl just completed her exams. Xavier was as proud as if he sat for them himself. Hey, congrats, Cara!" I hear her call up the steps. "Feel better soon, honey!"

With great effort, I drag myself over to the front window. I manage to pull at the window shade until one slat rebounds open. If Xavier looks up from the driveway, maybe he'll see the one shade up. Maybe he will understand that something has gone very wrong with our plan. In the meantime, I refuse to just lie back in bed and let Mama cart me away. I try to push myself forward but my whole body feels like it's operating in slow motion.

When the phone rings, I strain to hear the words bouncing through the house in Mama's sharp tone. "Why, yes, she is quite ill. She pushed herself to extraordinary lengths last week to keep up with your completely unreasonable exam schedule. Of course I will send a doctor's note. You can expect that by the end of business today. You can also expect that I will be contacting the superintendent and the school board. Thank you very much." Mama punctuates her words in the way that means the complete opposite of *thank you*. I hear pots and pans clatter and clang as if she has knocked down the entire kitchen in a tantrum.

Mama's footsteps creak up the stairs then and she steps into the room, looming over the bed. I pull the covers tightly around me. Her eyes look swollen from crying.

"I don't know what you're playing at. Cara Jean, you are a very sick girl. Do you understand me? You are very sick. You have no idea what you've set in motion. I can't do all of this alone. This is too much for anyone. If I have to call Dr. Eric over here to medicate you, I will."

I nod and cry and cower there and wish more than anything that I could take back all the little messages I sent out into the world, all the tiny requests for help. Mama has always said it: We are Wakely women; we don't expect others to come to our rescue. My brain moves even more slowly than my body. I didn't expect all those plans to unravel like this. I didn't count on the lack of emergency. I want to hang a white sheet like a flag of surrender out the window. And at the same time I want to spell out SOS on our roof.

The drop from the window is pretty steep. Even on my best day, I could not lower myself out the window without a serious injury. I try to imagine where Mama is keeping my cell phone, or if I can somehow access the computer without her knowing. I tell myself that Xavier won't give up. Mr. Brinks won't let my mom win. I decide I have to get to the first floor. I work my arms and legs into clothes and choose shoes that will allow me to make a run for it.

And then I don't have to.

When Dr. Abidi comes, she brings the cavalry.

I don't recognize her. For one thing, she's not like Dr. Eric—she doesn't wear a white lab coat everywhere. I just see some woman park her car on the street. Dark hair and yoga pants. At first,

I think it's Manuela, but this woman doesn't glide, she zooms. She gets out of her car and paces and then another car pulls up and parks behind her. Then a police car arrives, without sirens. Mama must be watching out the windows of the first floor because as soon as the squad car shows up, she bellows, "Cara Jean, what have you done?"

Her scream echoes throughout the house and I swear that outside, all those professionals must have heard it. Mama catches me in my doorway, fully dressed, and forces me back into my room. She grabs me by the shoulders and shakes me as she screams, "Cara Jean. Please. I have worked so hard to heal you, to find the right treatment. You don't understand how sick you are."

Outside, strangers knock insistently. As soon as the front door opens, my entire life will change. My mother stares at me the way I imagine a figure skater would stare out at the crowd, mid-spin, mid-leap, mid-flight, right before landing badly. I push past her and stumble down to the landing. I almost say, *I'm sorry, Mama.*

Then I let them in.

My mother makes a scene and I feel dizzy, so I retreat to my bedroom. As the police talk to Mama, Dr. Abidi climbs the steps with the social worker and finds me. She shows me my own note. I nod when she asks if I wrote it. They help me lift my mattress and I hand over the thick folder full of medical records—the treatments I didn't actually need, the diagnoses that had no merit. The social worker points to the name scrawled on the outside of the folder and I do my best to describe Dr. Eric. I tell them his phone number is in my phone downstairs.

I ask to see my mom. I ask for a bottle of water. I try to answer their questions honestly, but I have trouble with the truth. It's hard to talk about our life at home without mentioning symptoms. But I no longer know what counts as legitimate sickness. We talk about Munchausen's by proxy. They act surprised that I know so much but they don't have my study partner. They don't know Science Kid.

Then Mrs. Barnes arrives and I experience this flash of hope that she's come to get me. After all, she's always so kind. She seems to know exactly what to do. I just figure on staying at their house, even though it would be incredibly awkward to brush my teeth at a bathroom sink beside Xavier. But his mom doesn't offer me a place to stay. She's there to help Dr. Abidi explain to me that I'm headed back to the hospital.

"No way," I say. "Please no. Listen, I don't know what my mother told you, but I don't need to be in a hospital." I turn to Mrs. Barnes. "Please just ask Xavier. He'll tell you. I stopped taking all those medications and felt fine. I felt completely normal. I even walked home from the hospital."

But even I understand how ridiculous I sound. How worn down I sound.

"Where is my mom?" I ask.

"She's talking to the police," Mrs. Barnes answers.

"Is my mom going to jail?" I ask. "Has she been arrested?"

"Right now, we need to focus on your health," Mrs. Barnes says. "Let the police handle the rest of it."

Dr. Abidi takes over then. "It is very possible your mom has manipulated you and withheld some basic developmental and physical necessities. You are clearly underweight and malnourished and need a full, objective examination. Cara, there are psychological implications associated with your experience. We believe your mother may have manufactured significant health challenges in your life. We know you have been drugged. You've described a pattern of that treatment—we call that medical abuse. At the hospital, we can evaluate your current health. We can run a range of tests that will provide us with necessary information. And then we can decide what next steps to take."

My hand feels a phantom squeeze. I hear Mama's voice in my head, telling me not to believe them, telling me no one will believe me.

"What if I say no? What if I refuse to go to the hospital?" I ask.

Dr. Abidi glances at Mrs. Barnes. Mrs. Barnes says, "Cara, why would you want to? The doctor just wants to take care of you. From what I understand, you reached out to her. You knew you needed help. It must be very scary. You've recently gotten a little bit of control and maybe it feels like we're asking you to give that up. But it's just the first step in a lot of choices you're about to have."

I remind myself to feel grateful for the help I've been offered. I nod and go along. My first step down the stairs wobbles. My legs feel weak and watery.

I hear the murmur of my mother's voice, an insistent river running under everything. Even while she's crying, she lectures a police officer. He keeps interrupting her: "Ma'am. Ma'am."

My knuckles whiten while I clutch the banister. "Can I see my mom? Can I just say goodbye?" Mrs. Barnes looks to Dr. Abidi. Dr. Abidi looks to the social worker. The social worker looks to me.

As we are all considering, we hear Mama scream, "You have

no idea what my child and I have been through! She would be *dead*. It was just me, caring for her for so long. You cannot imagine the burden. She has become so manipulative—some of her medications cause hallucinations and psychosis. She doesn't know what she's saying. She is a very sick little girl."

It becomes easier then to take the next steps down, to slip by the living room, without even craning my head to see. I don't have anything to say to my mother. I take three calming breaths, brace myself, and leave.

CHAPTER TWENTY- NINE

The next step in my series of choices involves a private room in the ICU.

The social worker explains that they have added security on the ICU unit. It also means that Xavier can't visit me. Mrs. Barnes brings me a new cell phone so we can text each other. Mr. Brinks stops by to lend me a school laptop. I keep my street clothes and we order in Chinese food and at first it seems like a bizarre kind of sleepover. The adults keep starting all their sentences with the phrase "I'm sure." As in: "I'm sure you have a lot of questions." Or "I'm sure schoolwork might not be your first priority right now." Someone says, "I'm sure you know how worried we've all been. I'm sure none of us understand how circumstances could have come to this." And then finally, Dr. Abidi announces, "I'm sure Cara is exhausted. I think it's important that we let her rest."

I wish I could correct her. *I'm not sure I want to be alone*, I'd say. But that's not what you say when you are a Wakely woman, a wellness warrior. Instead, you sit on the hospital bed and thank all your caretakers for the needle sticks and rehydration and awkward conversation. When they file out, promising to come by tomorrow, you smile widely and tell them you sure look forward to their next visit.

Mrs. Barnes pats my leg as she leaves and nods at the phone on the bedside table. "I already programmed the first number into that phone, in case you need a tutor. Or a friend."

I hold the phone in my hand for a few minutes, thinking about what to write. I feel like from here on out, everything happens for the first time. This is the first night the breathing machine doesn't loom on my bedside table. An officer has packed it into an evidence box. It's the first night I'll fall asleep without Mama checking on me. This will be the first text I send that she doesn't read, with or without me knowing.

I go with an old standard. *New phone. Who dis?*

Just wait, Xavier texts back. *They're going to make you start going to gym now.* Then he asks, *How do you feel?*

I lie in the bed and try to decide. I stay perfectly still and wait for my bones to ache, for my skull to creak with pain. My scalp itches. 309

The bottoms of my feet are still tender from all the walking. My body still feels slow, from Dr. Eric's injected narcotics. *I feel numb,* I tell him honestly. *What do you know?*

I appreciate that Xavier doesn't try to shield me. *They arrested your mom. They can't find the doctor. My dad reached out to some support group, at the hospital. People there had concerns about that guy. Viewed him as predatory. Now they're looking for your father.*

My backpack sits in the corner of the hospital room. The framed photo is one of the only items I thought to grab. *That address in Aurora. On Uber? I went to see my grandparents.*

Ok for me to tell them that? That's the most awesome aspect of Xavier Barnes, Science Kid. When everyone else in the world just decides all my choices, he guards them for me. *What else?*

I went for pancakes. He knows that part.

But he writes, *What else can I do?*

You know how when I'm deciding what to write, you can see the ellipsis on the phone?

Yeah.

I can see those too. That's how I fall asleep on my first night on my own, with my phone right next to me. The three blue dots blink their proof that Xavier is out there waiting, still linked to me.

The next morning, Dr. Abidi shows up to check my vitals.

"You're still not wearing a lab coat," I say, partly to show how keen my observation skills are, partly to make sure she's a real doctor.

"Today's my day off," she says lightly. I watch her flip through my chart. "How's your appetite?"

"I'm hungry."

"Good, but we have to reintroduce foods slowly. We have plenty of time for Chinese food and Egg McMuffins. For right now, I'd like to monitor new foods very carefully."

"I know. I'm always really careful. I have severe allergies," I reply almost robotically.

Dr. Abidi stares at me. "We're not sure of that, actually. You don't have a medical history that we can accept at face value, Cara. The safest way is to simply start from scratch. Do you believe you're allergic to eggs?" I nod. "Then we're going to try eggs. Try not to be afraid. That's why you're here, so that we can monitor you and help if something goes wrong."

"But you said I'd stay in the hospital for a couple of days. If we rule out every allergy, one by one, I'll have to move in."

Later on, when Tessa the social worker shows up, I understand why we're not plowing through my nut allergies and gluten sensitivities. They don't have a place for me to stay. "We have several calls in. All of us hope to avoid an agency scenario. We've reached out to your paternal grandparents. I believe you recently had contact with them?"

"I wouldn't call it contact, really." I try to gauge exactly how much Tessa knows. They will no longer have to worry about housing me if I go to jail for breaking and entering.

"They would like to come see you."

"Are they angry?"

Tessa looks startled and glances at my chart as if my question functions as a symptom. "No one is angry at you, Cara." I am pretty sure Tessa has not interacted with my mother. "My understanding is that they have a complicated relationship with their son—your father. Do you remember him at all?"

I shake my head. My hands bunch, recalling the way I could grab tufts of his curly hair as I sat perched on his shoulders. I doubt the vague sense of broad shoulders framed in a hospital doorway counts as the kind of memory Tessa is after.

After Tessa leaves, they bring by a therapy dog. At first I am not so crazy about Theo. Mama has always warned me about the multitude of germs that exist in a dog's mouth. But he's a sweet animal, in a green quilted vest. And it is sort of calming to sit in the room with another creature and not have to field so many questions. After the dog leaves, an art therapist brings a flowerpot and some paint.

I sit there in the hospital bed and work out my feelings with terra-cotta. I dab yellow sunbeams radiating from the center with a design of ivy winding around the pot's circumference. It's not exactly enough to garner a gallery opening but I get involved in the process. It helps distract me from all the time I'm missing at school. I tell the volunteer about Mud Matters and how much I love pottery.

"That's so cool. *Very* cool." She says this in an overly cheerful voice that makes me think she's read my chart.

All of a sudden, I wonder what will happen to the vase that I gave my mom for Christmas. I picture it sitting in the center of the table, the flowers inside wilting. And just as I'm about to allow myself to wallow, I look up and see an older gentleman in the doorway, holding a brown paper bag. Of course, I decide it's Mr. Burton Wakely. But the man says, "Pat Neary here. I wondered if you might have a minute."

For a volunteer, the art therapist leaps to my defense pretty quickly, standing between the bed and the door as if this elderly gentleman might pose a threat. "Sir, this is a private room."

But I say, "Please—he's a friend of mine." And we nod at each other for a moment and quietly smile.

"Okay. I didn't know there was someone scheduled. I'm sure that's fine and your pot looks lovely. I'm going to leave it right on the windowsill. Hopefully, it will dry by the time you're ready to go home. To move on," the art therapist corrects herself.

I'm learning the power of just sitting quietly and sadly staring while good people scurry around and try to avoid saying the wrong thing.

The therapist says, "I'll leave you two friends to catch up. At the nurses' station, I'll just let them know you have a visitor."

"Thank you," I say, and then say to the man, "Thank you for your note."

"Of course. I was pleased to receive a response. It worried me a little, I'll admit to that. Nothing like a little unexpected mail to keep me on my toes. Are you all right?"

He asks so kindly. My vision goes blurry; my eyes fill up with tears. "This is a lot," I admit.

"What is a lot?"

I wave my hand around the room, graze my fingers against my head. "This."

"In your letter, you said you might not be sick after all." He sits down on the visitor's chair and looks up at the hospital ceiling. "It appears you are sick. Very sick."

"Not really. It's hard to explain." Pat Neary just nods and waits. "My mom pretended that I was sick, she ended up—"

"Making you sick." Now I nod. "Maybe making you a little heartsick too." I hadn't thought of that word before. It feels accurate. Mr. Neary pulls my letter out from his back pocket. It embarrasses me to see it in his hands. What was I thinking? He tells me, "Your letter struck me as desperately sad. And lonely. So I drove over yesterday, to your home. I knocked on the door, and a neighbor told me about the police cars. It sounds like quite a scene. Do you know the neighbor? Her name is Anya?"

I shake my head. "We don't really talk much to neighbors."

"That's what Anya said. She said she sometimes wondered about you, that she saw you outside so seldom. My niece works at this hospital. She mentioned seeing a patient the other day, a girl with very short hair who left a note for a doctor. I know there are many desperately sad and lonely teenage girls in the world. I just had this sense it was you. *Two letters*, I thought. *Same day, maybe same girl.* So I needed to investigate. Time on my hands. There is a distinction between sickness and heartsickness. Do you know what it is?" Again, I shake my head. "The remedy is different. The remedy for heartsickness is connection. You connected with me, with the doctor. Keep connecting, Miss Cara Wakely. You will heal more than yourself that way."

He rustles open the paper bag at his feet then and pulls out a teddy bear. It's white, with suede paws. It looks hand-sewn and seems fancy. "A gift for a child, I know. But flower arrangements just die, especially in hospital air. It's stale in here."

I've never seen a stuffed animal that's actually a piece of art. "I really love it. Thank you—it's so kind of you. Even to write that letter." But he holds up his hand to stop me.

"Would you keep writing me letters?" he asks. "I would like to know how the bear adjusts."

"I will definitely update you on its progress."

"All right, then. Get some rest, my friend. Tell them to stop making you paint flowerpots like some kind of child laborer."

"I will, definitely. They've scheduled me to sweep chimneys this evening. I will make sure to cancel." That's when Mr. Neary fires off finger guns and I think of Xavier, what a charge they would get out of meeting each other. When he texts promptly at three thirty, I tell him I met the kindest man.

If he tries to convince you that you have a rare autoimmune disorder, maybe question the crap out of that, Xavier types back.

It is so completely wrong that I have to laugh and then laugh even harder because Xavier immediately follows that up with: *Sorry sorry maybe not such a funny joke.*

I am over here pulling finger guns out of my imaginary holsters, I tell him.

My mom won't let me visit. She says you need time and space.

Maybe.

I'm sorry we didn't figure things out sooner.

No sorrys, I tell him. *Could you go to Mud Matters for me? Tonight or tomorrow?*

You want me to sculpt you a woodland creature?

I want you to tell Manuela.

Everything?

I just want there to be places where I can go afterward, where I won't have to explain.

Okay. Done, Xavier replies, and I sit back in bed and take inventory of all the other connections I've made and need to preserve.

On Thursday we confirm I'm allergic to neither gluten nor tree nuts and I order a peanut butter sandwich on wheat bread because I can. It's overly sticky and grossly sweet and teaches me that not all the missed childhood highlights count as deprivation. And then I meet my grandparents.

Tessa arranges for us to meet in a conference room so that it doesn't upset them to see me in a hospital bed. But then the charge nurse insists that an orderly push me down there in a wheelchair, so there goes that sliver of sensitivity. The first thing I say is "I'm sorry I broke into your house last week" and the orderly's hands tighten around the grips of the wheelchair and Tessa looks like she's swallowed a bee.

"That's just fine, dear," Grandma Wakely soothes . . . but really, what else would she say? Then she elaborates, "We understand that you came to us for help. You may not have known how to ask for that."

Mr. Burton Wakely speaks up then. "We wish you hadn't run. We could have stopped some of this if you hadn't—"

Tessa intercedes then. "I'm not sure that's productive. Cara has described feeling overwhelmed in that moment. She panicked. She didn't know that staying wouldn't be dangerous."

"We wouldn't have injected her with narcotics, I'll tell you that much." I sort of appreciate how cranky Burton is about the circumstances around our reunion. He makes it clear that he's up for grandfatherhood but he'd prefer not miss an episode of *Jeopardy!* for this whole business.

"Burton, please." I bet Grandma Wakely answers the final *Jeopardy!* question in her head every night, but keeps quiet so that she avoids antagonizing Gramps. She smiles at me. "We just want to help. We noticed you moved your photo. Did you remember spending time at that park? It's right near our house."

"No," I answer. She reaches in her handbag for a cloth handkerchief and dabs at her eyes. "I'm sorry. I remember this vague feeling of happiness, but nothing specific."

She dabs her eyes again, but smiles. "Well. A vague feeling of happiness is a positive place to start."

"What will happen to her mother?" Burton growls at Tessa.

"We're not here to discuss that." Tessa makes a note on her clipboard.

He continues, "That woman stole our granddaughter. Years with our granddaughter. She stole plenty of other things as well."

"Today, we're here to find ways of supporting Cara."

But Burton is on a roll now. He says, "Not to mention our son. The damage this woman has inflicted. You have no clue."

"I do, though," Tessa says sympathetically. "And obviously so does Cara. Please let's try to keep that at the forefront of our discussion. We will not continue this meeting if it upsets Cara. Cara, would you like to continue?"

"Yeah. It's fine." But I'm impressed. I wonder how long I get to keep Tessa the social worker. Navigating high school might be easier accompanied by Tessa on one side and Theo the therapy dog on the other. I feel bold enough to ask, "Could you tell me about my father?"

The look that passes between Mr. and Mrs. Burton Wakely carries a whole story and I'm suddenly regretful that I asked. "My mom wrote letters to charities. Programs for widows."

Burton snorts at that. "Well, that is rich. There's no end to her shamelessness, Maggie."

"Please. We've talked about this." Grandma Wakely reaches over to squeeze his hand and it reminds me of all the times Mama has done the same to me, reminding me to stay on script. "We love our son very much. But he is a troubled person. He and your mother did not help each other toward health in any way. He struggles with addiction; that's a kind of illness too. We believe—" She looks at Gramps again and gives his hand another squeeze. "We have long believed that Matthew felt very helpless in his marriage. He made his own choices. But perhaps his inability to protect you drove him to some of those choices. I know he feels an enormous amount of guilt."

Tessa peers up from her notes. "How much contact do you have with your son, Mrs. Wakely?"

Burton snorts again and receives another squeeze. Grandma Wakely answers, "Minimal. Once a year or so, he reaches out, usually to ask for money. We're not here representing our son." She turns to me then. "We can't make promises on his behalf. We're here today as grandparents for you. I'm very sorry if you have harbored the hope in a father who might show and make everything better. That's just not who Matt is. He'd like to be that, very much. But he falls short."

"Thank you for telling me. I took his picture. That's him, right?"

"A long time ago." Grandma Wakely smiles in a small and sad way. "He's different now."

"I didn't mean to just take it off your wall. I've just never had a picture of him before."

"Please keep it. We would love it if you came by and we could look at some albums together. Would you like that?" I nod and she dabs her eyes with the handkerchief again.

"Is Matthew aware of these recent developments in Cara's life?" Tessa asks.

Gramps and Grandma both shake their heads. "Not that we know of," Grandma adds, her voice steeled. "Matthew will not be able to provide any kind of reliable support, emotional or otherwise. We've discussed this at length." Grandma looks over at her husband again. "Cara, we've talked about this constantly from the moment we saw that news story. We want very much to support you. You are our granddaughter, even if that feels unfamiliar right now. We'd like to work on that." She looks intently at Tessa. "Maybe we should talk about living arrangements later on with just adults in the room?"

Tessa seems to consider this. "Our hope is that Cara regains a sense of control over her life. It's wonderful that you hope to rebuild your relationship. Difficult conversations can help with that. And I can help facilitate difficult conversations. So why not try now? If anyone starts to feel uneasy, we can step back and revisit the topic another day. How does that sound to you three?"

I press my lips together and nod. Mr. and Mrs. Burton Wakely agree as well. She clasps her hands in her lap and says, "Very well. We have the means to care for Cara in our home, but our home must also still remain open to Matthew, should he need to return. We also worry how our ages factor in—we know Cara will need support and structure. We have financial resources to help with her care. We also prefer not to uproot her from her school." They glance at each other again. "We wonder if there's a school friend or a teacher who might provide housing."

That stone tumbles along the bottom of the river again,

wearing down and scraping along the dirt bottom. *They don't want me.* The refrain ripples in my head. *They don't want me.*

"Cara, do you hear what your grandmother is saying?" Tessa asks.

I nod. *They don't want me.*

Tessa continues, "What do you think of that?"

I can't formulate words.

Burton leans forward. "I want this clear. I don't want her in foster care. Not my granddaughter." He slams his hand on the conference table and the rest of us jump back a little. "If that's the choice here, then honest to God, Maggie—Matthew can go to hell. He has been given chances. Many chances." Gramps Wakely sighs. He looks like he wishes he had a handkerchief too. "But if there's a better option, something that would end up being positive for Cara, then we will do whatever it takes to make that work. I'm very sorry, Cara." His gruff voice catches. "We told ourselves that your mother was making the best of a very difficult situation. We should have insisted on . . . I don't know. But we can only do better from here on out."

The ripples quiet to a still surface. I keep myself perfectly calm. Of course, Tessa doesn't let that stand. "What's going on for you, Cara? Do you hear what your grandparents are saying? It sounds like they are speaking from a place of great love. They want to continue to build their relationship with you. Do you hear that?"

"I'm so grateful," I say in the way I have been taught to. But then my composure slips, just a little. I look toward Tessa and manage to choke out, "I just don't know where I'll go."

"Oh, Cara. I didn't realize that you didn't know. I thought they would have already opened up conversations with you. We have some options."

EPILOGUE

Grandma Maggie puts the car in gear and guns it down the highway. I brace my feet against a stack of full Tupperware. Every Sunday goes like this now. I wake up in Aurora and the three of us go to church, which is not exactly my jam. But I sit through services because attending seems so important to my family. They park themselves on either side of me and make sure that the rest of the congregation catches a glimpse of their granddaughter. My hair has grown in enough that now people only stare because I am unfamiliar.

I still don't believe in all the talk coming from the pulpit. During the minister's homily, I watch my grandparents nod when the minister mentions faith or forgiveness and then we go to the

Comet Diner and they watch as I work my way through a stack of pancakes. We compromise.

Grandma spends a lot of time feeding me. On Saturday afternoons, we go to counseling and then we usually cook together. It gives us a chance to work and talk. It helps to keep our hands busy with a task while we tackle the harder conversations.

She doesn't believe Manuela knows how to cook properly, although she's careful not to say that. Instead she teaches me recipes and packs up leftovers for me to bring back to the apartment we keep above Mud Matters. Grandma and Gramps say that as I get older, I might want to limit our visits to Sundays. *When you're sixteen, you might find that you have dates on Saturday night. There might be young men circling, hoping to make plans with you.* She also calls Xavier my "gentleman caller" even though we mostly text.

I haven't yet spoken to Matthew Wakely, my father. In therapy, we talk about him, how I can't stand in as some substitute for their son, who went off the rails. They can't sort out their parenting mistakes with me. Mostly, I see how it saddens them to speak about him. It makes them as sad as it makes them angry to speak about my mom.

My mom can't put up bail; she still waits for the case to go forward at the state penitentiary. The fundraising platform froze her Caring for Cara account and returned whatever funds were left to the original donors—minus the money she'd already spent or paid to I'm-Not-a-Doctor-but-I-Play-One-in-Support-Groups Eric Andrianakis. Mama's lawyers keep delaying dates, claiming diminished mental capacity. The latest motion basically maintains that she's mentally ill and Dr. Eric exploited that. That's an easy argument to file when they can't find him anywhere.

Not all men disappear. Mr. Neary takes me to individual therapy twice a week and sometimes we stop and chip golf balls at the driving range. I am not at all good at that. But once in a while, the club smacks the ball right in the sweet spot. We watch the neon-yellow ball streak out across the range until it hits the back of the net and bounces down.

And then there's Xavier, who's not a man and completely weird and definitely not my gentleman caller, or boyfriend, or Science Kid romantic interest. By *definitely*, I mean that just because he is the first boy I've ever spoken to doesn't mean he'll be the first I kiss. Or the first I date. And just because he understands being sick doesn't mean he relates to how I feel now—seeing how much of my life was wasted. But Xavier is the person who checks up on me. He is the only one who will joke about Munchausen's. He is my connection.

Manuela is my landlord. She hates when I say that. But she's not my mom—foster or otherwise. She's my friend and my ceramics teacher and now she's my boss. Because now I get to run all the birthday parties at Mud Matters. At first, I would worry that I couldn't match Manuela's magical tone—her way of enthralling every kid. But it turns out the one thing you need to throw a really good birthday party is a love of birthday parties, and now I get to throw them every Friday afternoon.

I also run a YouTube channel for Mud Matters. Xavier came up with the idea. We feature instructional videos and run contests and even interview clients about the pieces they create. We're getting a lot of traffic, and not just the viewers whose curiosity surges every time Mama gets assigned a new court date. We have this whole marketing plan—Xavier says marketing qualifies as a scientific category because it implements lessons learned from research and data. I think he loves it. He just doesn't want to admit that it's more fun than mapping genomes and staring at a petri dish.

We are filming a different kind of episode for another channel today. Grandma Maggie knows what we're planning and she's tense about it. She passes cars on the road; her grip tightens on the wheel. She drives with a silk scarf tied under her chin as if a kerchief could function as a helmet. I like watching my grandmother handle the car. Manuela thinks it's crazy that each week she makes the drive on her own, dropping me off and then turning around to head straight back to Aurora. But Grandma Maggie is strong, just like me. We are Wakely women, after all.

I text Xavier so he knows I'm close by, and when she pulls over to stop, Grandma looks over to me in the passenger seat and says, "I'm very proud of you."

"I know." I reach over and pat her hand. It is soft and delicate, unlike ourselves.

"But, Cara, I also want to remind you that this isn't your mess to clean up. You don't have to put yourself out there."

"This is more like I'm putting myself away." We share a smile. "See you Saturday." I get out of the car then, balancing my backpack over my shoulder and the containers in front of me. Run up the steps and drop it all off. Xavier waits on the street.

"Your hair looks good," he tells me.

"Stop it."

"Lots of star power. Girls across the country are gonna be growing in their shaved heads, warrior style."

"You're ridiculous." I'm glad Xavier is the one walking with me back to my old street. It's almost warm out and the leaves on the trees are lush and green. The neighborhood looks more cheerful in the springtime. It even smells better, like fresh grass and hyacinths. No one has rented our old house yet. It looks dilapidated, even though it hasn't been left unattended for so long. I just never noticed the lopsided porch or the peeling paint on the shutters. We check around and I see the curtains move next door and wave to Anya if she's watching.

"You ready?"

I sit on the top step and Xavier crouches in the front walk, filming me with his iPad. I fix a smile on my face and begin, "Hello, wellness warriors. Cara here. It's been a while and a lot has happened since our last episode. I know many of you know about recent developments in my story. You might have heard about the reasons our channel has remained dormant. I've appreciated reading most of the comments you've left on earlier videos. Some of you have seen me grow up and your support has helped sustain me through really lonely times.

"You've also asked a lot of questions and I'm sorry that I can't answer most of them. No one else besides my mother can explain her decisions. It hasn't helped me to speculate about her motives. She's not going to be recording any more videos, though. You might have noticed that this morning we took the wellness warrior library of episodes down. Those videos are no longer considered public web content, but instead evidence. If you made any financial donations to the Caring for Cara website, thank you for your generosity. I have not nor will not have access to those funds. If you'd like, you may contact the Geauga County district attorney. She is working hard to return the money that has been recovered.

"I won't be filming anymore for wellness warriors. I'll be focusing on high school and hope to eventually apply to arts programs. My body has grown stronger and so have my relationships. I'm going to log off after this and focus on those connections in real life. Really, I just hoped to record one last video to let you all know that I'm okay. And that I wish you well."

My gaze stays steady, the way Mama once taught me. And then I nod for Xavier to stop recording.

"That's fire!" he says. "Cara, you smoked it. I can't get over how confident you are—you spoke so clearly. You hit all the notes we planned."

"We should post it for three days before we take it down."

"Okay." He nods excitedly. "I don't know—do you think we need to record one more version? Just to make sure?" I have to smile because Xavier is such a science kid. He thinks he can always make things make more sense.

"No, that's enough," I tell him. "Let's leave it at one take."

ACKNOWLEDGMENTS

Thank you to Cormac and Maeve, who have embraced all of this year's adventures and graciously shared my attention with these characters. You make every day an amazing story.

Love and gratitude to the Corrigan, McKay, Ryden, and Franzmann families, as well as to Anne Glennon and Steve Loy. Thank you for encouraging my leaps—both on the page and from coast to coast.

My deep appreciation for Rose Abondio, Barbara Corbin, and Ella Nowak for their friendship, as well as their loving care of my children.

Thank you to the incredible office team of Joe Chodl, Graig Domanski, Denise Ryan, and Meredith Santowasso. Together, we would have solved this mystery by the end of the second chapter.

I am grateful for my friends, especially those who talked through some of the connections in these pages: Sara Belyea, Yasmin Crystal, Nandini Dutta, Hannah Garrow, Lynn Hernandez, Elijah Kaufman, Stacy McMillen, Billy Merrell, April Morecraft, Mark Nastus, Sara Nardulli, Sherry Riggi, Nina Stotler, and Cora Turlish.

Christopher Stengel's striking design elevates my work. Thank you for showcasing this novel with such a careful eye. I appreciate it so much.

And special thanks to fellow writer Laura Barber; our weekly walks have helped Tacoma become home.

More than two decades ago, David Levithan chose my writing and changed the trajectory of my life. Every day I am grateful for his wise guidance and that extraordinary stroke of luck.

This past year has challenged me as both an author and an educator. Two exceptional communities have bookended the writing of this novel. Rutgers Prep's Class of 2020 and Annie Wright's Class of 2021: Your hard work, true joy, and immense strength endlessly inspire me.

ABOUT THE AUTHOR

Eireann Corrigan's novels for YA readers include *Creep*, *Accomplice*, *The Believing Game*, *Ordinary Ghosts*, and *Splintering*. She is also the author of the acclaimed YA memoir *You Remind Me of You*.